I0685852

A TURTLE ROARS IN TEXAS

An Al Quinn Novel

RUSS HALL

A Turtle Roars in Texas
A Red Adept Publishing Book

Red Adept Publishing, LLC
104 Bugenfield Court
Garner, NC 27529
http://RedAdeptPublishing.com/

First Print Edition: November 2015
ISBN-13: 978-1-940215-61-7 (Red Adept Publishing)
ISBN-10: 1940215617

Cover and Formatting: Streetlight Graphics

This is a work of fiction. Names, characters, places, and incidents either are the product of the author's imagination or are used fictitiously, and any resemblance to locales, events, business establishments, or actual persons—living or dead—is entirely coincidental.

Behold the turtle. He makes progress
only when he sticks his neck out.

James Bryant Conant

CHAPTER ONE

DARIN SANDERS TURNED HIS ELEVEN-FOOT Hobie kayak back into the wind. The accelerating breeze whipped his long hair straight back, tugging at it in jerks. Swells and white caps were forming as far out as he could see. Though the weather report had predicted ten-mile-per-hour winds, the gusts were closer to thirty or thirty-five. A cold ripple of fear ran up his spine inside his life vest. For someone in his twenties, he had way too many chores and far too few chances to get away to have to face such poor conditions when he finally did.

He was going to have a hard time getting back. Darin let the wind twist the kayak to one side, and he bobbed in the troughs long enough to adjust his paddle. He shifted one blade a quarter turn out of line with the other to reduce wind resistance. Then he dug the left end in deep and pulled, turning the kayak back into the teeth of the wind again.

He began to paddle hard. The nose of the kayak waddled slightly as he stabbed each blade deeper into the water, putting plenty of shoulder behind each stroke. He heard a noise and looked up to see a cigarette boat bearing down on him.

Damn! He didn't want to flash his paddle blades high because of the wind, but maybe whoever was in the boat couldn't see him for the swells. He raised the blades into the air with each stroke. The boat kept coming straight toward him.

What the hell? He dug in, trying to pull toward the far right so he'd be out of the way. When he looked up, he saw the cigarette boat adjust its heading so that it was bearing down on him again. The boat's driver was staring right at him... and grinning. The roar of the motorboat increased as the engine got more gas, and the boat surged forward.

Darin was still paddling as fast as he could when the other boat struck his, climbed right over it, and chewed it in half.

Wayon Gallard parked his unmarked car behind the sheriff's department cruiser. The uniformed deputy, Pudge Simmons, stood beside the two women a few feet away. Wayon straightened his tie and brushed at the sleeve of his suit jacket. He still wasn't used to wearing a suit on the job; he hadn't been out of a uniform long enough for it to feel natural. He hadn't been a detective long—barely a month—though he'd been with the department eleven years.

Lightning crackled across the far horizon beneath a low-hanging stretch of black clouds that seemed to ooze their way. But the woman's corpse dressed as a scarecrow and hanging on a wooden cross at the end of the row of peach trees topped the clouds for sinister.

He opened the car door. The dead woman's two surviving sisters were crying in big gasping wails. One of them had bent so far forward at the waist that she'd have fallen over if she weren't being held up by the back of her overalls by the other, who was crying just as hard. The second was barely able to keep her sister from crumpling to the ground.

Pudge, thin as a length of baling twine, his uniform hanging from him, came over, looking relieved to have another deputy present. He pointed a thumb at the body. "S'posed to be just a scarecrow, but someone went to some trouble to put the woman's body there. Hard to tell yet how long she's been there. The dead one is Gladys. The other two, the live ones, are Thelma and Millie. They're all in their sixties. Well, two of them are. One of them was."

The scarecrow looked like any other haggard example of its kind, though Wayon could make out the shape of a body slumped inside the tattered clothes. A gust of the whipping breeze tugged at the front lock of Pudge's short brown hair. He was supposed to have his hat on. As a detective, Wayon had rank on the deputy, but he didn't pull it.

Wayon scanned the area but didn't see anything out of the ordinary. "How do you suppose she came to be here?"

Pudge shrugged his bony shoulders. "They said she had a growing touch of the Alzheimer's. But I don't s'pose she killed herself and tied her own body up like that."

"You didn't touch the body, did you?"

"Of course not."

"The M.E.'s right behind me. Should be here in fifteen."

Wayon had spotted the sign for Three Sisters Organic Farm when he had pulled in off the two-lane farm road. He wondered for a second if they'd have to change the sign, with one sister being dead and all. He quickly shook off the notion. *Damned silliness.*

He looked at the surviving sisters. Their silver hair was tangled from the wind, their overalls dirty at the knees, their faces and hands chapped by the wind and sun. They had the rough texture of people who worked hard for a living. Their thin shoulders shook, nearly dislodging the denim overall straps. *Who their age wore overalls?* He guessed people who worked on an organic farm.

A square of white paper pinned to the front of the corpse rustled. Wayon went over and held it still with his suitcoat-covered forearm to avoid damaging any prints. Written in what looked like purple crayon and the handwriting of a child were the words "Never break the rule of threes!" He glanced at Pudge.

The deputy shook his head. "I asked. Neither of them has a clue."

Wayon walked toward the two women, thinking it was probably best to get them back to their house and calmed down before he questioned them. He could do that while the M.E. looked at the body.

A plume of dirt and dust sprang from the ground. A second later came the crack of a gunshot.

"Down! Everybody down!" Wayon yelled.

Pudge dropped to the ground. The two women stood paralyzed, eyes wide above wet cheeks, as they gaped first in one direction then another.

"Get them down!" Wayon shouted to Pudge.

Pudge rose but fell flat again when another shot sounded. Then he got up and scrambled to tug the two ladies to safety on the ground behind the thin trunk of a peach tree.

Couldn't be much of a shot, Wayon figured, to miss everyone, and with two of them still frozen there. He stared up the hill. He'd been on sniper scenes and didn't care for them. The guy was probably over two hundred yards up, he figured, given the time it took the sound of the shot to reach them after the first bullet had hit the dirt. Though caliber and muzzle velocity played a role. Wayon tried hard to see the textbook table for that in his mind then shook off the thought. He studied the terrain.

A lot of prickly scrub and loose rocks, probably full of snakes, lay between him and the shooter. He could go out and around, up that side lane along the fence line over there. That could take a bit longer. Or maybe not with the trade-off of not wading through the dense brush and possibly getting snake bit in the bargain. Shaking his head, he wondered if his mother hadn't been right way back when she'd encouraged him to become a dentist instead of joining the sheriff's department.

"Get those two back to the house, Pudge. I've got to go up there."

Wishing he'd thought to wear a vest, Wayon rolled to his right into an arroyo. Using the hint of cover, he sprang up and darted behind the row of peach trees, none of them with a trunk thicker than six inches. He fully expected to hear the crack of a rifle shot and feel the tug of a bullet hitting him, but he didn't pause. The best thing he could do was keep moving, fast and in irregular darts. He heard no more shots.

He got to the two rutted dirt tire tracks that ran along the fence line and started up the hill. The thick bramble gave him temporary cover, so he picked up his pace. Behind him, hurried steps gained on him. He spun and saw Pudge running up the slope.

"You nearly gave me a heart attack," Wayon said. "I thought I told you to herd those gals to the house."

"I just told them to go, and they were off in that direction like they had jet packs. You shoulda seen 'em. Besides, you need backup."

Wayon could have chewed Pudge out for not escorting them, but truth be told, he was glad to have him along. Pudge wasn't wearing a vest, either. It would have shown on his bony frame. Wayon signaled with his hand for him to slow down and follow, then he started back up the hill.

At the top, they separated, each sweeping around to the logical spot. But they stayed close to the thick stand of oaks and pecan trees as they skirted them.

Wayon eased around a live oak trunk and knew he was looking at the place where the shooter had stood. But no one was there. No shell casings, either. He stepped out to the edge of the spot, careful not to trample the scene. He signaled for Pudge to come out then looked down at the scarecrow. He could see it clearly from there, even though he didn't have a scope. Someone was standing beside it.

"Hey!" Wayon shouted.

Pudge squeezed off a shot.

Wayon snapped his head around, ready to yell at the younger deputy, but the gun was pointed in the air. "You're still going to have to write that up. Plus, buy me new underwear."

They rushed back to the path along the fence and ran down the hill. Wayon was puffing as he approached the scarecrow. The corpse was still there, but the piece of paper was gone.

Behind them, a van pulled up, and the M.E. swung his door open.

"Oh, crap," Wayon said. "This is not good. Not good at all."

In the distance, a siren grew louder. The place would soon be crawling with people, and that meant that it wouldn't be long before word got back to one unhappy sheriff. And the very last thing Wayon wanted to hear was "What would Al Quinn have done?"

CHAPTER TWO

AL QUINN'S EYES SNAPPED OPEN. People were in his house. There weren't supposed to be people staying in his house. He'd lived alone for years—well, since Abbie—but he could feel the other people there. His guests didn't make any noise, nor could he hear them breathe, but he knew they were there.

His bedroom was dark. The lapping of the waves on the lake outside came through the open crack at the bottom of the window. Maybe he could turn on his other side and manage to stay in bed until the dim light of dawn pushed through the corners of the closed blinds.

Nope. He was as awake as anyone ever got, and he could feel the presence of the other people as if they were with him in the master bedroom. He checked his watch: 2:47 a.m. Well, he'd slept. Sort of. Enough for him anyway.

He'd long ago come to the realization that everyone had his or her own sleep requirements. His brother, Maury, who was a year older than Al, needed at least eight hours, especially since he was recovering from a heart attack. Maury was probably heartily sawing logs in the basement spare bedroom. Bonnie, Maury's nurse, claimed she could stand getting ten to twelve hours, stand it and savor it, even wallow in it. The way Al figured, the whole thing averaged out so that the people needing more sleep balanced his needing or wanting less. That took the long way around and still didn't keep him from feeling he was becoming just a little neurotic about having other people in his house after living alone for twenty years.

Well, hell. He threw aside the sheet and light bedspread and got out of bed. He tugged on his jeans, put on socks for stealth, and eased the bedroom door open.

On his tiptoed way through the dimly lit living room, he came close to barking a shin on the coffee table, but he saw it just in time. In the kitchen, he poured some cold coffee from a thermos and gave the mug a minute in the microwave. He slipped back to his room without rousing Bonnie, the sleeping, blanket-covered lump on his couch, probably naked beneath that blanket for all he knew.

He set up his chessboard and started a game, spinning the lazy Susan each time so he could be his opponent, too.

When he had retired, he'd pictured himself alone in the house and quite enjoying it, savoring each day, the way he'd become accustomed to living in his post-Abbie years. Was it that brief business with Fergie, the short stretch of intimacy, that had rocked him off that base? He reached for a knight then stopped, hand hovering over the piece. *Damn.* He'd almost walked into a trap, one he'd set himself.

He heard his doorknob turn. The door to his bedroom opened, and Bonnie stuck her tousled curly blond head inside.

She winked. "Ah, caught you playing with yourself."

"Playing *by* myself. Big difference."

She eased into the room, closed the door, and came over to the table. "You can push around all the chess pieces you want, but in real life, people never act exactly like you want them to."

"Don't I know it."

She wore a fluffy, pink terry robe. When she bent over to look at the chess pieces, the top gaped open.

Al turned his head away. "Don't you wear pajamas?"

"What happened to living in the land of the free and home of the brave?" She gave her hips a shake but reached up and tugged the robe's lapels closer together to cover her tanned but loose and bouncy parts. "You're the only man in the world who'd look away. Maury would have been diving in, wearing a snorkel."

"I'm not Maury."

"I think it's your adjusting to being retired that puts you on edge."

"I am not on edge!" He realized he had snapped at her and softened his voice. "I'm sorry. Maybe I am a bit."

"I know several ways to hone that edge you claim you don't have right off you, Al, and one or two of them would leave your toes so curled you wouldn't be able to walk for a week."

He didn't have a quick answer to that. The house was so still he could hear the wind scratching limbs against its sides.

She nudged his arm. "Admit it. You miss the string bean."

"Fergie?"

"Of course, Fergie."

He'd been thinking about Fergie more than he liked to admit. Where Bonnie was frisky like some woodland creature, in her thirties, and buxom, Fergie was his age, stood six-foot-two, and was as lean as a rake handle, as Maury put it. Fergie also had the dignity and caution that went with being a city police detective. Perhaps that was why she'd headed for parts unknown after their last group flirtation with death. Well, that and maybe her house burning to the ground.

Years ago he'd been at a law enforcement convention in New York City, had thought, "What the hell," and had grabbed the subway all the way out to Coney Island in a break between sessions. The way he figured it, when would a chance like that come along again?

Rocking through lit tunnels and overpasses running through neighborhoods, he'd relished the surreal feel of it all. At the end of the line, he'd left the subway car and walked toward the ocean, drawn by the cries of gulls and the salty air. The Atlantic was a whole different ocean. He had been to the Gulf Coast near Port Aransas many a time but never so far east. Standing on an outcrop of bedrock that stretched down at a near vertical pitch to large, sharp rocks in a row of riprap along the shore, he breathed deeply and watched a tanker slide along the horizon.

He'd looked down and spotted a woman wearing what looked like a white sari. She carried a woven basket containing fruits—pineapples, bananas, mangoes, grapes—and some yellow, red, and white flowers. She waded out into the white froth of waves along the shore in the one place where a narrow sandy beach had formed. When the water was chest high, he worried that at any moment she might plunge under the swells that rose to meet her. *What would he do then?* He tensed up. He was too far away to reach her. Then, she stopped and pushed the basket away from her until the outgoing tide caught it and began to tug it out across the waves.

When she turned and headed back to the shore, he eased away from the lip of the cliff, not wanting her to see him, as if that might spoil her moment. Her skin was darker than his, and the sari made him think she was from some far away foreign place where the customs were different. He didn't understand what she had just done or why. It was incomprehensible to him, but he'd sensed in her some karma-leveling loss. It was the same way he had felt when, years later, Fergie had gone away.

———◆———

Bonnie tied her robe belt tighter. "You know what they say. If you like something, set it free. If it's supposed to be part of your life, it'll return."

"Who says that?"

"The usual fatheads, who are probably sitting around by themselves right now. You want to know what I think?"

He shook his head and didn't hear anything rattle. "No."

"I think you're being pulled in two directions. Part of you misses those days of solitude, and part of you doesn't. You haven't been right since Fergie came back into your life and rode you like Paul Revere's horse."

He tried to focus on the chessboard, but he could sense her waiting for a response. He looked up. "It wasn't like that."

"I could practically hear the two of you galloping across the wooden bridges."

"Is there anything else you wanted to say?"

"Don't want to talk about Fergie, eh? Want to talk about Abbie, then?"

Al pressed his lips together tightly.

"You want my five-cent psychiatric couch take on that, you've knowingly or unknowingly sabotaged anything like a relationship for all these years because you're scared Maury will butt in again, the way he wrecked your marriage with Abbie, and then you'd have to kill him or something. It's why you didn't talk to him for twenty years. It's why you don't think you can care for or need anyone. Am I close?" Her eyes opened as wide as they could get. She waited.

The phone rang. He glanced at his watch. It wasn't even three thirty yet.

"Saved by the bell," Bonnie muttered.

He darted into his bathroom to get the phone before it woke Maury, while she headed out of his bedroom and closed the door behind her. He kept the phone there so it wouldn't blast right in his ear during one of those middle-of-the-night calls. He picked up the receiver.

"I'll bet you're up and dressed already, Al," Clayton said.

"How'd you know I'd be up?"

"And restless too, no doubt. Sitting on your hands? Making out your bucket list? Playing with yourself?"

"Well, I was playing chess with myself."

"Sure you were."

Al didn't care to argue the point. "What do you want, calling at this hour?"

"I'd like you to ride along with Wayon for a few days."

"I'd rather not. I'm retired. When I was learning the ropes, I sure wouldn't have wanted some geezer riding with me, looking over my shoulder."

"You're no geezer. You're sixty-two. Too young to have retired anyway, in my book. I'm a fair bit older than that myself. Being idle doesn't suit you."

"His lessons will stick better if he learns them himself."

"I'd rather he not make any big mistakes just now. I'm asking the favor. Just a couple or three days."

"What do you think he's missing that needs honed up?"

"Maybe intensity, the way you attack projects."

"Me?"

"Anyone who's ever messed with a bobcat would

understand you, Al. You're easy to misjudge. You come across as calm, laid back. You're not really. You can be lightning in a bottle when riled."

"You want some of that in him?"

"Just enough of a taste to take him to the next level. He can get the rest of the way on his own. I want to make the horse thirsty. You know the saying: you can lead a horse to water, but you can't make it drink. But you *can* thirsty up the horse. Once he gets energized and pointed right, then all you have to do is get out of the way. We'll see if he has a chance to amount to anything, the way you did. Just that tiny little starter nudge, Al."

"Well, okay." Al glanced at his watch. He was about to ask Clayton what he was doing up at that hour, but he'd already hung up.

The thing about Clayton was that his simple request probably wasn't a simple request. He often had an agenda inside an agenda. A guy like him, with three hundred deputies and nine hundred correctional facility employees, as well as tactical and investigation teams, didn't need to be quite so hands-on. He also had a chief deputy, three majors, and eight captains working under him. Some people didn't get why the man would occasionally climb out from behind his desk to handle one or two special cases and mingle, especially with his detectives. Al figured it all stemmed from Clayton's mother-hen need to protect the citizens of his county, but it didn't do any good to probe for an ulterior motive. For Clayton to make that call, something must have been tickling deep in his gut.

Maybe it had to do with Wayon, maybe it didn't. Wayon had the training, but perhaps he did need a touch more supervision and guidance. Al's twenty-five years in the department, much of it working for Clayton, had predisposed him not to leap to quick conclusions.

He went back to his chess game, but the pieces began to blur. He was thinking about a bucket list, something he was too young to be mulling over. He wondered what had started that train of thought then tracked it back to something Clayton had said. Most of Al's pals his own age had kids, grandkids, wives, and ex-wives. A few of them were still, amazingly enough, married to their original spouses. He couldn't begin to imagine what lives like that were like.

So what did he want? What should he do before it came his time to shed this mortal coil? He shrugged. He'd opened the chess game with a Ruy Lopez against an open defense, not too challenging. He would see where it took him until the sun made its way up.

Al stepped out onto his front porch. Steady beads of water dropped from the ends of tree limbs, catching a sparkle here and there as they fell. Sunbeams speared through the thick green growth of trees, lighting his house in a spray of moving, swaying yellow spots. A post-rain moist breeze swept across his face. It felt as if the world were taking a moment to sigh. He took a deep breath and thought, not for the first time, that it would be nice to share that moment with someone.

He walked to the shed, where he scooped some deer feed pellets from the fifty-pound bag. He carried the full bucket to a wide-open area packed hard by many hooves. The place was circled by a tight green wall of mountain cedar, live oak, mesquite, vitex, and one stand of agarita taller than Al. But the thickness of the living curtain didn't mean he wasn't seen and watched.

As soon as Al stepped into the feeding spot, the deer began to move toward him through the underbrush, some steady with eyes fixed on him, licking their lips, others leaping his way in sprints from at least three directions. There were a dozen does, half as many fawns, and at least three young bucks. The biggest buck, Spikey, three years old and with only two points but foot-long antlers— nothing to be proud of since they were as thin as bent knitting needles—crowded especially close and began to eat. Al could see Spikey's ribs and knew that as soon as he stepped away, one of the does would poke Spikey in the haunch with a front hoof and he would move back from the food. Al stood there for a bit longer so Spikey could grab a few mouthfuls.

"I don't know, Spikey. Someday, you're going to have to grow you a pair. Maybe you'll make up for all this in the rut season."

The doe that moved in to displace Spikey was Nora, his twin sister. She had two fawns of her own that were just losing their spots. She raised a front hoof to jab at Spikey.

Al stepped a little closer to Spikey. Nora paused and didn't poke. As much as he worried about Spikey being pretty much a wuss, he was more troubled about what a bully Nora had become. He called her "Nora, the queen of all deer," but there wasn't much queenly about the way she dominated the area just because she and Spikey had been born there within sight of his lakeside house. She lowered her hoof and looked up at Al with big eyes that could seem sweet, even innocent, yet still had a stern touch of Queen Victoria to them.

He heard the crunch of gravel and looked up. A car pulled up along the drive, swung in the curve in front of the house, and stopped. Wayon Gallard sat behind the wheel of the sheriff department's car, the same vehicle Al had driven before retiring. With its push bumper on the front, searchlight, and tax-exempt license plates, it was hardly an unmarked squad car, though it might seem that way to some civilians.

Al finished sprinkling the feed in a wide pattern so all the deer could get some without too much assertion of hierarchy. That gave Wayon time to get out of the car. "That's it for today. Now play nice."

Al moved away from the deer so Wayon wouldn't feel obliged to come closer, which would frighten them. Nora jabbed Spikey with her hoof. Spikey gave Al a look as if asking for help.

"You're on your own," Al said. "Stand up for yourself or go hungry."

"I heard that you talk to deer. Is that what retirement does to a man?" Wayon's grin had a mocking edge he didn't try to disguise.

"That doesn't mean they understand. It just means it comforts my soul to do so. Probably makes me feel needed too, like having unthankful kids."

Al had jogged twice that week and hit the free weights yesterday at the gym. He was feeling pretty taut, fit, and ready for someone his age. Wayon seemed as tight, almost *up*tight.

"Even Clayton says you think you really talk to animals."

"I've heard you mumble to yourself while inspecting a crime scene, Wayon."

"At least I have an intelligent audience."

"I don't know about that. Sheriff Clayton didn't seem to agree when he asked me to ride along with you. Leaving a crime scene? Really?"

Wayon lowered his head, mouth tightened. Then he struggled to grin. "We all learn, don't we?"

"Sure. I guess we do."

"Was Clayton kind of pissed when he called you?"

"Oh, I don't know. He always sounds like a grizzly

someone roused from hibernation. He did ask the favor, though."

"Does that mean you're to handle the case?"

"Of course not. Just so you know, I'm as unhappy about this as you are. I'm supposed to be retired. But Clayton asked the favor. I'm just to go along for the ride, do a bit of mentoring if the need arises. Otherwise I'll stay shut up. That work for you?"

"Thanks. Anyone else but you and I'd be worried."

"What's that mean?"

"You aren't on any mission to prove anything. It's all about results. A lot of detectives think they're building a legend that's going to get them added to Mount Rushmore."

"Not me."

"There you go."

———◆———

They'd gone a few miles down the road when Wayon asked, "Is that skirt-chasing brother of yours still staying with you?"

"Maury? He's still at my place, recovering from the effects of a small heart attack, if that's what you mean. His nurse, Bonnie, is still on board, too."

"Didn't he get the heart attack from Viagra?"

"A couple or three of them someone slipped him."

"Death by Viagra. Now there's a tombstone marker for you."

"That's my brother you're talking about, Wayon. Besides, he wouldn't have taken them on his own. Bad heart. Old news now. Sure, he was a bit of a chaser, a womanizer, a player. But he's doing better, and he's working on his urges, too. Bonnie helps. She carries a small cast-iron frying pan in case he feels frisky. That tones him down."

"That'd do it for me."

They stayed quiet for a stretch, the only sound the raspy hum of road passing beneath the wheels. Al reached for the radio and turned it on. Wayon glanced at him. The station was in the middle of a country-western song. Al fiddled with the tuner until he found the classical station he listened to at home. "Ah, Smetena. That's *Má Vlast*, his best work."

"You know composers by name?"

"Yep. That's Bedřich Smetana."

"Now you're just yanking my chain. Bed-rich?"

"Nope. That's his first name."

"What's he do, come over to your house and visit?"

"Well, he did." Al paused a couple of ticks. "Until he died in 1884."

Wayon snapped his head to raise an eyebrow at Al then turned back to the road. He gripped the wheel tighter. "Can't believe you'd know a name like that."

"Hard to forget. Take Thackeray. His middle name was Makepeace. William Makepeace Thackeray. Or hell, take Tiger Woods. His real name is Eldrick Tont Woods. Once you know a thing like that, it's hard to get shed of it. No big trick to any of it if your memory works at all."

Wayon's glance that time took a bare second.

Hmmm. Clayton had sensed something was going on with Wayon, and Al was getting a touch of it, too. All he wanted was for Wayon to be off balance enough to give away his tell, then Al could mentor him. A really sharp cop would have caught on to the nudging. Wayon seemed deep in his own thoughts. The quiet was okay with Al. He listened to the orchestra float down Bohemia's Vltava River.

Wayon tilted his head. "What do you make of the rule of threes?"

Al reached out and turned off the radio. The piece was

wrapping up anyway, had made it through the musical rapids. "Look, to be up front here, I thought there was something hinky about the note from the get-go. It's not the kind of thing that happens at a crime scene. It feels cheap, manufactured. Often as not, something like that's a red herring. But the part about someone coming back to get the note, now that makes it interesting."

"Still, what could the damn thing mean?"

"Depends on whether you're talking about photography, medicine, math, the Wicca religion, a play, writing, economics, statistics, diving, Christianity, memory aids, or basic survival. And that's just some of them."

"Whoa. Get out of town! There can't be that many rules of three."

"Well, there are. Blame it on the memory trick that it's easier to remember three things than, say, nine or eleven. In the case of survival, it's three minutes without air, three days without water, or three weeks without food. Though I've heard it another way, where the second is three hours when improperly dressed for extreme heat or cold. Hypothermia, I'm told, is a bitch."

"What is wrong with you? You can't possibly remember that kind of detail."

"Wayon, it's more of a curse than a blessing. I'm a very curious person, and I have a better-than-average memory. So stuff sticks. The thing is that the more likely the information is to be useless, the more likely it is to stick." *Yeah, he sure couldn't forget. But could he forgive? The jury was still out on that.*

"What does this rule of three seem to mean here?"

"Well, in the case of photography, it applies to the fact that the human eye is drawn to a place about two thirds up in a photo. That's usually where you want your subjects for a pleasing effect, instead of dead center in the picture.

If your subject is in the sky, then you want your horizon a third of the way up from the bottom."

"How's that fit?"

"Probably doesn't." Al ignored Wayon's exasperated sigh. "Hell, it's a farm. One rule of three might be a succotash field. That's where you plant corn, beans, and squash or pumpkin all in the same field. The succotash I ate as a kid was a combo of lima or kidney beans, green beans, and corn. But I've heard there are a lot of variations."

"Come on, Al. What makes sense for this woman's murder?"

"Killing little old ladies rarely makes sense to me. Earlier, I asked Bonnie what sprang to her mind, and she came up with the rule of three for happiness, one I'd never heard of."

"Hard to believe," Wayon muttered.

"That one is love what you have, build loving relationships, and love what you do."

"What a load of cow droppings."

"Why did you want to become a detective?"

Wayon clenched the wheel even tighter, glanced at Al, then turned back to watching the road. "Are you trying to change the subject?"

"Same subject. Different agenda. Well?"

"The pay's better, and the job's more challenging, less dull. That makes it more enjoyable, or at least endurable. Was it the same for you?"

"Not really. I didn't have a family or kids by the time I made detective."

"Well, I do," Wayon said. "I'm going through a messy divorce that costs a fortune. But the money wasn't the motivator for you?"

"Naw. I was just a nosy sort. When I was younger, I had missed a detail or two in a case, and that made me rabidly curious to always know what's going on." He thought of Abbie but saw no need to mention her.

"And that includes all this detail about the rule of three?"

"Nope. I just find that interesting, in a Rubik's Cube sort of way." Al studied Wayon's profile. "Sure you don't want to hear any more?"

"Not without a barf bag." Wayon clenched his jaw, the muscles twitching as he ground his teeth.

Something about Wayon, maybe his being a little over-eager and slightly full of himself, made Al enjoy the needling more than he should have. He'd just been trying to get a rise out of the deputy to get a feel for how the man was at doing his job, how his mind worked. Al had mentored younger men before, and he'd found he needed to take a different approach with each individual. Clayton had been onto something. Wayon wasn't what Al would call relaxed. Wayon would need to work on that if he was going to be able to go with the flow of the everyday disruptions of being a detective while still achieving the objectives.

The radio squawked, saving Wayon from the brain aneurism that seemed to be looming in his near future. Julie Ann, the dispatcher, shared that a cigarette boat had run aground by a boat ramp. No one had reported it stolen, but the department was calling the owner.

"Hey, that's near here. Almost on the way," Al said. "Why don't we swing by?"

"Are you kidding? I hardly think a stolen boat trumps a murder. We're on the way to investigate a homicide."

"Exactly. One that happened on the same day, in the same general area. Call it a hunch. The murder can keep. The M.E. probably has the body back on a table by now. There'll be plenty of time to poke around at the farm."

Wayon sighed and pulled into a driveway. He reversed

out and turned the car around. Pulling back onto the road, he made a show of checking his mirrors, probably hoping Al would think he needed to concentrate on driving and conversation would be a distraction.

Al realized he was humming "Maggie's Farm" and made himself stop. He stayed quiet to give Wayon time to get back his equilibrium. Everyone had buttons.

During Al's first year as a detective, he and his partner, Barrett, had arrived at a crime scene ahead of the M.E. and the tech crew. Milt Steven was dead. That was a cold fact. The first deputy on the scene had found him in the barn. An owl's head could rotate as much as two hundred sixty degrees. But when an owl turned its head one way while twisting its body the other, it gave the illusion it could rotate its head three hundred sixty degrees. People's heads couldn't do any of that, though Milt's head had tried. Plus, he was under a ladder when the thing should have fallen away from him.

The first thing Clayton had told Al about being a detective was that he would have to look at the whole picture and exhaust all possibilities if he was to present the best case to the district attorney, one the D.A. could win. The opposite of success, as Clayton put it, was to make a homicide arrest and have the suspect found not guilty because of the lack of thoroughness in the investigation.

As soon as he stepped out of the cruiser, Al noticed that the victim's nineteen-year-old son, Terrant, had a black eye. "How'd you get that?" Al asked.

"I could say I fell, but you're going to find out. Dad and I got into a fight, a public one. I went to confront him at the Pig's Whistle, a pub about three miles from here. He was drunk. No surprise there. We got into it."

"What about?"

"I'd rather not say."

"I'm afraid you're going to have to."

Terrant shrugged.

"You inherit the place, right? Three hundred acres or so. Not a huge spread, but your dad made good money selling hay."

"I'm not going to say anything else."

The crime scene crew was still going over the barn, but there was enough to take the boy in for questioning. Heather, the fourteen-year-old daughter, had long blond pigtails and a splash of freckles across her nose. She cried when they put Terrant into the cruiser.

"Please, please." Heather grabbed Al's forearm and squeezed. "He couldn't have done it. He was the nicest boy in school, in the county. Ask anyone. He just needed to get away from here. I tried to get him to enlist, anything. Sure, Dad could be rough, but he loved us in his own hard way."

The hard country way. Al dismissed the thought as not being fair since he hadn't grown up on a farm and couldn't really know anything, just guess.

Heather squeezed harder and looked up at him through her lashes in a way that should have niggled. Her eyes were red, her cheeks shiny with tears, but those pale-blue eyes held a hint of invitation. Then he decided he was mistaken. She was just a grieving young girl.

Some prints found on the ladder, the fight, and the motivating inheritance were enough to hold the son overnight. As if that wasn't enough cake, Terrant later confessed on tape during his interrogation. Icing. Two hours after the young man was returned to his cell, he managed to hang himself with his own T-shirt. That slammed the file closed on the case.

"Would have been a slam dunk anyway," Al told Clayton.

"Nothing—I repeat, *nothing*—is ever a slam dunk." Clayton seemed irritated, but Al didn't know why.

Al spent the next nine years trying to figure out what had bothered Clayton. What had happened with Abbie and Maury should have taught Al to trust nothing. His big-picture antennas should have been ramrod stiff and perking when years ago he'd been fresh at that crime scene at the barn. But he'd missed it way back then, and he'd missed it with her.

Heather sold the farm and traveled the world. She returned looking thirty years older and carrying a methamphetamine habit that had made her eyes blank, her cheeks hollow, and her once-cute face pocked with reddish scabs over droopy skin. No more pigtails. She had cropped her hair short, and it was thinning. She looked as though she hadn't slept in five days when Al found her at Easy Bob's, a flop of a motel that had fallen on hard enough times that she could afford it.

They sat in the room and talked for almost an hour. He told her how it must have gone down, the only way he could figure it after years of playing the same record, going over the details again and again. Her father hadn't abused her. She'd just gotten impatient and greedy, and had seen a path to the money. She nodded and looked up at him. As she leaned closer, he saw a brief hint of invitation in those pale-blue eyes—haunted eyes that had lost their ability to reel anyone in—and thought he had seen something similar at their last meeting. "You must be a very unhappy young lady."

She nodded.

Al took out his wallet and withdrew two hundred-dollar bills. *That ought to about do it.* Money in the hands of someone as far gone as she was wouldn't provide groceries and a fresh start; it was drugs and lots of them. A binge. He put the bills on the chipped credenza, next to the bolted-down television. "I hope you find peace."

Late the next afternoon, he heard they'd found her in a coma and that she was DOA by the time they got her to a hospital. She'd killed her father, had been the one to push the ladder, sending him to his death. She'd let her brother be taken in for the crime and had as good as killed her brother. And Al had killed her as sure as if he'd given her a gun and pulled the trigger himself. Yet he read the department report and newspaper account of her overdose with a little weasel of unsatisfied curiosity gnawing at his innards.

He went to her funeral and watched the faces. He stayed while her body was lowered into the ground.

Years later, he was still mulling over that case, still working it out in his head. In all the cases he'd turned inside out, in all the stories he'd told or heard anyone else tell, the single function of each had been the same as the driving purpose of his life—to find the truth. Never fun, often painful, and sometimes the opposite of what he hoped.

———◆———

"Hey?"

Al looked over at Wayon and noted the tightened forehead. "Yeah?"

"You were just drilling for a nerve there earlier, weren't you?"

"Yeah," Al said. "Let's say that."

"Okay, then. We're cool."

CHAPTER THREE

THE PARKING AREA WASN'T CROWDED, just three pickup trucks with empty boat trailers lined up in the gravel lot. The lake that stretched out from the boat ramp was marked by sharp lines of waves cresting with whitecaps. A sheriff's department cruiser was parked near the beached cigarette boat, a thirty-eight-foot white Top Gun with a red racing stripe.

"You live right on this lake, Al," Wayon said as they got out of the car, the wind tugging at his short brown hair. "Ever see one like that before?"

"All the time. Way too many of them. But I don't recall this one in particular. Not my kind of boat. Mine's for fishing."

"Giant plastic penises, my ex-wife calls them. Ego boats. Compensation for something. Wouldn't want the fuel bill, though."

"You said it." Al nodded. "One like this could burn a hundred fifty gallons an hour at a hundred miles per hour. At full throttle, more. Tank holds three hundred gallons. At four or five dollars a gallon when buying on the lake, that's a bite. Do the math. That's some pretty expensive penis waving, if you ask me."

Wayon shook his head. They walked toward the water.

The deputy, Bob Hancock, stood by the boat, looking at it as if considering whether to buy one like it. "Owner's on the way. He's plenty pissed off. It was supposed to be in a locked marina slip. Forensics is on the way, too. Take a look." He pointed at the bow that had been run onto the sand and riprap of the shoreline. The owner was going to be plenty ticked off about that too. But one step at a time.

Al bent over to look at the marks along the waterline of the bow. He didn't touch, and Al pulled back Wayon's hand when he started to reach out.

"Looks like blood," Wayon said.

"And some sort of blue polyethylene. Probably a kayak."

"An accident, do you think?" Simmons said. He hung back but watched them closely. "A hit and run?"

"I don't think so," Al said. "But let's find out more first. Still, a stolen and abandoned boat? Smacks of use as a temporary weapon."

"Sheriff Clayton is firing up the department's boat," Hancock said. "Someone will go out and take a look around."

That's a good idea," Al said. "Now we've got to go to a farm. Right, Wayon?"

Wayon looked up as a black Silverado 1500 skidded to a gravel-spraying stop in the lot, stopping just short of the ramp. A small man, about five-four, in a pink-and-yellow polo shirt and black jeans hopped out of the truck.

"Compensation," Wayon muttered. "Didn't I tell you?"

Al and Wayon skirted around the approaching man to let Hancock deal with the irate owner. He was probably going to jump a foot into the air when told his boat needed to be processed for a possible homicide. Some boat owners were touchy that way.

By the time Al and Wayon pulled into the drive at the organic farm, Gladys's body had already been taken away.

The wooden cross that had once held a scarecrow stood like a makeshift religious icon in the middle of its ring of fluttering yellow tape. The forensics crew was still digging for bullets and casting around for any usable footprints.

Al didn't expect much from that. "Let's go on to the house," he said.

Wayon nodded and parked near the front door of the farmhouse. He turned off the car and reached for his door handle.

Al held up a hand. "Just a minute." He punched a number into his cell phone. "Hey, Julie Ann. Can you look something up for me?"

"Can you hold on?"

He put his hand over the mic and told Wayon, "They always ask you to hold on but never tell you to what."

Wayon rolled his eyes.

Al lifted the phone again at the sound of a voice. "Yeah, still here. What I want is for you to see if you can give me anything on the Three Sisters Organic Farm. Yep. Our crime scene. Well, one of them."

"Sheriff Clayton had us start a file on it that's right here."

He took a small notepad out of his back right pocket and a pen from his shirt pocket. "Go ahead."

"The place is twelve hundred forty acres. But they only farm on twenty acres of it."

"Doesn't seem like much." He was writing away.

"Oh, and the sisters are Thelma, Millie, and Gladys Sanders," Julie Ann said. "The M.E.'s working on Gladys right now."

"Okay. Well, I doubt I share that with the other two." Al closed his phone.

"I could have told you most of that," Wayon said.

"It's a bigger spread than I thought."

He'd seen the rows of rounded plastic covers over some plants, more shaded coverings for others. A few peach trees stood in a grove along the side where the scarecrow had been. A chicken coop ran alongside a big shed that acted as barn and cover for where the tractor was parked. The farm wasn't anything to get rich on. Al knew the sisters sold most of their goods directly to the public instead of to stores, so their margin was better than some farms'. He'd seen their stand open on Saturday mornings at the nearby intersection, and they usually participated in one or two of the farmers' markets in Austin. He'd bought green onions, zucchini, arugula, escarole, and fresh greens from them, all very good stuff. A little pricey, but he didn't mind since it was fresh and going to support a farm like theirs. He was trying to think back to whether or not he'd ever met Gladys, but he wasn't sure.

Al looked around the farm as he and Wayon went up to the farmhouse, a two-story wooden home with one of those white-latticed porches that wrapped all the way around the first floor. A row of three rocking chairs teetered on their own in the breeze. Wayon walked past them and rapped his knuckles on the wood of the front door.

Pudge Simmons opened the door, his eyes widening when he saw Al. "Doesn't Clayton trust you, Wayon? Had to call in the pro from Dover on this?"

"I'm just here to pitch in as it helps," Al said. "Just a fly on the wall. Wayon here is still on point." Pudge had a bit to learn about tact if he was going to last long in the department. He might as well eat something, too. Man was as skinny as an upright zipper.

The two sisters sat on a couch in the living room. He didn't see a television, so they probably read or played music in the evenings. The couch looked like their usual spot to roost. They had gone to it because it was a comfortable home base to them. People did that when they lost someone close.

Wayon perched on the matching love seat at a right angle to the sofa. Al chose the wooden rocker, and from the way the two of them flinched, he guessed that was where Gladys usually sat. But he stayed put, figuring that would make the fewest waves.

Both ladies wore denim coveralls with white blouses. They had on slippers, but Al had taken in the matching rubber boots by the front door. There had been room for another pair in the row. Their once-bright-red hair was frizzing into silver tangles, and their faces glowed the rough reddish hue of people who worked outside a lot. It would be clear to anyone that they were sisters.

Wayon indicated the one on the left. "This is Millie"— he gestured to the right—"and that's Thelma. Gladys was their older sister, but they were all born within a year of each other and were pretty close."

Al nodded to each then rocked slowly.

Wayon took the cue and said, "Can you think of anyone who might have wanted to harm your sister?"

They shook their heads. Millie lifted an embroidered handkerchief and rubbed at her cheek the way she'd erase a stubborn mark from a chalkboard, as if a little angry at herself for crying. Thelma clenched her hands into fists.

"You told Pudge, Deputy Simmons, that she'd had a few symptoms of dementia lately. Is that correct?"

"I'm the one ought to be checked," Thelma said. "I have enough senior moments for all of us. I go to feed the chickens and end up watering the radishes. It's a wonder anything gets done right. It's a good thing the younger help is around to make sure we aren't a danger to ourselves."

Al had them figured for maybe just a few years older than he was. Being outside all the time might have weathered them more, but they seemed like solid country stock. Though Alzheimer's could sneak up on anyone.

"She said she was seeing things," Millie said. Her voice quivered. "People coming up out of the ground. Another time she saw people up a tree."

"Is there any chance she could have really seen those things?" Wayon asked.

"Are you kidding?" Thelma pursed her lips and cocked her head. "She was bongo in the Congo. I think that's the technical term for it. At least they weren't little green men or anything."

"You say some other hands work on the farm. How many?" Wayon glanced toward Al, who nodded. The questions were coming in the right order.

"There's Betty, Rheba, Roger, and Darin. Darin is Gladys's son. She's the only one of us married, and it didn't last." Millie started to hiccup.

Thelma patted her shoulder. "She didn't have Darin until she was in her late thirties. Maybe that took something out of her. I wouldn't know about that sort of thing."

"Did any of them see any of these things? People coming out of the ground and such?"

"Of course not," Thelma said. "That's why we had an appointment to get Gladys checked. A checkup from the neck up. We heard there were meds that might help. Heaven knows we already take plenty, what with the aches and pains of working for a living. And now there's going to be more for all of us to do."

Millie's crying picked up, and Al was going to wave Wayon off, but his phone rang. He got up and went out on the front porch to answer it.

"Clayton here. I'm in the boat. You got any ideas?"

"Why not swing by closer to the organic farm? A stretch of it runs along the shoreline."

"Is this a hunch or something solid?"

"Hunch right now."

Clayton clicked off. Al went back inside.

Al waited for a break in the questioning then asked, "Does anyone here own a kayak? A blue one?"

Thelma nodded. "Darin does. Why do you ask? We've been trying to get him, but he's not around. We figure he went for a paddle."

"Is his kayak blue?"

"Yes. Why?"

Wayon glanced at Al. Al gave him half a headshake. Al's phone rang again. He apologized and stepped back out on the porch, closing the front door behind him.

"Clayton here. We have pieces of a blue kayak and an ID for Darin Sanders that was in the vest. Haven't found a body yet, but we've got blood."

"Sounds like it's Gladys's kid, Darin."

"You're right there at the farm, aren't you?"

"Yep."

"Depends on what we find, but it doesn't look good. We may have to break it to them their nephew's dead, too. I'm sending down divers. I confirm anything, I'll be heading that way in a blaze. Those ol' gals have sure had a day of it, haven't they? Use kid gloves for now. But if this all hangs together... well, you know what we'll be up against."

He hung up. Al looked out at the peaceful farm. He couldn't see the forensics people at work. But if things were shaping up the way they looked, the quiet farm and the poor rattled ladies were in for a real media shit storm in short order.

CHAPTER FOUR

CARL FRANKLIN LET HIS SON out before he pulled his Dodge minivan into the garage and hit the button on the visor. The door rolled down into place behind the vehicle. He turned off the engine and reached back to get the gun, a 30-06 Browning Bar Safari rifle with scope that had been his father's. The spent brass casings rattled in his shirt pocket as he got out of the vehicle and swept a caressing hand across the rifle's scroll engraving. He'd sure hate to lose the gun, if it came to that.

Still in the garage, he opened the gun safe and put the gun back into place next to the Winchester Model 12 shotgun his father had given him when he'd turned twelve. He went inside to the kitchen. Roger pulled the folded paper from his pocket, crumpled it, and tossed it into the plastic-lined trash can beneath the sink.

"Are you simple?" Carl said. "You need to burn that."

Roger sighed, an elaborate moan of breath, and retrieved the paper. He held it over the sink, took a Bic lighter from his pocket, lit one corner of the paper, then let it drop once the flames neared his finger and thumb.

"Don't look so surprised I have a lighter," he said. "I smoke. Get over it."

"You don't think I could tell when you smell like an ashtray?"

Roger turned on the water, swirled the black ashes

toward the drain, and flipped on the garbage disposal. "There." He dried his hands on the towel that hung from a hook beside the sink.

"Next time don't do something so stupid."

"Next time..." Roger started to say in a mocking whine.

"Oh, go to your room."

"I don't go to my room anymore, Dad. I'm twenty-four now. I don't have to do what—"

"Then get out of my sight for a while. I have to get ready for a funeral." He wondered what Clarisse would say about the way her son had turned out.

Carl went through his master bedroom to the bathroom, washed his hands once with rubbing alcohol, then with lotion, and again three times with soap to get off any GSR. Then he took off the clothes he wore and went to his closet for his suit. He changed quickly and went into the bathroom to take a look at himself. He made sure his clerical collar was square in front, where it should be.

On the way through the house he grabbed his Bible and put it on the seat beside him when he got into the minivan. He was already rehearsing what he would say as he backed down the drive to head for the funeral home.

<hr />

Al let Wayon lead the way as they hiked up the hill to where the shooter had been. He doubted the guy had come up this way. The forensics crowd had tromped up this way too, or Al would have looked around more closely for signs of anyone else using this way up. Almost certainly a guy. Few women are rifle snipers, though he couldn't rule anything out yet. Whoever it was hadn't hit anybody, though that could as readily be good shooting as bad.

Al hated to admit it, since he'd pitched this as something of an ordeal and bother to himself, but he was enjoying the crunch of gravel and snap of dead sticks beneath his boots, the strain on his calves as they walked up the hill, and the breeze that swept across the lake and tousled his hair. He took deep breaths and absorbed all the details he could as they hiked upward. His enjoying the climb, even given the circumstance, made it a guilty pleasure, so he savored it all the more.

As they came to the place where the shooter had been, the hilltop spread out with more rock, but some green sprinkled through it now too.

"No shell casings and no footprints," Wayon said. "Although one of the techies who fancies himself part Native American followed a faint trail of bent grass and broken limb tips of mountain cedar to the parking lot of the adjacent park."

"I'd like to follow that trail once we've looked around." Al turned and looked about from the same spot where the shooter had stood, getting the perspective. It was a beautiful scene to take in, though he doubted the sniper or even Wayon was able to enjoy it as much as Al. Being retired makes a difference. To his left the lake formed a border that ran along the far side of the property. The farm lay nestled in the valley below the hill. An equally steep hill climbed up to the same height on the far side. These hills that formed bookends to the farm both turned into rocky cliff faces when looked at from the water. Al could make out the sheriff's boat and a couple of diving boats with their red "diver below" flags, still working the scene where they hoped to find a body, or parts of one. The wind was stacking up vigorous wave sets that had to make the work out there a challenge.

The breeze tugged at Al's own hair as he took in the farm buildings, the land closest marked by rows of plants sheltered by arching rows of plastic. A stand of peach trees ran along the side of the road where Gladys's body had been. To the farthest right he could make out the corner where the organic farm had a stand across from an old-time general store turned convenience store. A country pub occupied the opposing corner, a place called Fuzzy's, much favored by the bikers who liked to traverse the winding road and stop there for refreshments. A row of three or four bikes and two pickups outside the door showed there were patrons present even at the early hour.

The sheriff's department had made a number of visits to Fuzzy's. One of the most colorful recent ones while Al had still been working in the department had been when an off-duty city cop, Bart Haley, peeled out from inside the bar, leaving skid marks across the wooden floor. He and his wife, Daryl, also an off-duty city cop, had flown back on the highway toward Austin. Only thing was, when they came to the first sharp curve, Daryl had really flown, going straight over a cliff with a hundred-thirty-foot drop, still screaming and gunning her Katey Jo Road King Classic Harley as she sailed out of sight. Bart had to loop back and find where she went off. Three cars and a sheriff's cruiser that happened to be going by also pulled over. At least two of the auto drivers claimed they had heard her final screaming. Bart hadn't. The barmaid at Fuzzy's claimed she hadn't wanted to keep serving Bart and Daryl, but they were cops for heaven's sake. Hard to say no to that. She hadn't thought it odd at all, she said, that Bart and Daryl had ridden their bikes inside and had peeled out to leave from there.

"Okay, let's see this trail your scout found." Al turned and let Wayon have the lead again.

Wayon led the way. "You don't think Clayton has lost faith in me already, do you?"

"I may have known Clayton for twice as long as you,

but he hasn't changed any. He was and remains the most cautious bear in the circus. Few cases we handled were slam dunks, but he always wanted every *t* crossed and every *i* dotted. That's just business as usual for him."

"Yeah, but for him to call you in. That means I screwed up major, doesn't it?"

"Wayon, maybe he just wants you to keep an eye on *me*. Who knows? I can tell you one thing. If you keep a tight focus on just this case at hand and don't worry about yourself, you're going to earn a secret smile from the sheriff, even if he's the last person to ever show it."

Wayon stayed quiet the rest of the way to the park's parking lot, which was fine with Al. It gave him the opportunity to hear the chatter of quarreling mockingbirds, and later the excited sound of a blue jay that must have found a pile of acorns. The live oak trees grew closer together, and the thick ones were well over a hundred years old. The mountain laurel grew in thick green clumps close around their trunks. It was easy for Al to see why a trail had stuck out. Few people came down this path congested with vegetation, and it was hard to pass through without brushing aside limbs and leaving some indication you'd been there.

The woods opened beside a row of low, foot-wide, round cedar posts with steel cable stretched along through them. They lined one side of the asphalt-and-gravel parking lot of one of the Travis County Parks. That was good. The park charged admission to enter unless the vehicle's owner had purchased an annual sticker. In either case, the gate attendant might remember something. Al glanced toward Wayon.

Wayon shook his head. "Kid was only half paying attention. Said they were slammed. This is the upper parking deck. There are two more parking levels, one all the way down a winding road to the water, where there's a boat ramp. Half the vehicles pulling in were families with boats wanting to use the boat ramp. The rest were cars, trucks, vans, you name it. Some paid, some had stickers. That's all we could get from him, and he's probably wondering why he has a minimum-wage summer job."

"Hmmm."

"What? There's no camera surveillance on those coming in. You think I should have fingerprinted every bill in the till?"

"I would have."

"Why?"

"Maybe to wake the kid up, piss him off a little. But there's a one-in-a-hundred chance we could get a print of the shooter. That's better odds than we have at the moment."

Al stepped to one side and kept his grin to himself while Wayon made the call, sent someone from forensics to get the bills. What Al hadn't mentioned, maybe didn't need to, was that Sheriff Clayton would have expected it. He was prone to saying, "When I mean turn over every stone, I mean *every* stone."

Wayon closed his phone. "Anything else?"

"Well, you could take me home so you can get started. I'm sure there'll be more to do if the department turns up a body in the lake."

They made their way back down the hill toward where Wayon had parked the car by the farmhouse. Al started to whistle to himself then thought better of it and stopped. It was a long, quiet walk back, with barely a bird peeping.

CHAPTER FIVE

WAYON PULLED THE DEPARTMENT CAR up as close to Al's front door as he could.

Al sat for a second or two. Wayon had been chewing the inside of his mouth for most of the trip to Al's house, not saying anything. Al wanted to tell him not to worry, to be self-confident, assertive. But those things come to someone like Wayon on their own, or not at all. Al thought Clayton had made a good choice in Wayon for the detective spot. He had the right training and background, though they both knew Wayon could be a little enthusiastic, over the top, gung-ho. You can't teach patience and deliberation, but it can be learned. Wayon just needed time, and more experience. The thing about his job was that experience was inevitable, as long as he kept showing up.

"See you," Al said. He got out and hadn't gotten to the front door by the time Wayon had eased out of sight.

Al opened the door and went in. "I'm home. Hello?"

No one answered. A muffled mumble made him turn his head. Maury sat on a straight- backed chair facing the corner. Al thought he was naked at first but realized as he got closer that Maury was wearing white jockey briefs. He was also fastened to the chair with silver duct tape. Strips of tape looped around his ankles, wrists, and upper arms, pinning him to the chair. When Al was close enough for

Maury to twist his head toward him, Al saw a strip of the tape across Maury's mouth. Al sighed. He eased the strip off.

"I'm having a time out," Maury said before Al could ask.

"What did you do?"

"Nothing really."

Al reached for the tape that went around Maury's right wrist.

"Leave him there. He has fifteen minutes more to go." Bonnie stood just outside the bend that took the big open room around to the kitchen.

"I'm innocent," Maury said in a voice no jury would believe.

Al stood up and headed toward the kitchen. "And I had so much hope for you." He shook his head.

"I am getting better," Maury said.

"Healthier," Bonnie called from the kitchen, "but not better. In fact, I vote for worse."

Al followed Bonnie around and through the dogleg at the end of the living room that swept into the kitchen.

Bonnie was cooking. She had his Cuisinart stock pot on the stove and held the lid in one hand while she stirred with a long-handled wooden spoon. Smelled like corned beef and cabbage. Well, that was *kind of* more vegetables. Al preferred to do all the cooking himself, but living in a house with others had made him bend, make concessions. He got his turns at cooking, and she got hers. But he'd had to talk to Bonnie, whose cuddly build and cute little round belly hinted at her regular dietary choices. He'd tried to talk her out of making comfort food as often as she'd like. A batch of her cheesy potatoes had sent Al to the gym to work out, just when he'd thought his gym days were over. Her mac and cheese was to die for, as was her lasagna. If

Al was to get around without a little wheelbarrow for his stomach, he needed to stay clear of that sort of thing on a regular basis. So he'd started encouraging salads and more vegetable dishes. Corned beef and cabbage must have seemed like meeting in the middle to Bonnie.

"What did he do?" Al asked.

"I was taking a shower in your bathroom. You know, that really nice shower of yours with the glass all along one side."

Al sighed.

"I look up, and there's Mr. Ogle himself leering through from the other side. I gave a scream that could have gotten me a role in *Psycho*. Then I grabbed a towel, wrapped it around me, and went out to wrestle him to the earth and convince him he needed a time out."

"He's recovering from a heart attack, Bonnie. You're a nurse."

"He's recovering just fine. Too fast, in fact. I may have to start sneaking saltpeter into his food."

"We both know he has sort of a problem regarding women. I'm glad you're able to keep him under control. But he's not hurting out there tied up like that is he?"

"My first choice was bolt cutters for a little do-it-yourself castration, Al. He's ahead in the bargain."

"I'm going to take a shower," Al said. "I'll talk to him later, if you like."

"I think he understands well enough. He just needs regular convincing, and I'm just the person to do it."

"I believe you are." Al started down the hallway toward his bedroom. Since coming to stay with Al, Maury had been living downstairs in what Al called the "guest quarters." Bonnie was supposed to be sleeping down there, too, but had moved to the upstairs couch, as she put it, "to be safer." But a couple of times Al had awakened to find her in bed with him, gently spooning. He was used to living alone. These little variations from that norm rattled him to his core. But what scared him more was that he sometimes suspected he might be getting used to being rattled.

Bonnie watched Al cross the room toward his bedroom. His stride was confident, not weary at all, but his head was down. He was obviously thinking hard. He cracked her up. Sometimes he came in from work or being outside and he seemed like a knight in rusting armor waiting to be called off on some quest, even if a reluctant one. Other times he was like an injured bird she'd found as a little girl, holding it in her hands so it wouldn't hurt its wing worse flapping to escape. Men get to a certain age and they know some things very well, know them to their aching bones. Other things, things they knew very well once, have become hazy: the old philosophical arguments about why they do what they do, how to act around women, why the sick, dark things that happen around them even matter or affect them, and why they care what others think more than half the time.

Now Maury—hard to believe these two were brothers— he was stuck in some time warp where it was cool to send nude pictures by cell phone, like that congressman who got busted. Or Bill Clinton—smart but not always with the right head in charge. She'd liked Clinton but doubted she would have agreed to get under that desk. Maury had a good heart, though, not dangerous. Just frisky. Guys were funny sometimes. Just when you thought it was all yuk, yuk, they could snap and you could get hurt, hurt bad. Her husband, bless his pea brain, had been that way until she'd known she had to get away, or kill him. *Men.*

She opened the lid on the pot. Hot cabbagey steam

surged up at her. She stirred with the long-handled wooden spoon, and her hair went *pling*, instantly curly. One of her genetic advantages, hair that permed itself in steam rooms and kitchens.

That bird, that hurt baby bird, was a mockingbird. She had nursed it and fed it by dropper and splinted its wing until she'd held it warm in her hands, taken it outside, turned it loose, and it flew away. She was pretty sure it was the same one she watched build a nest in the backyard loquat tree behind the family house weeks later. When she heard little chirpings in a few days, she eased up quietly beneath the tree, stood on her tiptoes, and tried to see up into the nest. Whoosh. A bird buzzed her, close. Then back the other way; this time it pecked her—on the back of the head as she dove, grass-staining both knees as she rolled, the bird pecking away at her, wings fluttering. She'd babied it, turned it loose, and it had turned on her. She knew it didn't hate her, was just going through confused defensive motions. That was Al in a nutshell.

He was wrestling with something. That was for sure. It made her want to strip down, oil up, and wrestle with him.

She rubbed a hand over her round little Buddha belly, smiled to herself, and felt a warm glow tingle down to her toes. More than once she'd been asked if she was early on in a pregnancy. She wasn't. She just liked food, and it liked her.

⊷⊰⊱⊶

By the time he was clean, dried off, and dressed in khaki slacks, burgundy loafers without socks, and a long-sleeved blue cotton shirt, Bonnie was yelling for him to "Come and get it."

The dining table sat between the kitchen and the back

end of the living room. Windows ran all along that side of the house. Out past the upper-level porch, Al could see the lake every day, and he glanced that way now. The orange rays of a setting sun caught the ripples the breeze was still stirring across the lake. Maury already sat at the table, dressed. He'd washed up too, but a faint pink rectangle showed around his lips where the tape had been.

"I'm glad you two could settle your differences." Al sat down.

"Settle them? How come that always means she wins?"

"Let's face it, Maury. Your intentions aren't honorable. Maybe you should work out more too, muscle up a bit."

"But she shoots people as well."

"Well, that's true enough." Bonnie approached the table and put a steaming plate of corned beef and cabbage in front of Al and another in front of Maury. She spoke over her shoulder as she headed back to get her plate. "My daddy taught me to be a crack shot so if the need to take potshots ever came up, I could hit what I was aiming at. Or miss, if that was my intention."

Al chuckled.

"What's so funny?" Bonnie asked.

"Just the case I was called in on. Someone was shooting at Wayon and Pudge. The thing is, the person missed every time. I think he meant to."

"It can be done."

"I think whoever did the shooting was good enough to miss on purpose. That's the point. Anyone else might've accidentally hurt someone."

"Why would they do that? Shoot at people and mean to miss?" Maury already had a forkful of cabbage halfway to his mouth but had paused to ask.

"To lure them away. Make Wayon and Pudge come up the hill."

"Why?"

"So the person doing the shooting could be long gone while an accomplice was retrieving a note that had been left on the corpse."

"It worked, then. Right?" Maury said.

"Yep."

Bonnie sat down.

"Would you have traipsed up that hill?"

"Nope. I'd have stayed back and waited on the younger one."

"Why younger?"

"Who leaves a corny note like that on the corpse of an old lady?"

"Old lady? I thought she was your age," Bonnie said.

"Sure, I'm old too. Just because I sparkle in a radiant glow doesn't mean I haven't piled on the years. Still not as old as Maury here."

"I'm only a year older."

"But your odometer has been turned over a couple of times, Maury. Hate to say it. You've lived hard. Been rode hard and put away wet. Too many times. That's why you have a nurse here to take care of you."

"Tied me to a chair. That's how she takes care of me. Hey, I'm fragile."

That delightful turn of the conversation could have gone on if the doorbell hadn't sounded just as Bonnie sat down.

"I'll get it," Al said. He dabbed at his face with his black linen napkin, put it down beside his plate, and rose to head for the door.

He swung it open, and there stood Fergie.

Ferguson "Fergie" Jergens, a retired city cop, a detective, who years ago Al had taken to their high school prom. Not his finest hour. They'd been in the same class. She had worn high heels on top of being six-two and had towered over his five-eleven. He'd looked at the thin string of her shoulder strap stretching across her pale white skin and had just handed her the corsage. He'd never so much as kissed her good night. Not quite a year ago they'd made up for that, and he could still picture her walking naked across the room from his bed, with steps like a panther. Then she'd drifted away again, like a leaf floating to earth, the same way she'd come back into his life.

Her hair was still long and red, though she probably helped it there these days. Still, her skin was that of a twenty-year-old, until she was without makeup, and then she still looked half her age. He'd been able to detect only the finest lines around her eyes. Fergie's eyes were purple—red flecks deep inside a dark blue when he had been real close to them—but possessed of an inner fire, an excitement that could set anyone close to flames. Al wasn't all the way reluctant for that to happen.

His heart bounced around inside his chest like an electric volleyball, but he stayed calm on the outside. "Come on in. Have you eaten?"

She shook her head.

Bonnie looked up as Al and Fergie approached the table. "Well, if it isn't our Olive Oyl friend, retired from the city fuzz."

"She's not all that thin," Al said.

"Must be like making it with a broom handle." Bonnie winked at Maury.

Maury missed the wink. He was leering at Fergie as if Al were bringing a dessert to the table.

"There's something wrong with you, Maury," Al said. "Seriously. You too, Bonnie."

"Good to see you two as well." Fergie settled into the chair Al held out for her. He went to get her a plate. "Smells good. Your cooking, Bonnie?"

Bonnie nodded. "Haven't seen you since our last happy times. You haven't had any more to do with Los Zetas, have you?"

"No. Since retiring I've avoided all gun battles. Also, since my house burned down and I collected the insurance, I've been traveling. But I got called back by the department. That's the something else I have to discuss with Al. A favor."

"Uh-oh." Bonnie glanced toward Al.

"I can do it," Maury offered. "As long as it doesn't involve getting shot at again."

"The task doesn't come with any fringe benefits, Maury."

"Oh. Then I decline." He went back to eating his cabbage.

"If it in any way might put these two at risk, you might as well go ahead and spill it, Fergie," Al said. "I'd have to tell them myself when you're gone. They might as well get it from the. . . the lovely mouth of the former city detective." Good save. He'd nearly said "the horse's mouth." She shook her head. She hadn't missed where he'd been headed with that.

Fergie waited until they were all done with the main course and had moved on to peach cobbler and coffee. She cleared her throat softly, and all heads turned toward her.

"The thing is, IA has called me in. They think they have the vise grips on me because my last partner was bent as a stepped-on pig's tail and I never ratted him out. I had to plead ignorance, but they never entirely bought it."

"Walsh Turbin. We sure know about him," Maury said. "But you're retired."

"A retirement they can take away. They hinted, in their usual firm and obvious way, that they would sweep all that under the rug if I'd help them with something."

"That's never good," Al said. "Working with Internal

Affairs. Can't help but alienate you from your friends still on the force."

"Truth be told, I don't have that many friends left, at least who haven't hit the retirement trail too."

"What do they want?" Al said.

"There's a guy, a sergeant, who's been investigated by IA ten times in the past twelve years. Squeaked through every time. Motorcycle cop, one who doesn't mind letting it be known among his close pals that he isn't above rounding up a little 420 for amateur glaucoma sufferers."

"What's 420?" Bonnie asked. She took a sip of her coffee, and for a second or two Al watched her. She tended to take each sip of her coffee with cream as if taking a bite, then chew it, and swallow hard like it was a pill.

"That's the street lingo these days among the semi-hip for marijuana," Al said.

"Really? A cop who brags he can score weed?" Bonnie shook her head. Her blond curls bounced about.

"Well, it's kind of the wrist-slap sort of crime that doesn't register so high on the concern scale these days," Fergie said. "Some think the stuff is half a step from being legalized widely. The thing is, there may be some gang connections. Biker gangs. This guy's been through a personal tragedy and is walking wide and wild, IA hears. But they just can't pin anything real on him. If IA could get anything firm on that, they could kick our guy off the force the way they'd like to." Fergie took a sip of her coffee. Looked over the rim at Al, measuring his reaction.

"His name wouldn't happen to be Bart Haley, would it?"

Fergie nearly spit out her coffee then carefully lowered her half-full cup back to the table. "Now, how in pluperfect hell did you know that?"

Bonnie banged around the pots and plates more than usual as she cleared the table. Al had watched her giving him sideways glances ever since Fergie had arrived. She could be a little protective and territorial. He wasn't sure which was at play at the moment. Al had volunteered to help with the dishes, but she had insisted, nearly snapping at him. He let her, since he sensed smoke coming out of her ears. Any minute now. Tick. Tick. Tick.

Fergie sat across from him at the dining table, and Maury sat to one side. They sipped from freshly filled coffee mugs.

"What is it?" Al said at last.

Bonnie spun and rubbed at her hands with a dish towel. She spoke to both of them. "The thing is, you got a guy who Internal Affairs can't pin down, who's likely to be tangled with gangs. This sounds like the sort of thing the department can't handle on its own, so they cast about for a low-risk way to take another stab at it—someone expendable, so there's no downside . . . for them. Got it so far?"

Both Fergie and Al nodded. Maury tilted his head in thought.

"That's pretty astute of you," Fergie said.

"Don't talk down to me," Bonnie said. "I didn't just fall off the rutabaga wagon, or whatever passes for a turnip truck out in these parts."

"Sorry, I—"

Bonnie interrupted, "Then you take a guy who may seem hard on the exterior, but is soft enough of a sap to be the kind of guy who feeds deer, and one who's apt to put out twice as much food if one of the deer is limping. You add to that he's the type to prefer cozying up to a reluctant rake handle before he'd go for someone willing and voluptuous and right damn here in front of him every damn day, and I see two suckers rushing off to something that could mess up all of our lives. That's all I'm saying. I realize they may have Fergie in their vise grips, but her coming here all limping deer sends up more than one blue warning flare. That's all I'm saying."

Bonnie slammed the dish towel onto the counter and took off at a run past the table and down the hallway to Al's room. She slammed the door behind her.

"Hmm," Fergie said. "I wouldn't really call that passive aggressive."

"No. She calls them as she sees them," Al said. "I'd better go talk to her."

"Nope. Better me." Fergie rose and headed down the hall.

"In all the time you were a world-class skirt chaser, Maury, did you ever figure women all the way out?" Al asked.

"Nope. I don't really think it can be done, by anyone." Maury waited a few ticks and said, "You know you might have to give Bonnie a poke to calm her."

"If I do, then who's going to calm me?"

"Come on. Bonnie's a dumpling. But that's not really the problem, is it? You still have a thing for Fergie, don't you?"

"Why do you say that?"

"Well, you've taken three sips from a coffee mug that's been empty for five minutes."

Al looked down into his mug and sighed. "What's the one person you don't want to come to your house but are glad when they do?"

"You mean a fireman?"

"That's how the riddle goes, but in this case, I mean Fergie."

CHAPTER SIX

A L'S EYES BLINKED OPEN. FOR part of a second he thought he'd awakened to the retirement life he'd once pictured. The house to himself. Alone. Taking the bass boat out early and moving from point to cove, casting, not much caring if he caught fish but enjoying being on the water, taking in the smells, the texture of the breeze. Nothing on his agenda but maybe feeding the deer and reading a book in his chair that evening. Then he realized he was on his sofa and that Maury stood in his blue plaid robe, staring down at him.

"What's happened to you?" Maury said. "You used to be the cool one."

Al struggled to sit up, let the covers fall off him. He wore just his boxer shorts. He reached for his shirt, which lay crumpled on the floor, tugged it on, buttoned it, and found his pants behind the couch where they'd fallen.

"I was never the cool one. And why are you concerned with me being cool all of a sudden? I'm retired. I don't have to be cool. In fact, it's probably best if I try not to be."

"Well, you're succeeding."

"Is something bothering you, Maury?" Al felt a little grumpy edge creeping into his voice.

"Sometimes when you talk to me it's like you're talking

down to me. I'm your older brother, not some comic-relief figure."

"I come home and find you tied to a chair, I get led astray. But I'm sorry. That wasn't right. Besides, if anyone is going to be the comic relief around here, it looks like it's going to be me." He glanced to the end of the room, but neither Bonnie nor Fergie had emerged from his bedroom yet.

"Seems odd," Maury said while Al got his pants on and reached for his boots. "You judge me and give me a hard time about being with more than one woman, and you have two at once."

"Yet you notice where I slept, Maury." Al waved to the blanket and pillow on the couch.

"Yeah, that is funny."

Al busied himself folding the blanket. "Yet you don't see me laughing, now. Do you?"

"If you had to choose, which one would you pick?"

"What?"

"Between Bonnie and Fergie. And, oh yes, I'm just as surprised as you are that here we are, of all people, having a talk like this. Go figure."

Al looked up from where he was pulling on his boot. He felt his brow tighten into furrowed rows.

"I mean, they both have a lot to offer," Maury said. "Fergie sure has the looks, though don't forget, she kind of betrayed you by not telling you everything about her partner, Walsh Turbin. And putting aside Bonnie's earthiness and her tendency to tie people up, she has a lot of sparkle. Plus, she's young with plenty of bounce. As I've said, a real dumpling. I've seen her naked, and I can . . ."

"What the hell is wrong with you, Maury? Seek help."

"It's just that I've never seen you quite so, well, off balance. I think you're emotionally drawn to at least one of these women, maybe both, whether you want to admit it or not."

"I can't believe I'm hearing this relationship stuff from you. Aren't you the one who once said of women, 'I just want to fuck them'? At least that's the way I remember it."

"That was a long time ago, on the day of your wedding to Abbie."

"We agreed not to talk about Abbie. Ever." After the long silence between them over what had happened, Al didn't think that was so much to ask.

"Before all that was over, she hurt me as much as she had hurt you. Well, okay, I wasn't married to her. But . . ."

Al felt a flush of anger rush in a fiery surge all the way through him. When he'd been in crisis situations, he'd let that take over, and he'd done things he wasn't altogether proud of, letting his training and physical conditioning take over. He'd surprised quite a few men bigger than he was that way. He'd sworn he'd never let that loose on Maury, and that was one reason they hadn't spoken for twenty years.

Maury must have seen a glimmer of that cross Al's face because he nipped off whatever he'd started to say.

Al pulled on his other boot. His mouth opened then closed again; he was still too full of quiet rage.

— ◆ —

Al was still mulling over the deep waters that ran in his house a few moments later while standing in front of his place. Wayon's car came up the path and swung to a stop in front of him.

Al slid into the passenger seat.

"You take care of feeding and watering your pet herd of venison?" Wayon asked.

"Yeah, and they were talking about you. They shared

some evil deer giggles that said, 'You know, we don't have to be vegetarians.' Then they licked their lips, and your name came up. Very Alfred Hitchcock."

Wayon let out a deer-like snort as he shifted gears and backed the car out of the lane.

"Clayton find anything out there on the lake?" Al asked.

"Pieces of the kid. Enough to identify. Darin Sanders. The son of the woman hanging there as a scarecrow. Clayton doesn't think it's a coincidence. Nor do I."

Al started to say something but stopped himself. Far be it from him to get in the way of these little epiphanies. Wayon was learning to piece things together. What he needed most now was enough slack rope to do so. "What about cause of death on Gladys Sanders?"

"Strangled. Neck broke. M.E.'s still writing his report, but that's the preliminary. Helluva thing to happen to a little old lady. No idea why yet."

Little old lady? Al almost reminded Wayon that Gladys was nearly the same age as Al. He thought better of it. "It's a helluva thing to happen to anyone. What's the plan for today?"

Wayon kept both hands on the steering wheel, stared ahead at the road. "Talk to everyone there. I called, and they're working. Can you believe it? Day after their sister and nephew are killed. I guess organic produce needs constant attention, no matter what."

"From what I've heard, that's true," Al said. "It's not just shove seeds in the ground and sit around waiting to count the money."

———◆———

Thelma got up from the ground so slowly Al thought he could hear her knees creak. She lifted her foam knee pad as she rose, then sidled a few steps to her left and lowered herself again. The sun was up but nowhere near hot yet at not quite eight o'clock. It cast her shadow across the row of spinach she was weeding.

"Why don't you use a hoe so you can stay standing?" Wayon asked.

Al winced but said nothing.

She tilted her head up and glared at him. "Don't you think I've already hoed? Can't hoe any closer or I'll be taking out as much spinach as weeds. Weeds mix inside with crops. You can't hoe that. Weeds won't pull themselves, so I have to go in after them."

A fairer question Wayon might have asked was why didn't she have one of the younger hands do this chore that involved so much getting up and down on knees that were almost certainly arthritic. Al figured Thelma was the sort of person who thought she was the only one who could do things right.

Both the surviving sisters seemed big-boned gnarly women who had never been immensely pretty young women. Farm girls, with rough, happy giggles, big eyes, and some of their current homeliness even back when they were young. Life had probably shuffled from a mean-hearted deck that dealt them setback after setback—even for Gladys, who had married— until the sisters folded into a defensive posture of leaning and depending only on each other. Now the tight group had lost one of its only pillars, as well as their only child. Yet here Thelma was, working away in a sun that was soon going to be relentless. She squinted up at Wayon as if he were a snake that had slithered through the grass, and maybe to her he was. She was working as hard as she was to forget, not remember.

"Of the sisters, Millie seems more emotional and you more logical," Wayon said. "What kind of person was Gladys?"

Thelma yanked at a weed as if its roots went all the way to China. "Young man, I don't appreciate anyone patronizing me or condescending to me, or, in your case, assuming you know enough about us to pigeonhole us after knowing us for so short a time."

"I . . . I . . . I'm sorry." Wayon glanced toward Al.

"If you must know, Gladys was the logical one, the most organized of us. Not that it matters a hill of beans now." She looked through the fields around them for a moment, as if looking for her sister or lost in seeing something they couldn't. "She provided for us with this land, you see. Married into it, and we kept it, despite any squawking on his side of the family. It was in his will. Everything to her. Hadn't been for that, we'd be hand-to-mouth. We've all three of us bled from the ends of our fingers to make this farm grow and work. Her loss is a terrible, terrible thing. You have to realize that. Then Darin on top of that."

She choked for a second, and Al thought she was going to break into tears. But she straightened her stiff shoulders and blinked her eyes and held it back somehow.

"I'm not sure how safe it is for any of you to be out here in the open," Wayon said. "That sniper . . ."

"Land sakes. Don't you think if he was shooting at us we'd be stretched out beside our sister?"

Al looked around from this perspective, taking in the whole little valley where the farm nestled between the road and the lake. The soil had been enriched—compost, manure, and mulch—and drip irrigation lines fed fields that had once been arid wastelands. It had taken a lot of work, and an outpouring of love, to nurture this little pocket of green. Sure, their prices at the stand were higher than those in the stores, but their produce had been picked fresh, often that morning, and the taste was nothing Al could get at the supermarket. The regular crowd of local fans, Al among them, always rushed to get their products.

Wayon glanced toward Al but got no sympathy, so he turned back to Thelma, who was attacking the weeds with vigor again. Yanking them, not just easing them, from the dark soil.

Elsewhere in the county, people were rising—some putting on coffee pots, others turning in bed for a snuggle that would soon turn into more. Birds were calling, and in the far sky toward the lake, Al could see an osprey carrying a fish in its talons. Life was going on, but it probably didn't seem so to Thelma. A slow trickle of a tear had started down her dusty left cheek.

"Do you mind if we talk to the other farm employees?" Wayon asked.

She shook her head. Didn't seem to be up to speaking.

Wayon and Al eased away and headed toward one of the buildings, where they could see a girl with a pitchfork tossing something up into a spreader. The breeze swept across the farm in the other direction, and Al felt glad about that.

They went up to her, a young black girl in coveralls, a blue blouse, and large rubber boots. She was forking what looked and smelled like horse manure into the spreader. When she saw them coming, she poked the tines of the fork into the edge of the pile and leaned on the handle, waiting. As soon as they were up to her, she said, "You know, when I was living in Austin and saw an ad for a chance to work on an organic farm at 'low pay but with satisfying work,' I leaped at it. Who knew that animal poop is organic?"

Wayon shrugged.

"I didn't care for horse manure at first, but I've grown to think it has a healthy, natural odor," she said. "I don't see much chance for there being an Eau de Horse Droppings coming on the market, but I'm just saying, it's something I got used to. Stop me if I'm rambling. I'm rattled, jangled. What's happened has me a wreck. I didn't sleep a wink."

She had the smooth, taut skin of someone in her early twenties. Her hair was pulled into a bun at the back. The sun glittered in its black sheen. She blinked at them. "Awful thing about Gladys and Darin. What can I do to help?"

"Have you noticed anything abnormal going on here at the farm?" Wayon asked.

"You mean other than one of the sisters being hung dead as a scarecrow and her son chopped up by a speed boat? Oh, and someone shooting a rifle down at the farm?"

"Yeah. Other than that." There was no fazing Wayon. "Do you have any theories? Know of any motivations?"

"Other than that the world's just suddenly gone crazy, no. I hope you catch whoever it is, and you have my permission to open a can of whoop ass on them. I know a lot of people fret about police violence, but I'd look the other way just this once."

"Gee, thanks," Wayon said. "We'll get back to you if we think of anything else to ask."

Al thought of a few things to ask but didn't sense she was the one with the answers. When he glanced back as they moved away, Betty was still leaning on her pitchfork, staring off into the rows of crops. Al followed Wayon on around the barn.

They came across Roger next, Darin's best friend according to Wayon's notes. He was kicking the tire of a large tractor, an antique John Deere with as much orange rust as faded green paint. He yelled at the machine then turned and saw them coming his way.

His eyes were red and swollen. He looked like he wanted

to reach up and rub them but kept his hands down limp at his side. "Stupid machine. Everything here is old."

He had limp dirty-blond hair grown long and shaggy, the way some kids were wearing it these days, and his face had rounded from eating anything he wanted, yet he'd still managed to stay fairly trim, probably from all the rigorous farm work. But give his metabolism a chance someday, Al thought, and he was going to end up perfectly round. He wore a short-sleeved denim shirt and tattered jeans—the first person Al had seen yet not wearing coveralls on the farm.

"What's wrong with the tractor?" Al asked. Wayon gave him a glance. He'd expected to start the questioning.

"Hard to tell. Piece of junk. Last time it was the carburetor. Had to take it apart. I found thirty years of gunk in there."

Al walked around it, looking up and down. "What happens if you get mud in the exhaust pipe?"

"What?" Roger rushed around to the back of the tractor. "Oh, good lord!" He picked up the sort of stick he might use to stir paint and dug into the end, tossing chunks of mud aside and digging again.

"Try it now," Al said.

Roger climbed up onto the tractor and turned the key. It fired up. Not the smoothest rattle Al had ever heard, but hearty and ready to get to work. Roger turned the key again, and the engine stopped. "Well, I'll be damned." He started to grin then remembered a cloud that seemed to hang over his head.

Al nodded to Wayon to question away now.

"I'm surprised you're at work. Darin was your best friend, wasn't he?" Wayon said.

"Yeah." Roger swallowed hard. "Dad says it's best to

work in times like this, take my mind off all that's going on."

"Your dad have a big work ethic or something?"

"He's a preacher." The church was on the other side of the property—church on one side, park on the other.

"Oh." Wayon glanced toward Al.

"What kind of person was Darin?" Wayon asked.

"The best."

"How so?

"Well, he was all about everyone else. A giver. And honest. Why, he couldn't take a grape in the supermarket. One of *those* kinds of people—transparent and real. Not too many of them around, at least in our class, or the world, for all I know."

"Is it likely he was messed up in anything that might have given someone reason to want to harm him?"

"No way. He jogged. He paddled his kayak. But he never bugged anyone. Not a soul."

"This is a big place," Al said. "Twelve hundred acres. You don't farm it all, do you?"

"Oh, good lord, no. We do twenty, and that's too much, especially now that we're shorthanded. We'll be glad if we can just keep everything alive and get it to market. With that in mind, I'd best get to work, now that I've got the tractor running."

He turned toward the tractor then back to Al for a second. "Thanks."

"Know where we might find Rheba?" Wayon asked.

Roger pointed past the chicken pen toward a white building made of concrete blocks. One end was open, a loading dock. Inside, a redheaded girl with long pigtails and wearing an orange rubber apron and elbow-long gloves held a hose above an oversized strainer filled with leafy greens. She didn't hear them approaching over the roar of water and gave a start when Wayon was close enough to reach toward her. She turned off the water and tugged off the gloves as she turned to them.

Her pale face was covered with freckles. Green eyes flashed in the bright overhead lights. Al didn't think she looked the least bit frail. She was perhaps the stoutest of them, a real Pippi Longstocking. She gave them a polite smile and held out a hand. She had a handshake Al thought would be good for cracking pecans. Only about five-seven but sturdy as banded steel.

Wayon started to say something, but Al held up a hand. He stepped closer—close enough to see that the girl's hard edge extended to her eyes. "Let me ask you something. Does this farm make money? I mean, with this much acreage, property taxes must be dear."

She tilted her head, and then the corner of her mouth tugged up. As sad as the day must feel to her, she couldn't fight back a grin. "I've thought about that, a lot. We hands don't make much, but the sisters make less. I've seen the way they eat. What they can't get by living off the land, they buy cheap. And here's why. They could probably make more if they were in jobs where their main question was, 'Do you want fries with that?' There are kids making sneakers in sweatshops in the Pacific Rim making more an hour. But they keep at it, because they love it."

"Do you think Gladys had insurance?" Wayon asked.

Al would have handled that differently. He would have checked on the side first.

Rheba frowned at Wayon. "I doubt it. When your fashion statement is wearing clothes you buy from the feed store, I doubt you pony up for big-bucks insurance policies. That would be money out the window to the sisters. They can squeeze a penny until Lincoln squeaks in Chinese."

"They don't rent out any of the land for grazing?" Al asked.

"There was talk of it. But the rest of the spread isn't grassy enough. Half of it is in the rocky slopes heading up to those hills on each side. Cattle wouldn't find enough for any quantity of them to do well here. Goats are out because they'd eat everything down to the roots and beyond, and if they ever got loose in the crops it'd be a disaster. So, no. No one's renting any of the land. Gladys walked about on it some, but the others left it the hell alone."

"Gladys was a hiker?" Al asked.

"More like someone who would wander off in a daze and reappear hours later covered in stickers and with her hair in a tangled knot." Rheba looked across at the farmhouse. "She might've been batty enough to fill half a dozen belfries, but I'm gonna miss the dear old coot."

When they were walking back to the car, Wayon said, "Sounds like I have a lot to check up on, but very little to go on."

"The joys of the job, Wayon. You'd better learn the thrill of mostly unproductive digging. It will be ever thus. The job isn't as exciting as some think."

For a moment it looked like Wayon had something he wanted to say. But then he thought better of it.

CHAPTER SEVEN

BART HALEY LEANED CLOSER OVER the bar, watched Peggy pour lager carefully over the back of a spoon into a tall glass that was already half full of dark ale. In England it would have been ale and porter. The Fuzzy's way might be more American, but Peggy still wrangled together one of the best arf and arfs Bart had ever tasted. She finished, set it in front of him, then went down the length of the bar to round up a couple of light beers for the two truckers playing pool. Bart curled a lip and took a sip from his glass. He called light beers "comedy beers." He wasn't on any damn diet, which is why he'd taken his uniform in to have it let out a bit just this week. Belly and all, he was about two sixty now, but the bike could still hold him. With his wife Daryl gone he didn't see any reason to cut corners or be careful. Her passing had made him a dangerous man, like Doc Holliday hanging out with Wyatt Earp. Doc had had TB and thought he should already be dead, so he wasn't afraid to shoot it out with anyone. That's the tightrope walk Bart danced these days. Didn't really give a rat's ass. It showed. Most people steered clear of him, when they could.

He listened to the truckers laughing at the pool table. Couple of assholes.

Bart stood up and lifted the leather saddlebags from the stool where he'd been sitting. He flipped them over one shoulder and headed for the men's room. When he opened the door, he could see the stars between the shifting clouds above. The bathroom area had no roof and was enclosed by a chest-high cedar fence, so he could check on his bike while taking a whiz. The breeze tugged at his hair.

A long tin trough filled with ice served as a urinal and ran along the side nearest the road. He hadn't come out here for that, but because of the footsteps he'd heard approaching. The bathroom area was lit by a bare red bulb. He waited until he could see a face before he moved closer to the fence.

"How're you doing, Larry?" Bart held out a hand.

Larry wore black biker leathers, had a Harley tattoo on the side of his neck, and wore a handlebar mustache that hadn't been trimmed in a long time, maybe never. He had a belly and looked like half the other bikers Bart had ever seen out on the road. Larry reached over the fence and plopped a bulging envelope into Bart's hand. Bart shoved it into one side of the saddlebags. From the other side of the bag he took out a clear-plastic-wrapped thick brick and handed it to Larry, who tucked it inside his jacket in one motion. It was dark enough anyone standing twenty feet away wouldn't have seen the exchange.

"You gonna be here next week?"

"I don't know who's gonna stop me." Bart winked.

"Well, there's always someone wanting to be the bigger kahuna."

"You let me worry about that. You're here with me because I'm still the best deal in town. Don't you forget it."

Larry was already walking away. He waved a hand without looking back. "Whatever, dude. See ya."

He closed the clasps on both sides of the saddlebags, flung it back to rest over his shoulder, then thought, "What the hell? As long as I'm out here." He stepped closer to the row of ice and started to unzip.

The first shot slapped against the cedar fence with the sound a flat board would make if someone swung it with all their might. Bart dove and rolled as close as he could get to the ice-filled trough, was against it by the time the second, third, and fourth shots pounded through the wall. They slammed into the outside of the trough, sending a spray of shattered ice into the air to sprinkle to the gravel around Bart like heavy flakes of snow.

His fingers curled tighter into the gravel. He hugged the ground, trying to pull himself closer to it.

A few moments went by with no more shots, then came the screech of a pickup truck's tires and the sound of an engine fading as the vehicle raced away. Bart took his first full breath in a while.

———◆———

When Al saw the flashing red and blue swirls of light ahead, he slowed his truck and glanced toward Fergie, who sat in the passenger seat, unaware she was leaning forward slightly, eager.

When he turned off the engine, he sat there. She waited too, turned to look at him.

"Does this mean you agree to help me?"

"It means I'll keep my mind open to thinking about it."

"Is it because I didn't sleep with you?"

"That would have been fun, but I doubt it would have made a difference."

"I want to be sure, too, that you're not grabbing at some scrap of your own history you think you can revive, relive differently, some unfinished business from your youth."

"Fair enough. I had a twinge of the same concern," he said. "You ever think this was how your leisure time was going to be spent once you left the force? An evening visit to an exotic place like this?" He nodded toward the sign that shouted "Fuzzy's" in fading neon.

"I didn't know what to expect. I don't knit, and traveling alone didn't turn out to be as much fun as I thought. You're asking what I want. I don't really know myself. I feel like I've been thrashing around, trying to make sense of all the free time with no real purpose in mind."

"You're preaching to the choir," he said. "Amen, sister."

"People our age, Al, who aren't attached, were never attached, or are just coming out of a second divorce, cast about and start thinking about whether or not they want to be around someone with whom to grow old gracefully, to be more understanding, to learn to bend more. But you and I, Al, have grown rigid and comfortable enough in our own skins to savor spending more time alone than with someone. Yet there's always that tiny itch and niggling curiosity. Are we doing the right thing? Are we really happy? Who knows?"

"Isn't retirement a bitch?"

"Roger that."

Al parked behind Wayon's car, which was bathed in the rotating lights of the sheriff's cruiser in front of it. They got out and walked into the blue-and-red dazzle.

A state trooper stood just outside the front door to Fuzzy's. He held up a hand. Al and Fergie slowed. Then the big shoulders and shaggy head of Sheriff Clayton leaned out of the front door and waved them forward. "What took you so long?" He looked like he'd already been in bed and had had to pull on his civvies to come to the scene. He wore Red Wing work boots and a hunter-green windbreaker over jeans. He didn't need a uniform. Everyone knew who he was, and no one seemed amazed that the sheriff himself was out at night at a piddly little shooting. He was like that.

The inside of the barroom was one open wide space, with a pool table off to one side under a fluorescent light. A few tables were scattered between it and the jukebox on the far side. Two doors flanking the bar led to what served as restrooms. All tired and worn, smelling of dust, cigarettes, stale beer, and a touch of burnt rubber, though that could have been Al's memory playing tricks.

Wayon sat on one of the bar stools next to Bart Haley. One of the knees on Bart's jeans had a scuffed tear, but otherwise he looked fine. He sipped at a cup of coffee the barmaid had slid there.

"I'm Peggy. Any of you fellas want a cup? I just made a fresh pot. Figured company was coming." The barmaid's eyes swept over each of them.

Al held up an index finger. Fergie and Clayton shook their heads.

"You're a lucky man, Bart," Clayton said. He stood in front of Bart, towering over him. "Live through a drive-by like that."

"Yeah, well, folks call me Lucky Bart."

"I'm surprised you'd come to this place, one that has a history, memories." Clayton glanced toward the floor, as if looking for the skid marks where Bart had peeled out that night his wife had died. The floor had been buffed since but looked dirty again, with an occasional cigarette butt tucked back where a casual broom might miss it.

"Fellows by the pool table said you were sitting on a saddlebag," Clayton said.

Peggy filled a plain white mug with coffee, held it in one hand, and lifted a bottle of bar brandy with the other. Al shook his head. She put the bottle down and slid him the coffee across the counter. He went over to get it and was near enough to smell the hint of brandy from Bart's breath.

"Their heads are up their asses. I didn't have any saddlebags. Did I, Peggy?"

She shook her head. "Not that I saw."

Clayton nodded to Wayon, who rose and went out the front door. They waited until he came back a minute later. He wore white latex gloves and carried a vintage set of black saddlebags.

"These yours?" Clayton asked.

Bart's eyes narrowed, but he managed a smile. "Nope."

"Damnedest thing," Clayton said. "Found them halfway up a juniper tree out back. You suppose they blew there off the road?"

"I'd be guessing if I said." Bart panned all of their faces, didn't see one that believed him. But he'd probably bluffed his way out of worse fixes than this.

"I'll just put it in the department lost and found," Clayton said. "After forensics gets done. Maybe they can identify the owner from any prints."

Bart didn't even squirm. Al gave him points for having ice running through his veins. Bart was a cop himself, a sergeant. He'd been through this plenty of times, though usually on the other side. But he knew what to expect, and how much they had, or didn't have.

"My prints might be on it, but it's not mine," Bart said. "When I hit the gravel, I saw it on the ground and pitched it over the fence in case it was a bomb or something. I didn't have a bag. Just ask Peggy."

Al wanted to grin, but neither Clayton nor Wayon smiled. Al kept his thoughts to himself and watched Peggy polishing some glasses that didn't need polishing. She wasn't a pretty woman but looked handsome in a grown-up farm-girl way. Dirty-blond hair in a ponytail, brown eyes that rarely blinked, and a build that said that while she was no gym rat, she was no couch potato either. Al imagined she might've been a shoulder to lean on after Bart had lost his wife.

"Nothing in the bags is yours, then?" Clayton asked.

"Nope." Bart started to grin and stopped.

Clayton jerked his head, and Al, Fergie, and Wayon followed him until they had all moved as far away from the bar as they could get. They formed a small huddle around the sheriff in a corner of the room out of Bart's hearing. Clayton spoke low. "What's in the bags, Wayon?"

"An envelope. Five thousand in cash."

"Really? The deal was already over then. Had to be more than a brick."

Fergie cleared her throat. "Not if it was locally grown. The stuff from Mexico may only wholesale for twelve to fifteen hundred, but you know that domestically cultivated cannabis has a much higher tetra-hydrocannabinol level. Even more so if it's grown indoors. It really kicks butt, and almost always brings a higher price. It could go for five G a brick."

Clayton looked at Fergie then toward Al. His head swung back to Fergie.

"Young lady . . ."

She released a short puff of air. "Young lady?"

"Take the compliments when they come," Clayton said. "You look young and frisky to me." He glanced to Al then back to Fergie. "I want to know. Are you official on this?"

"No. I'm retired. Just like Al."

"No one's just like Al," Clayton said.

"Some of us have our little dreams," Wayon said.

Clayton started to say something but stopped himself. Al had always admired that about the sheriff. He had the ability to dismiss all he thought he knew about his county and open his mind to what he could learn. "I doubt we'll get anything more from him." Clayton nodded toward Bart. He kept his voice low. "We've done county-wide air sweeps looking for anyone doing any cultivating here. That doesn't mean we know everything. Most of what comes into the county, to smoke or snort, is coming in across the border. Certainly the coke, heroin, and meth. The cartels down there are scrapping with each other and the law, but it's still a multi-billion-dollar problem. I hear tales of some locals with ties to the cartels squaring off. What I want to head off is what happened in El Paso where the Barrio Azteca gang started acting as enforcers for the Juárez drug cartel. If one of the groups like the Bandidos start doing the same here, or that new bunch, Tango Blast, we're going to have a real shoot-up on our hands." He ended up looking at Al.

"That may have already started," Fergie said.

Clayton's head swung to her, but he waited a moment and decided not to speak.

"You're going to have to cut him loose, aren't you?" Fergie said.

Clayton nodded. "But that doesn't mean someone"—he looked at Wayon—"can't stay on his case like stink. There's a lot I don't like about all this, don't like it one damn bit."

―――――◄◈►―――――

Al and Fergie stood beside Al's truck outside Fuzzy's, the truck doors open. The blue and red lights still swirled. Cars slowed as they went past, the drivers rubbernecking, wondering what was going down at the bar this time. Then the headlights picked up speed as they went away, slashing beams into the dark of night.

The first sign of a shift inside was the state trooper

stepping away from the bar's door and climbing into his lit-up cruiser. He turned off the lights, eased back onto the road, and was soon out of sight.

A few moments later Bart came out, alone, apparently free to go. He didn't say a word, just headed for his Harley. When he was almost to it, he turned back and pointed a forefinger at Fergie, thumb up and stiff. He let the thumb snap down, like a shot being fired from a gun. He may have winked as well. He stood too far away in not very good light for Al to see. Bart turned back and climbed onto his bike, started it, and was off into the night in a small spray of gravel.

"What do you suppose he meant by that?" Fergie asked.

"I guess we'll have to wait and see," Al said.

CHAPTER EIGHT

AL PULLED HIS TRUCK OUT onto the road. They rolled their windows halfway down, and the smell of juniper and dry Texas dirt swept across them. Soon the flashing swirls of red and blue lights faded in his rearview mirror and disappeared. The night closed around them like a black fist. Not many people were about at this hour, and most of those on the roads weren't up to any good. It felt like old times to Al. Another trip to another inglorious nightspot where the parking lot gravel was likely littered with broken teeth and broken dreams. It probably felt like that to Fergie too. He glanced her way.

The lights from the dash lit her in a dim green glow. She often smiled to herself when her face was at rest, but not now. She looked to be grinding through the gears of deeper thoughts. Her long red hair swept past her smooth cheek and neck in the breeze. He knew they were the same age, but she sure didn't show it, even with her clothes off. He looked back to the headlight beams slicing the road ahead. He still had that pretty distinct high-definition memory of Fergie walking nude from his bed to the bathroom, with those long athletic legs and a delicate roll of her hips. For a second he pondered if there was any meaning in the fact that his most frequent recollection of her that way involved her walking away from him. Thinking about that wasn't doing him any good.

She glanced toward him. "Does this mean you agree to help me?"

"No. It means we have a mutual interest just now, one we can look into together. We'll see about the other later."

"You know, I'd give you sex again, if that's what you want. I'm sorry about how it all turned out before."

"Forget about it. That's old news. Over the dam."

"I never told you," she said, "but I really respect you for taking your brother in after his heart attack." She was looking out her window into the dark night.

"After someone tried to kill him."

"I realize he can be a handful. It's a big deal, and it showed me who you really are."

"Yet you decided not to stay around."

"That's, as you say, old news, and nothing's carved in stone. You needed time to adjust to Maury and Bonnie being around so you didn't go wackadoodle."

"Is that the technical term?"

"I know how you are about having your own space. You also needed time to figure out whether you were selling yourself on the notion of a more-than-casual relationship just because Father Time is standing over your shoulder with a scythe. Now, about this deal of helping Wayon. You know you don't have to do that just because Clayton asked."

"Is that supposed to make me more inclined to help you instead?"

"Look, I probably shouldn't have asked, knowing how chivalrous you can be. Tackling this chore of trying to get something on Bart is plain stupid on my part. I should just tell IA to take a long walk off a short pier. He's made of Teflon as far as they're concerned, and you saw how smug he is about it. And he's dangerous."

"You think he was serious with that gesture? It only

gave him the boyish, arrogant look of someone seeming to be clever. As for dangerous, I'm not so sure he isn't all swagger. I'm more curious about whoever was shooting at him."

She started to say something, but he held up a hand.

A flicker of light appeared in his rearview mirror. Then another, and two more.

Fergie glanced back. "Oh, shit."

"That's what I was thinking," Al agreed. "Glove box."

She popped it open and took out the Glock, jacked a shell into the chamber, and handed it to him. He held gun and steering wheel in his right hand long enough to lower his window all the way then drove with his left hand while holding the Glock across his lap. He eased the safety off.

Fergie reached down and took a small, black .25 automatic out of an ankle holster hidden under her jeans. "It's only for emergencies," she said. "And this qualifies."

Al raised a quick eyebrow at her tiny gun then kept his eyes on the road and rearview mirror. There were seven of them now, single headlights, coming up fast.

Most bikers these days were harmless enough hobbyists who liked the feel of two wheels gripping the road, the wind in their faces, and the occasional bug on their grinning teeth—nothing like the riders Hunter S. Thompson had portrayed in his *Hell's Angels* book. Al had been part of the disciplined law enforcement effort to clamp down on any of the law-breaking gangs. They were rarer these days but by no means eradicated.

The first of the bikers rocketed past, got in front of Al's truck, and slowed enough they could read the back of his jacket.

"Bandidos," Fergie said. "Crap."

"Crap, indeed." Al's hand clenched the wheel tighter, and he willed himself to relax. Though a paramilitary group with a tendency toward violence when defending their territory or drug routes, the Bandidos had in recent years been making an effort to turn public sentiment in their favor by organizing events like charity runs and gathering toys and clothing for kids. This didn't look like one of those community-embracing activities.

Fergie had her cell phone out and was punching in a number when a biker pulled up beside them. Al glanced left, looked into the end of a gun's barrel that looked like the mouth of a fifty-gallon drum. So much for the motorcycle gang's positive PR.

"Down!" he yelled, but he needn't have bothered. Fergie was already hugging the floorboards. Al ducked and swung the truck hard left just as the biker fired. Glass exploded across the front seat, and wind rushed in through a gaping hole in the windshield. Al felt the thump of his fender slamming into the biker, sending that bike across the opposing lane and up a slight grassy hill into a tangle of brush along a fence line.

Shots came from behind them, fast enough to suggest an automatic—a Mac-10 or something like it. The next biker to come up near Al's side had a gun held out but never got to fire it. Al led him and fired, shooting three times back across the man's body. The bike tumbled into a roll the biker probably never felt. Al pressed the gas pedal to the floor and heard the hearty engine roar. He swept up on the bike ahead. The rider saw him just in time to swerve right and off the road into a spray of gravel as the bike fell on its side.

Al could hear shots slamming into the metal of his truck, but for a second he thought he might be able to pull away. Then he felt a lurch as the right rear tire blew and the truck settled onto its rim. He could see a spray of sparks when he glanced into the side mirror. The truck got harder to handle. He slowed, saw a shoulder ahead that opened into a short, wider stretch of asphalt and gravel at the end of a ranch home's lane. He steered into it and hit the brakes. As soon as the truck skidded to a stop, he and Fergie rolled out the passenger door. The remaining four bikers pulled to a stop, formed a semicircle on the other side of the truck, and started unloading everything they had at the cab.

Crawling on elbows and knees, Al and Fergie veered off to the right, through a stand of sumac and tall, scratchy bunch grass, away from the path of any bullets passing through the shambles of what had once been a pretty nice and fairly new truck.

Al and Fergie backed in under the low limbs of a tight stand of mountain cedars and lay pressed close to the ground. A bed of fallen brown needles that smelled faintly of juniper carpeted the ground beneath them. He waited until the shooting stopped as the bikers paused, came to look inside the truck, then raced around the vehicle. Al shot the first one to come around in the knee. He dropped, screaming, to the ground. The others ducked back around to the safety of the other side of the truck. Al heard them shoving in fresh clips. Not an encouraging sound.

One by one they began popping up, each in a different place, to pepper the slope with shots, some trimming off cedar limbs that fell down onto Al and Fergie, with one shot slicing a groove right between where they lay. It was only a matter of time.

Al fired back enough to keep them from charging, hoping all the while another vehicle would come down the road. Nothing. A head rose above the truck's bed, and Al fired. The slide stayed back. His gun was empty. He glanced toward Fergie, a last look perhaps.

The bikers seemed to sense the meaning of the quiet.

One darted out around the front fender and ran toward them. He had a rough idea where they were from the gun flashes of returned fire, but Al could see him peering into what had to be dark gloom for him.

He was a burly fellow with a taut beer belly and dark hair beneath a do-rag. Fergie waited until the biker's face lit up. He'd spotted them, and he started to lift his automatic. Fergie fired, every shot in her gun. Al saw the slide open and stay back. Empty.

The .25 had little stopping power and not much accuracy either with its short barrel. The biker rocked back a couple of times, hit at least twice, but not hurt enough to keep him from raising the barrel of his automatic again.

Al glanced to Fergie. She shared the same look he probably wore, that goodbye one that comes from knowing they'd played every card they had and even getting up and running was not going to save them. He leaned closer and realized he was going to kiss her, a kiss goodbye. She didn't pull back. He heard a siren, distant but approaching fast. Their heads pulled apart. The biker nearest them spun and ran toward his bike. The noise of the sirens grew, and he could see bursts of the lights flickering red and blue into the treetops just over the hill.

The bikers left as quickly as they could. The one who had been nearest them was already pulling away. The other two dragged away the fellow Al had shot, got him on the back of one of the bikes, then took off. The sound of their mufflers faded around the next bend in the road that Al knew sloped down into a sharp hill. The first cruiser, the sheriff's, pulled up behind Al's truck. The next one, the state trooper, kept going, in hot pursuit after the bikers. Wayon's car followed the trooper's, two red lights going in his back window.

Al took a deep breath and realized he'd stopped

breathing altogether for a few moments. Fergie was already scrambling to her feet. He did the same. She held a hand down, but he got up without it.

Sheriff Clayton got out of his cruiser, carrying a long-handled flashlight.

"Three of them down back there," Al said, pointing to where they had gone off the road.

Al went to his truck and got a flashlight out of the glove box. There was a spare clip in there, one he had been wishing he'd grabbed earlier. He reloaded his Glock and felt better right away. Fergie was bent over, slipping her small automatic back into its holster.

They followed Clayton back up the road and came to the spot where one bike had gone off the road. Al held his flashlight in his left hand and his gun in his right. He noticed Clayton was doing the same. Some of the bikers had been sporting automatic weapons. Back when he'd been drawing a pay slip from the department instead of a pension check, Al would have called for backup before doing this in the dark.

"I've called for the K-9 car and backup already," Clayton said. "Ambulance too. But we can still nose around."

"Were you reading my mind? I was dying to have a closer look at these guys."

"Don't have to read your mind, Al. You were as good a procedural deputy as I ever had."

"They came out of nowhere and came fast. They were already in place and poised. But for what?"

Clayton turned and waved a hand to indicate they should follow him.

Fergie moved closer to Al. She held neither a gun nor a light. "This does feel odd. Something wasn't right. Didn't have much time to ponder it while it was going on." She followed their steps through the gravel between pavement and scrub growth.

"I'll bet Al was pondering the dammit out of it while it was going on," Clayton muttered without turning his head back to them.

They came to where the bike had gone off the road.

Clayton led the way. The bike had tumbled, so it hadn't gone far. It lay in a tangle of twisted metal that was never going to roll down any highway again. Same for the biker. Clayton felt for a pulse. Shook his head. He pulled the jacket away from what was left of the biker's crushed chest. Al bent closer to look in too.

"Hmm." Clayton stood up. "Better get the M.E. headed this way too. Guess I may not need the K-9. Thought some of these guys might be in the wind. But you do thorough work, Al. Don't touch anything. Let's see about the other two you mentioned."

More sirens approached from the other direction, the direction the escaping bikers had taken.

They backtracked and found the other two, dead as well. One from bullets, the other a testament to not wearing a helmet. Clayton looked up from the third one to Al. "I see a pile of paperwork in your future. Gonna need statements from both of you."

"Hey, I'm out a truck here," Al said.

"Better call your insurance company. You can bet we'll have a report, if you need it for them. But don't be surprised if they drop you." Clayton turned away from Al as the caravan of flashing lights pulled up. He stepped out into the road to meet them. He pointed to where each biker lay and had a few words with the crew. Then he came back to Al and Fergie. They all three stepped off to one side, out of the way of the bustling crews.

Clayton focused on Fergie. "Back a short while ago you told me you weren't official. Yet you were carrying."

"I always carry these days, after what I've been through. I have the license for it."

"I'm gonna need the piece and the paper." He shook open a plastic evidence bag from his pocket.

Fergie dug the license out of her pocket wallet and dropped it and the .25 into the bag.

Clayton shook another bag open and held it toward Al, who shrugged and dropped in his Glock, which still felt warm to his touch.

"This is a helluva time to leave us without protection."

"Oh, come on. I know you still have your Sig, and Annie Oakley here will just move up to something bigger than this pea shooter."

"There's that," Fergie admitted.

"You notice anything about those bikers, Al?" Clayton asked.

"Yeah. Hard to miss."

"What?" Fergie asked. She'd seen the bodies too. Three very dead Bandidos. That was going to send ripples.

"First one had a tattoo of the capitol building. Same with the other two."

"That means the bikes and the jackets may be Bandido, but these guys were all three Tango Blast," Al said.

"Oh," Fergie said. "I'll bet the Bandidos are mucho pissed off."

Clayton had a couple inches on Fergie. He had to bend around her to watch the other deputies marking off the crime scenes. A few cars had trickled down the road even this late. They were being held back and were starting to build up. It was going to be a long night, for everyone. "I can't imagine Tango Blast is very damn pleased just now either," he said.

"This is going to be one tough knot to untangle," Al said.

"Not for you."

"How so?"

"Because you're off the case, as of now."

"Oh, come on. After years of following the regs, this is the first time the job is really starting to be fun."

"That's part of what worries me. You're off the case now. That's official and not subject to discussion. If you were still in the department, you'd be riding a desk until we have a handle on this. All standard procedure. You know that."

"I thought you wanted me to help Wayon."

"That was before all this." Clayton waved a hand at the crews scrambling around the spots where the bikers had fallen.

"You think this means it's an easier case to handle now?"

"No. But I won't have a civilian, retired deputy or not, at this level of risk. Someone's trying to make a point. They may even know who you are. Until we figure out just who it is, you're to stand down, stay retired. Look, you get visible in this, and right away, in seconds, you've got Tango Blast all over you. A coincidence? I don't think so. You've got one big-assed bull's-eye painted on you right now, and I need time to figure out who's put it there and why. I'd tell you to go fishing or something, but I want you and your crew to go to my nephew Skinny's place. It's for sale since he passed. It's all prettied up enough to stay in. I still haven't sold it, and you'll be as safe there as anywhere. And you're to stay put. I'll have a car go by now and then to keep an eye out. You're out of it, for good. Got it? That's an order." Clayton's eyes narrowed. Now he was the riled bear roused from his cave. "If this goes the way I think it might, from biker gangs to cartels, I'm gonna have my hands full with people like your pal Jaime Avila with ICE. So you have to stand down, as of now. Got it?"

Just thinking of Jaime and ICE, Immigration and Customs Enforcement, sent a shiver through Al. He could see Clayton's jaw tighten when he said the name, and he hadn't been the one jumping out of a low-flying helicopter the last time Jaime had been around. Al had.

"Well, I won't argue with you. But the decision may not be ours. For whatever reasons, I already seemed to be centered in their crosshairs, and tonight's little episode can't have endeared me to them much," Al said.

CHAPTER NINE

THE MOTORCYCLE'S ENGINE SLOWED TO a low burble. Bart pulled off the road and eased past a mailbox and up a short gravel stretch until he came to the gate. He got off the bike, resting it on its kickstand, engine still going, and went to the left end of the gate. The padlock was locked to the other end of the chain, and it had just been looped around the post twice and dropped into place. He lifted the chain, swung the gate open, then went back and took the bike through. He paused to close the gate behind him, dropping the chain back into place the way it had been.

Bart took his time going back down the twin ruts of the lane that led all the way to the house. He never knew when a fox or armadillo would shoot in a blur across his path. Once an entire pack of coyotes had tumbled past, right in front of him, wrestling with some potential victim. He'd swerved to miss them, and they'd scattered the moment they saw him. But his heart had still been beating pretty good by the time he'd gotten to the house.

He could see lights on downstairs as well as in an upper window. Alone in the dark, with the moon mostly obscured by shifting clouds, the gravel seemed to crunch louder than usual as he took the bike slowly around the side of the house and tucked it into the open shed that served as a three-vehicle garage. He left the bike there and headed inside.

Peggy looked up from the dinette table. She held a mug, and he could smell fresh coffee. Her hair was down, and she wore a worn red terry robe, belted tight at the waist and pulled snugly together just under her neck. Her eyes seemed worn and tired, and they lacked any sparkle. "What the hell went on down the road?"

"I have no idea. Had nothing to do with me."

"Don't give me that crap. Just about everything around there has something to do with you these days. I thought we'd be ready to get out of here by now, to bug off to Buffalo, or wherever."

His lips tightened. He wasn't in the mood. He was never in the mood. Besides, he'd never said a damned thing about Buffalo. Too cold up there. Maybe a spot in New Mexico. He could picture that. "We stay. I'm almost there, but I need one more good batch."

"We have enough."

He shook his head.

"You know, you're just being a risk junkie now. You should quit. We should go. Do you think you're just plain bulletproof?"

Bart stared at her, hard enough to burn holes if his eyes were lasers.

He spun, went to the cabinet, and yanked out a half-empty bottle of Black Jack. From another cabinet he took down a glass jigger. He carried them into the living room, which was dark except for the light coming in through the kitchen door.

After a few minutes, she came into the living room but didn't turn on any lights, just stopped in front of him and looked down at him. He sat on the end of the couch, leaning back. He reached and poured until the glass was filled.

She tugged at the knot at her waist, struggling with it for a second before getting it loosened. Then she let the robe fall open. His eyes went up, then down, and up again until they locked with hers.

"Come to bed," she said.

"Make me."

"Oh, I'll make you all right." She shrugged, and the robe crumbled to the floor.

She stood there for a moment, naked, then turned and went to the stairs, quietly making her way up to the second floor.

Bart sat staring off at a corner of the room in the dark. No sense mulling over any more possibilities or probabilities. Things were getting chancy, and he had to take that chance. He thought about the five thousand for a second. Just a drop in the bucket. He needed a helluva lot more than that.

The wind outside rasped at the old wooden house. It had picked up since he'd gotten there. He lifted his glass then put it down without drinking. He tugged off his boots, stood, and headed upstairs.

———◆———

Deputy Bob Hancock drove, with Fergie in the passenger seat and Al in the back, where there were no inner door handles. It gave Al a taste of the other side he could have done without.

Bob pulled up in front of Al's house and parked behind Fergie's car. He got out and opened Al's door.

Al climbed out, took in the house. It looked eerie at this hour, going on four in the morning. Some of that could have been what he'd just been through. Being shot at, being on the cusp of dying, can bring out that surreal feeling about everything that once seemed so normal. Bob got back into the cruiser and looked up at him from the driver's seat, his head cocked at a slight angle.

"Want a cup of coffee or anything?" Al asked.

"Sorry, I've gotta get right back there. Clayton is still making sure we help the crime scene people be as thorough as possible. Your truck will get taken in to be processed, not that you were going to go anywhere in it real soon. But you knew all that already."

"I could help with all that," Al said.

"You know how Clayton is. He says no, he means no. He takes it personal if any of his deputies are injured or killed on duty. If someone who was retired got shot, I don't know what he'd do. It would be way uncool. You don't want to be uncool for Clayton now, do you?"

"Heaven forbid," Al said. "Uncool's the last thing I'd wish on him." Bob had as little sense of humor as anyone Al had ever met, so there was no sense prodding him, especially at this hour. Bob put the sheriff's department vehicle into gear and pulled around Fergie's car and away into the night.

"I hope you don't mind, but I'm too pooped to drive home. That and I'm wound up at the same time," Fergie said.

Al looked for that sparkle in her purple eyes, but they appeared grey in this light and looked flat and tired, not eager for anything he might have wished to read into her statement.

"Okay, come on inside," he said.

Late as it was, Bonnie heard them come in the front door. She'd left the lights on and came out into the living room while tying the belt of her thick, pink terry robe.

"I thought you were just gonna be gone a few minutes?"

she said, fluffing the curls of her hair as soon as her belt was tied.

Al figured she had already rested far more than he was going to this night.

"We got shot at on the way home," Fergie said. "I think Al's truck is a goner."

"Oh, my stars. I thought you were all done with that shoot 'em up stuff, Al?" Bonnie looked them over. "You're not hurt, though. That's good. Let me put on a pot of coffee or something."

"Not right now, Bonnie. I think we could both use some rest. We'll sort it all out in the morning."

"Okay, just a sec." Bonnie spun and was off to Al's bedroom, where he suspected she already had the sheets warmed.

She came back into the living room with a pillow, a blanket, and a sheet. She handed them to him. "Fluff up the couch, sweetie. Tired as you are, I doubt it'll matter. Come on, Fergie."

Fergie shrugged to Al and was tired enough she followed after Bonnie without a word.

Al stood in the living room, lights on and the couch right before him but not looking all that inviting. How's this sort of thing even happen?

He kept coming back to the same thing, wondering what happened to that picture of the carefree life of a retired man living alone and puttering about the house, sometimes going fishing. Sleeping in his own bed, too. He sighed, dropped the bedding onto the couch, and started to unbutton his shirt.

———◆———

Alejandro Elizado and Lance Rodriguez helped Jesus Vasquez hobble through the open warehouse door.

Rolando Linzen looked up from the table where he was cutting adhesive tape into strips and gauze into squares. He indicated the cot he'd set up while they were on their way.

The two helping him eased Jesus onto the cot. Lance started to reach for Jesus's belt buckle, but Jesus snapped, "I can do that."

They did have to help him remove his boots and slide his jeans off. When he shrugged out of his Bandido jacket, Alejandro tossed it crumpled to the floor. He and Lance each tugged off their jackets and tossed them there too, making a small pile.

Juan Madrigal walked the remaining bikes inside, one by one, then hit the button to close the gaping warehouse door on the black outside. He tugged off his Bandido jacket, revealing a bulletproof vest beneath it. He laughed, plucked two .25 bullets out of it, and flung them hard against the wall.

Rolando held a steel pan of water and swabbed at the entry wound with a wet piece of gauze. He spoke in Spanish, with the soft, feathery prison voice he'd acquired during two longish stays at the John B. Connally state prison in Kenedy, Texas. "Hell, good news, Jesus. Through and through. Could'a been right square in the kneecap."

"Yeah, that's me. Happy to be hopping. Thought this was some harmless old dude."

"Who knew he'd be packing?" Lance said. "It's a lesson for those we left behind."

"You ever notice it's the brave ones get shot or wounded first?" Jesus glanced toward Alejandro and Lance.

"We had your back, hombre," Lance said.

"Someone should'a had my front." Jesus winced as Rolando took a deeper swipe across the front hole in his thigh with the gauze. "Hey, man, you got nothing for this pain?"

Rolando nodded toward a stack of cases of booze next to televisions, stereos, and other goods still in their boxes. Lance tugged a case of Jose Cuervo tequila off the stack, ripped open the box, and handed a bottle to Jesus, who twisted the top off and took a long gulping drink that emptied a quarter of the bottle. "Now you're talking, man."

Rolando finished taping the entrance wound. He gave a hand flip to indicate Jesus should turn over onto his stomach.

Jesus took another long pull from the bottle and put it on the floor before turning. "Don't you be thinking of doing nothing silly when I'm like this."

"Not me," Rolando said. "You must be thinking of Ramon. He's the one always wanting to bring in young wannabes who didn't even do any hard time."

Ramon came out the back of a rusting white panel van with an armload of new cell phones in bulk boxes. "I'm just saying," he said, "we lose a few, we gain a few. Lotta people still think the *Mexikanemi* and the Texas Syndicate rule. We're gonna need numbers to convince them otherwise."

Lance reached into the case and took out another bottle. "Hell, case is open." He opened it, took a hearty jolt, and held it out to Alejandro, who reached for it.

"You ain't wrong." Alejandro took a swig then wiped the back of his hand across his mouth and held it out to Rolando, who shook his head. Not yet. So Alejandro handed the bottle to Juan, who had just peeled off his bulletproof vest and had been holding it up to look at it.

Rolando finished taping the exit wound. "You're good to go, but take it easy for a day or two. And get your pants back on before Ramon gets ideas."

"Hell, I'm too old for Ramon," Jesus said, but he tugged

on his pants, wincing. Beads of sweat dotted his tanned and dusky forehead. He reached for the open bottle.

Rolando held out a hand, and Alejandro passed him the other bottle. Rolando took a long drink from it. When he lowered it, he looked around at the others. "Well, you may have taken losses, but you were supposed to stir things up, and you sure as hell did that."

Jesus looked up from where he was struggling to get his boots back on. He grinned. "If you ain't blasting, you ain't lasting."

"Every business gotta grow," Ramon said. He waved a sweeping hand that took in their *silla*, their home base seat. "We don't stop till this place is busting-ass full, then we get another place. What you say?"

The others chorused, "I hear that" and "You got that right." One drunken "Kill 'em all" came from Jesus.

The warehouse, their little slice of heaven opening to an alley off East Seventh Street, was half filled with goods, mostly stolen, along with cases of ammo, an assortment of weapons, and some tightly wrapped packages of coke and marijuana. They were handling some of the hands-on end of local business for the cartels, but not nearly as much as they wanted, or thought they deserved. There's always room for more profit to share.

<hr />

Al's eyes blinked open. He thought he could smell coffee, though it wasn't light outside yet, then realized it was his imagination playing tricks. He felt a shape looming and in an eye-popping déjà vu moment looked up to see Maury wearing his blue plaid robe. He was bent over the side of the couch to push at Al's shoulder.

"What?" Al asked.

"Bonnie and Fergie say you've got to hurry," Maury

said. "It's nearly daylight, and we've got to get the hell out of here. It's a good thing you and I never had kids so our grandchildren will never have to hear how we came to live in a matriarchy. It's just like your damn deer."

"It feels like I just fell asleep." It was only yesterday he'd been patting himself on the back about needing so little sleep.

"Maybe so, but you've got to hustle. Fergie says your truck is gone too. What happened? Who'd you piss off this time? Wait. You can tell me later. You'd better grab your bathroom while you can. I've got to go shower up and pack."

He spun and headed for the stairs down to his room, the ends of his robe belt flapping behind him.

Al pushed himself up off the couch and got back into his clothes.

As he passed the dining table and kitchen, he saw Bonnie loading supplies from the fridge and shelves into a couple of cloth grocery bags. Fergie sat at the dining table looking like she was wishing for a cup of coffee. The long expanse of windows was still dark enough to reflect the kitchen, dining area, and that end of the living room.

"We can eat when we get to our new digs," Bonnie said. "From what Fergie tells me, we'd best make tracks out of here, skedaddle first and think it out later. Now step lively. You hear?"

Al watched her grab some paper plates and plastic utensils from one cabinet and put them in a bag. At least she added a few real mugs. He wished he could pause to cook a proper breakfast and sit and savor a cup of joe. But the two of them were right. They should get going. In fact, they should all have left in the night, though he was glad for the hour or two of sleep he'd snatched. Still, he felt a disturbing strangeness to what had once been his comfort zone. He'd come to view his home lately as a place he was visiting. The upward tug at the corner of Fergie's mouth said she understood but also enjoyed seeing him squirm as he walked past her on his way to the bathroom.

The aroma of mixed perfumes still dominated his bathroom as he brushed his teeth. He took a five-minute shower and felt more awake. He reached for his cell phone and made a quick call. When he hung up, he headed out, hoping for the smell of coffee, only to be disappointed again.

"So your truck is gone," Bonnie said as she carried two bulging bags of supplies to put beside the door where her small bag already waited. "Fergie says it has gone the way of the Dodo."

"It got ventilated pretty good," Al said. "We're just glad we weren't as well."

"Sounds like the craziest mess I ever heard of." Bonnie headed back to the kitchen to do a walk-through, make sure she hadn't missed anything she'd regret not taking.

"Not really," Al said. "Everything's random, until you think it isn't."

"Oh, come on," Fergie said. She sat with one elbow on the table, still waiting. "You trying to tell me you've figured all this out?"

"No. But in any case, you need just a tiny bit of thread to start the unraveling."

"And what, Sherlock, is your bit of thread?"

"There's that note on the scarecrow corpse."

Fergie let an indelicate snort escape. "That was just stupid."

"Exactly. It *was* stupid," Al said. "Let's accept that. Now all we need to figure out is who does stupid things."

"That's gonna be you if you don't get a shake on," Bonnie said. "Fergie tells me Clayton's got a house where we're to stay until whatever is going on calms down. You can catch us up on your theories when we're there."

Al started to say something but shook his head instead. He went back to his room to pack as little as possible. He knew Maury had almost nothing to pack, Bonnie had only her one small bag, and Fergie had nothing, so they should be out of his house in a flash. He glanced at the rumpled bed as he once again entered his bedroom.

Fergie had risen from the dining table, and she followed him into the room. She hovered by the door. He took out a small bag, and the first thing to go in it was his Sig Sauer and a box of 9mm ammo. With his Glock in a sheriff's department evidence bag, it was all he had for now, or he would have given Fergie a gun.

"I don't care much to be on the run," Al said, "but once I know Maury and Bonnie are safe, I can poke around a little on my own."

"Poke around? How? And why on earth would you expose yourself to these guys who just tried to kill you?"

"You're the one who asked me to help look into Bart."

"I didn't ask you to get yourself killed in the process. So, why poke?"

"What can I say? I'm a very curious person, especially when someone is targeting me and the people around me."

"You're an angry person then, Al. I know you. You're not as careful as you might be."

He shrugged. "I don't expect to live forever, but I do expect to do so standing up and with my head high."

"As a target." Fergie sighed. "I know, I know. I asked the favor, so I'm to blame as well. All I can say is for a person having to move out of his home, you seem to be rolling well."

"I'm rolling. I wouldn't say well. I'll feel better once I get busy again."

"Are you sure Clayton will be okay with you doing any poking?"

"He's not my boss now, Fergie. He doesn't have a say in what I do on my own time."

"Clayton was a little gruffer and more snippy than usual. Did he see something in your eyes?"

"It's what he didn't see."

"What's that?"

"Nothing. All he saw was a big dose of blank nothing in my eyes. I wasn't upset at all about killing three worthless former prison gang bangers who wanted to kill me. I guess I should be, but they didn't give us much thought, so it's hard to feel I owe them any thought either."

"It's indeed a new sad, brutal world we live in," Fergie said. "We all of us will have to be made of tougher stuff if we're to survive."

CHAPTER TEN

A L SAT IN THE BACK seat of Fergie's car with Maury. Bonnie had called shotgun and was in the front passenger seat.

"It'll be nice to all spend time together," Bonnie said. "We can think of it as a vacation, kinda."

Fergie glanced into the rearview mirror at Al. "I doubt if Al will be with us for the duration. You apparently don't know the look of a hound that's stirred up when it thinks it has a sniff of the scent."

"What's she saying, Al?" Bonnie asked.

Al shook his head, felt Maury looking at him too. Bonnie turned around in her seat to stare at him.

"Haven't either of you ever heard the story of the blue boat?" Fergie said.

"Hey, I have," Maury said. "That's from a while ago." He paused before going on. "When Al and I weren't talking. But I followed it in the papers. That was one gripping story of relentless pursuit."

"I never heard about it. Tell us, Al." Bonnie twisted back to look at him again.

Fergie glanced at Al in the rearview mirror.

One morning Al's water heater had conked out. He'd had to take a cold-water sponge bath and shave himself with a sink full of icy water while the razor dragged and gouged, and he'd enjoyed that more than he did sharing details of anything others might call exploits. He shook his head.

Fergie cleared her throat. "Quite a while ago, three young high-school-aged boys were fishing in a wooden boat at night. Part of the fault was theirs. Just a lantern. No running lights. But what happened shouldn't have. A boat came along at top speed and plowed right over them. The person in the boat never stopped. By Texas law that's one of the worst offenses, failure to stop and render aid in any kind of accident. But the guy took off. A hit and run. Two of the boys were hurt but made it to shore. The third boy was dead. So now it was manslaughter too. The Parks & Wildlife people and the sheriff's department knew the speeding boat was blue, but that's about all they had. They looked everywhere but found nothing. How long did you look, Al?"

"Eight years. Not my finest hour."

"Actually, it was," Fergie disagreed. "You never hesitated, and. . . you never stopped."

"Eight years does seem a long time," Maury said.

"But there were no clues, nothing." Fergie watched the road ahead but kept talking. "Every law enforcement group, city, county, and state checked for blue boats getting repairs. Nothing. They cast a bigger net to look for any blue boats at all. Still nothing conclusive. But eight years later Al got wind of women talking at a social gathering and one of them had said, 'Didn't ol' Jim Bob Grady used to have a blue boat?' That's the tiny bit of string Al was looking for. Since he was still going around, asking the same questions eight years later, it's the piece of string he found. He checked the records, and Jim Bob Grady had owned a boat, but its registration had not been renewed, nor was there record of a sale. The sheriff's department can't run witch hunts, but Al finally had enough probable cause together for a warrant. Jim Bob had an eighty-acre spread he'd inherited from his mom's side of the family. Al went over the property with his finest-toothed comb then went over it again with a metal detector. That's when he found it. They brought in a backhoe and dug up that boat from its six-foot-deep hole, still in its trailer, with forensic evidence on it. Jim Bob had lived with that guilt all those years."

"That's what gave me enough," Al finally said. "When I went to talk to the man, he was, as Tennessee Ernie Ford used to put it, twitchy as a long-tailed cat in a room full of rocking chairs."

"Well, I think it's a fine story," Bonnie said. "Though it does come back to Fergie's point about relentless pursuit. I suppose you do have a snout full of some kind of scent by now."

Al didn't answer, and they all rode in silence the rest of the way.

The sun had started to come up as they skirted Austin and crossed the county to get to the house. Traffic got lighter as they passed open fields where cattle had nibbled the bottoms of trees as high up as they could reach, rounding the trees at their tops and flattening them at their bottoms.

"This is the place," Fergie said. She turned at the mailbox into a long lane that led back to a two-story wooden house that stood alone on a slight rise. There wasn't a tree in any direction on the property.

"Holy crap on a cracker," Bonnie said. "It's like the dead opposite of your place, Al. No lake. No trees. Nothing but grass in all directions. And no deer to eat it."

Al felt his own eyebrows rise. The only thing that looked safe about the place was that he could probably see someone coming from any direction. Other than that, it was just a different place to be, where no one knew they would be staying. Well, almost no one.

They got out of the car and went inside. The three who had small bags dropped them in the living room. It was furnished the way someone might who's getting ready to sell the place. Everything was new and a little pricey but didn't look especially comfortable. There was just enough furniture to show potential but not get in the way of any prospective buyer's own vision. Fergie carried the grocery bag of supplies they'd brought from Al's house into the kitchen.

"Good, there's a coffee maker," Bonnie said. "I think we could all do with a cup and a proper breakfast. You just sit, and I'll get right to it. No better way to warm up a kitchen that doesn't feel like it's been used in a while."

Al didn't argue. He and Fergie sat down at the kitchen table, a long square-edged affair made of what looked like mango wood with matching straight-backed chairs. Maury hustled off to explore. He was back in two minutes.

"Bad news for you, Al. There are only two bedrooms. But on the plus side, the couch looks especially cushy." Maury sat down at the table. They could smell the coffee perking away.

The doorbell rang. Al started to stand, but Bonnie waved him back to his seat. "Now who the hell could that be? We're barely in the door. Well, hell. Might as well see. I'm already up."

Al heard her open the front door. Then she yelled, "Hey, Al. It's your pal Jaime Avila with ICE. He says he brought you the bike you asked to borrow. It seems you called him from back at your place."

Fergie's eyebrows shot up when she looked at him. "Really? Of all the people in the world, why did you call him?"

"Yeah," Al admitted. "This is something I may later regret."

Al rose and went out into the living room, with Maury and Fergie crowding close behind him. At the far end of the room, Bonnie stood beside Jaime Avila, whose compact, muscular bullet of a body filled the shoulders of his brown leather jacket. He always looked like a ticking bomb to Al, though he was five-six and not a great deal taller than Bonnie. His dark hair glittered, as did his eyes. He always entered a room like a racing greyhound that had just spotted the rabbit, full of energy and urgency.

"Did you bring it?" Al asked, coming across the room with his hand extended.

Jaime shook hands, his grip firm enough to crack walnuts. "It's outside, in a horse trailer. You don't want to haul a Harley around on an open trailer. You just get laughed at."

"Where'd you get it?"

"Impound lot. Owner isn't going to care. He lost a hell of a lot more than his bike, but he did get a swell new place to stay. Small, but at no cost to him. Solid too."

"Maybe you'd better explain what all this is about," Fergie said to Al.

Jaime looked up toward Fergie. She was a former cop, but he was current ICE. That made him an active player for Homeland Security, and a ranking one at that, head of the nearest field office in San Antonio. Her tone and her towering over him didn't faze him.

"You recall Fergie, Bonnie, and Maury, don't you?" Al said.

Jaime nodded.

"Why don't we move this festival to the table and have coffee while I try to pick Jaime's brain about a few things?"

Al nodded to Bonnie, who scooted on ahead of them to get the fresh pot and a few mugs out of the bag she'd packed.

He watched Jaime's eyes track the wiggle of her hips as she left the room. Jaime was on the road a great deal in his work, and Al knew he'd had a dalliance or two. Al had once kept him from getting caught when Jaime's wife was coming home early. Jaime's wife was a very jealous woman—and no stranger to guns. Al might've saved Jaime's life that time. But Jaime had returned the favor, had saved Al's. So their accounts were square to the present moment.

Once they all sat around the table, with Bonnie leaning against the granite counter by the sink since the seats were all taken, Al leaned forward, letting the steam from his cup curl around his face, and said, "I want to know how deep the shit is I'm in, Jaime."

"Deep enough to need a safe house," Jaime said. "Though I could have supplied one better than this."

"I've been in one of your safe houses before," Al said. "Didn't go well. No thanks. I just want to know, am I wearing a bull's-eye?"

Jaime took a sip of his coffee and winked at Bonnie. "*Bueno.*" He turned back to Al. "It all depends, you see. The truck used for the drive-by shooting at the off-duty cop was white. Your truck's white. Could be somebody just got confused about who they were after. But I don't think these guys get confused much. Of course, it's hard to ask the ones you left out there by the road." His mouth tilted up at the corner in a twist. "Nice work on them, by the way."

"Any idea of what's going on out there? The cartels and their soldiers are your cup of tea."

"At the core of this, it's not about the local gangs, though they're a real enough danger should you come up against them. But they're the pawns here, puppets if you prefer. You can't always determine what's up by looking at the actions of puppets. You have to search for the motives of those working the strings behind them. The real deal is the cartels, and that means what this is about is money. Big money. Wrestling for sale territories and supply and demand. The cartels are businesses, rough and big, and making quite a bit more than ExxonMobil. I need to pick at the threads on this end, Al, to get to them. *Comprende?*"

Al nodded.

"Another thing you can do is rule out the Bandidos. Believe it or not, they're the victims here. They've taken plenty of heat, mostly around San Antonio, but they're busting their chops to shift public opinion. You probably know about that. It doesn't mean they aren't active and don't traffic and deal a bit, but they're generally trying hard to look like they're keeping their noses clean. Plus, most of the newbies they're recruiting have no prison records. It looks like some of the Puro Tango Blast gang stole their bikes and jackets. Now that should tell you something, a group tough enough to rip off a biker gang."

"That's who shot at Al and Fergie?" Maury said. "Are we all in real danger now?"

Jaime nodded. "You sure as dammit are. Hard to tell if they expected return fire. If they were after the bangers who shot up Fuzzy's, they had to be expecting return fire, though. From the reports, they didn't act like it. So I'd be cautious."

"I guess it's time to start carrying again," Bonnie said.

"From what I recall, you're a crack shot. Normally, I'd discourage it. But this time I'm looking the other way." Jaime lifted his cup and looked over the brim at her. "I'd have brought along some spare guns, but Clayton doesn't even know I'm helping you this much, Al."

Bonnie's lips tightened into a grim line.

"Maybe Bonnie and Maury should pack up and head for somewhere safer, maybe out of state," Fergie said. "Is that what you're thinking, Al?"

"I wouldn't be against it. The reason I asked Jaime to borrow an appropriate bike is so I can nose around to see what we're up against, find out if we're really in the crosshairs, and determine how much time we have. I can't very well drive up looking like myself and start asking questions. I have to be a little more round about at this."

"Al, don't you dare tell me . . ."

He interrupted Fergie. "Yeah, I'm going to have to do a little undercover work. And, Maury, spare us whatever 'under-the-covers' gag you were getting ready to share."

Al glanced toward Maury, whose mouth had already started to open. It closed, and the elfish glee of his dark side went with the smile as it faded.

Fergie frowned. "I can't believe you're even considering this, Al. I take back asking for your help."

"Too late. That ship sailed when those Tango Blast riders started shooting."

"I have a kit with me," Jaime said. His shifting of the subject wasn't lost on Fergie. "Realistic fake tattoos, do-rags, leathers, and everything you're going to need to fit in but not accidentally side with Crips, Bloods, or anyone else out there wearing colors."

"Hey, if someone has to ride bitch to boost the reality, it had better be me and not string bean here," Bonnie said. "Everyone knows bikers like boobs."

"I've heard that," Jaime said. "But maybe this once Al should go alone. This is supposed to be just a quick reconnoiter, a fact-finding probe. I'd do it myself, but I'm known in certain circles."

"Don't you have anyone inside the gangs?" Al asked.

"Did. Don't now. A temporary thing I'm fixing. Want details?"

Al shook his head.

"I've got more men trying to work their way inside, but they're not there yet. That's why I'd be glad for anything you can gather in the meantime, Al."

"It sure seems," Maury said to Al, "that everyone is wanting your services these days, but no one is paying for it."

"This is for mutual gain," Jaime said. "But if Al here wants to put a chit in for his services later, we'd be glad to pay. Well, the taxpayers would. That is, if he learns anything of value. First let's get you up to speed on the big picture, Al."

He turned to Bonnie. "There isn't any pie in the ice box, is there?"

"No. But I've got plenty more coffee, and I was just starting to whip up a good country breakfast."

Jaime held up his cup. "Okay, we'll go with that."

When Bonnie had refilled all their cups, Jaime took a sip of his and leaned back. "First thing you need to know is that there's a war going on."

"And, of course, money is the prize," Fergie said.

"Usually is." Jaime looked around at each of them. "Now, you can read the papers or catch some of this on television, but let me give you a snapshot of what's going on as it pertains to here."

Nothing Jaime had said so far gave Al a bigger chill than that. It was very unlike Jaime not to play his cards very close to his chest. For him to open up said he thought something very serious was about to hit the fan—and that it might affect Al.

"I'll keep this brief because no one wants the complete

detail on this picture right now. A hazy snapshot will have to do it. Okay?"

Bonnie and Maury nodded. Fergie and Al waited with stony faces.

"We all know about the craziness going on in Mexico. Cartels are fighting it out with each other as well as the armies and agencies, in many cases with military weapons and equipment. It's a poor country, and the money to be made from coke, meth, and marijuana is huge. Some say bigger than the country's budget. My own guess is that the wholesale earnings from just the drug sales are around thirty to forty billion a year. The law here and especially in Mexico has clamped down all it can, but the arrests of key cartel leaders in the Tijuana and Gulf cartels have actually just increased the violence as the rest struggle in the fight for control. That's what's behind the brutal killings, beheaded bodies, and women and children sometimes caught in the crossfire. I've been down there, Al, and more goes on in one week these days than you maybe investigated in your whole career. Same goes for you, Fergie."

"Who is the top dog now?" Al asked.

"Doesn't matter." Jaime leaned closer, and his brown eyes got bigger. "It's whoever didn't get caught, sold out, or killed by the competition. And that's only good until next week. It's a regular revolving door. But that's not what concerns us here. There will always be cartels. You need to sweat who's working for them way up here."

"I'm surprised their tentacles reach this far," Maury said. "I thought our tangle with the guys from Los Zetas was a one-time thing."

"Oh, hell. The Mexican cartels reach to Chicago, New York City, even to Seattle. Forget about San Diego, Laredo, or anything touching Mexico. We're still finding tunnels.

But the ones you need to worry about right now are the Texas Syndicate, the Texas Mexican Mafia, also known as the *Mexikanemi*, and your recent acquaintances, the Tango Blast, or Puro Tango Blast."

Al had been out of the department only a short time, but the scene had sure shifted. La Familia had been a player when he was active, but they had been shut down and virtually eradicated. One goes down, another springs into place.

"So there *are* three," Maury said.

Jaime frowned. "No. Not just three. There are several others, like the *Mara Salvatrucha*, and a bunch of other badasses. But there are at least three that affect what we think is going on here."

"Isn't that what I said?" Maury looked to Fergie and Bonnie.

"I've known about the three main biker gangs all along, Maury." Al rubbed a hand across his chin. "What I didn't know was the 'why' and 'who' behind the note. Still think that's plain hinky. Just let him talk, or we'll be all day at this."

Jaime shook his head and took a sip of coffee. "The *Mexikanemi* got hit real hard in 2009, with a whole batch of arrests, mainly in San Antonio, some of my doing. They're getting back up to full strength, though, and we think they're dealing with cartels like the Gulf, Sinaloa, Jaurez, and Los Zetas. They also do burglaries, some drug trafficking, and extortion. Their gang is highly organized and operates under a strict paramilitary structure. They're like an armed military business, if you can imagine. These are serious dudes. Don't doubt it. They're kind of known as guns-for-hire for some of the cartels. They and Los Zetas got into a tangle in Laredo, and some serious blood was shed.

"Now, the Texas Syndicate members do a lot of trafficking but also go for robbery, murders, and some burglaries, particularly of other drug dealers. They are on the serious grow. They're connected to cartels like the Sinaloa and Gulf cartels. These are also real violent dudes, and they've been jostling most with Tango Blast.

"Tango Blast is a prison gang, but the big difference is no hierarchy. That makes them officially unorganized. Hard to lop the head off a monster like that. All the guys you knocked off the road, Al, were Austin members. We could tell that from their tats. Dallas members, the D-town bunch, often have a Dallas Cowboys star. The Houston members, the Houstones, use the Houston Astros symbol. But since Austin doesn't have a major sports franchise, their bunch, the *Capiruchas*, are stuck with getting the area code, 512, and images of the capitol building as their tats. At least one had the 16-20-2 tat, which stands for Puro Tango Blast. The numbers represent the letters PTB." Jaime paused to take a sip of coffee. No one spoke in the silence, letting him keep the floor.

"Members in the Tango Blast are usually recruited in prison and go through a beat-in. That's where a prospective member fights several of the Tangoes, and if he doesn't call out *"no mas,"* he's in. Almost all of them were from the system, but because of recent losses like the three you did in, Al, they are accepting some willing recruits these days from the eager faces of the young who think the gang is cool. They start to imitate them, even getting the tattoos. Some of them, eager as they are, don't make it through the initiation. Just the way it is. These are major violent dudes. And they're growing fast. They're already twice as big as the Texas Syndicate. The two of them were having a huge bloody war until a truce in 2007, but that's been fragile. It could erupt into full scale again at any second, and the Tangoes are hungry enough, and numerous enough, to want that."

"Real bad boys?" Bonnie said.

"When these groups fight, it's no holds barred. There are guttings, beheadings, castrations, and that's just instead of handshakes. Then they get really serious about their violence."

"You don't think I could get the best of them if it comes to that?" Al said.

"Let's face it, Al. You'd scare these kinds of guys as much as a turtle's roar. They're young, crazy, and as mean as your worst nightmare. Meaner."

"Clayton thinks I'm more bobcat material," Al said.

Jaime suppressed a chuckle. "Don't let him sell you the soap, Al. I say turtle, terrapin, tortoise."

Al shrugged. "How's knowing all that about them supposed to help us?"

"It isn't. It's supposed to scare the bejesus out of you and make you want to run far and run fast and hide deep. Then I and my men will take care of what needs taking care of, the way we're trained and prepared to do. *Comprende?*"

"Why loan Al the bike, then?" Fergie asked.

"Because I've known Al a long time. A very bright man, a first-rate detective. But he has a head like a brick. I can say 'duck,' and I can quack duck, but until he sees it waddle, he's gonna have doubts. I want to remove those doubts as quickly as possible."

"I don't know," Fergie says. "This still sounds like you're kind of eager to hang Al's ass out there."

"Yeah," Bonnie said. "We're supposed to be at risk now. We don't want more risk, especially for Al."

Jaime looked at Al and shook his head. "You sure do have a posse here looking out for you. I guess that's a good thing."

"I could go instead," Maury said.

Jaime looked him up and down. "I doubt it. Only reason I'd trust Al is because he's got thirty years of service and a good deal of common sense to boot. Plus I've seen him fight. He's pretty good, even for a turtle."

"That common sense should be telling him not to do this," Fergie said. "Clayton and his men can sort this out on their end, and you on yours."

"Suit yourselves. But this is one or two quick in-and-outs. You must be familiar with that concept. Al should see minimal risk, and we might get a scrap of intel that helps. It's just as likely we don't get anything and he gets a few beers and a motorcycle ride at my expense. But you're suspecting my motives, so let me lay my cards on the table for you. Okay?"

He looked around at each of them, held the look until every one of them had nodded.

"Just so you know, our interest is in the cartels. These gangs are a local problem, except where there's trafficking. Then the DEA has an interest. But getting to the cartels isn't easy, and it doesn't always satisfy when we do. There was this head of the Tijuana cartel, for instance. Benjamin Arellano Felix. This is a guy who led a cartel that smuggled hundreds of tons of cocaine and marijuana into the United States and, for novelty, dissolved bodies of its rivals in vats of lye. He only got twenty years after pleading guilty to racketeering and conspiracy to launder money. Why? Because of a plea bargain deal we had to take. If we wanted to get all the time we could against him and put him away like the dog he is, we'd have had to take the twenty-one plea bargains of those willing to testify against him. Maybe someone will shank him real good while he's inside. More than likely, though, his gang will just protect him in there."

"That bites the big one," Bonnie said.

"What would you prefer?" Al asked. "Termination with extreme prejudice?"

"I wish. You know we can't do that, Al." Jaime spoke through nearly clenched teeth.

"Too bad," Bonnie said.

Jaime nodded. "Meanwhile, the public is busting our chops because it seems like we only respond to situations, that we aren't more proactive and going after these sons-a-bitches with everything we have."

"Is that what this is about?" Fergie asked. "Putting Al in jeopardy just to jostle something into action?"

"You're already in jeopardy or you wouldn't be sitting here in what amounts to Clayton's safe house. All I'm doing is helping Al with a request he made. Like I said, we had a couple of people inside these gangs, until they were tumbled. We've got more trying to work their way inside. We're not asking Al to do anything like that. That sort of thing is what we do, what we prefer to do. We'd be glad for any tidbit Al can pick up for the moment, and if the slightest thing comes of it that we can use, we'll get him out of the way and step in and take the brunt of it. Okay?"

"I guess so," Fergie said.

Maury and Bonnie nodded.

"Now," Jaime said, "who wants in on the fun of making Al look pretty so he can get all this over with as soon as possible?"

All three—Bonnie, Maury, and Fergie—held up their hands.

Al leaned back in the chair, his eyes closed and a towel around his neck, while Bonnie and Fergie tried to suppress giggles as they applied the makeup.

"Come on, think biker." Bonnie frowned at their work so far. "He's starting to look more like a pirate."

Maury and Jaime even chuckled a time or two. Al kept his mouth and eyes closed, tried to think about anything else. Austin and bikers. And drugs. Not a necessary and logical connection, but a possibility to keep open until disputed.

People who visited the Austin area, or even those who lived smack dab in the middle, might have no idea about the drug dealings flowing in and out as well as passing through the growing town. A few social workers might, or cops, or some federal agency guys like the DEA, and certainly any of those in scrubs who work in any of the many ERs. Nor would any visible ties between drugs and any bikers have been obvious. That's because thousands and thousands of bikers were on the roads year round—hobbyists, enthusiasts, and folks in their first leathers on their first bikes. Texas is warm most of the year, and a lot of the people who prefer two wheels over four get to wheel about all twelve months of the year, taking day trips and having harmless fun, for the most part. In a way, all the friendly biker traffic made for perfect camouflage. To the average driver on the road, one biker looks pretty much like another.

Once a year, just after Labor Day, the Republic of Texas biker rally takes place in Austin. Five-to-six thousand bikers and their glittering, usually well-kept machines ride into town for what the city realizes is a revenue-generating good time. As many as thirty-five thousand other people pour into town for the related events and to bask in the window-rattling roar of the modified tailpipes of Harleys and Hondas. No public figures ever make an effort to discourage the event. Aside from a lot of bikes parked in front of a lot of bars, and a lot of beer going down road-dusty throats, not much happens. That is if you don't count a dozen or more dust-ups in parking lots, a couple hundred DWI arrests, and as many as five deaths a year caused by drivers of four-wheeled vehicles not used to there being so many bikes on the roads.

So it wasn't fair to think of bikers as being generically bad. But a tiny percentage of them were as bad as they can get. These prison-gang sorts of bikers could be a whole other kettle of fish. Nothing to take lightly, and Al was about to head into the heart of them.

Bonnie and Fergie both chuckled out loud again. Al's jaw tightened. He was far from in the mood to chuckle along with them. Then all the tension eased out of him, and he relaxed.

Aw, come on, he chided himself. Whatever glue they were using on his face for the beard was tightening his skin into a taut drum beneath the scratchy fur. *You've stood on the curb yourself with the other slack jaws and quite enjoyed the rumble of the bikers parading in droves of twenty or thirty at a time up one street and back down again, revving. Those pot-bellied bikers with bug stains on their teeth from smiling while they ride are an invigorating sight. It's different, and it doesn't last all that damn long. A brief colorful flicker in your life. And, yeah, there's going to be some danger and risk. Sure there is. But right now you're in the mood for something dangerous, aren't you, if only to make you feel just a little bit more alive. So, bring it on!*

CHAPTER ELEVEN

Joaquin Zambada "El Chapo" Arellano sat in the worn passenger seat of a 4 x 4 Dodge Ram 2500 with crew cab. It wasn't his truck, nor did it belong to Heriberto Alonzo, his *segundo*, who had driven them there. The imprint of a rear impressed into the seat was much bigger than his own. Someone's *esposa* was getting ahead on her *sopapillas*. Heriberto had acquired the truck earlier that morning, before the sun had come up. Through the darkly tinted windows, Joaquin watched the house. He wasn't the only one. At the house to his left, a venetian blind at the front window lifted a fraction of an inch then dropped back into place. They knew, but didn't want to know any more than they had to—probably went back into another room and turned the television up loud. The whole neighborhood was closed down now, curtains and blinds pulled. Not a kid playing. Barely a dog barking. The one behind the house, it was barking. Then it stopped, never to bark again.

Two of his men came around from that side. Heriberto on the left. On the right, with a slight limp, plodded Benito "Viejito" Huerta. They were going about it just the way they'd been taught when in the military.

Heriberto got to the front door and didn't hesitate. He kicked it in. El Chapo thought he heard a scream, but he could have imagined that, or desired it. After a few more beats, Heriberto came to the open doorway and nodded. El Chapo got out of the truck, stepping on the running board with one careful cowboy-booted foot before hopping to the ground. He wasn't a big man, but it comforted El Chapo to know he was a very powerful one.

The doorjamb had shattered at its hinges, the door hanging off to one side by the time he got to the house. He glanced around at the preternaturally still neighborhood then stepped inside the house. Viejito stood behind the man, who was on his knees. He seemed to be praying. When he lifted his head, El Chapo could see the long flash of Viejito's knife stretched across the neck, its tip just grazing flesh.

"Por favor, Jefe. Por favor. Diez años."

From the next room, Joaquin could hear the whimper of the children, and the woman. The corner of his mouth twitched up. A smile. It was like the chorus to a song, one he could dance to or savor on a drive through his turf.

Stealing is stealing, and ten years of loyalty or not, no one steals from the *Mexikanemi*. And a member who steals is not a loyal member.

El Chapo glanced toward Heriberto and nodded. They both stepped back to avoid splatter. Viejito's knife slashed, and the head rocked back like a puppet's head falling to one side, except for the visible scraped bone. Blood sprayed from the severed carotid artery. The whimpering in the next room grew. El Chapo lifted a hand and with a pointed finger made a circular motion that meant *"do them all."* That would normally include the dog, but El Chapo had a hunch Heriberto was ahead of him there. El Chapo turned and went back outside.

It was turning into a beautiful day. Maybe some pork *carnitas* for lunch. He patted his round stomach. Then there was the business of finding who was holding out on the "dime" that should be theirs. Probably those Texas Syndicate hombres.

He started to walk toward the truck and glanced back to the inside of the house, but all he could see was a dark rectangle behind the gaping doorway. Heriberto would be finishing the job. *Bueno.* But Heriberto worried him. He was an ambitious man. Soon he would be wanting El Chapo's spot, at the top. Maybe Heriberto should go on a mission, an impossible one. El Chapo thought about it as he slid into the passenger seat of the stolen truck and closed the door. Maybe those Tango Blast members had the right idea. No top dog. Just a relentless horde of them, growing fast and becoming more dangerous with every new day. But no top dog meant El Chapo would have to give up what he had, and he didn't really want that at all. Not at all.

———◄◄◆►►———

Al used the bathroom mirror to check and straighten his black Harley do-rag. He turned his head. The tattoo of a skull in a spider's web on the side of his neck seemed a bit much. He wished he'd had time to let his beard grow for a few days so Jaime wouldn't have encouraged them to stick on the theater stubble that itched like dammit.

He came out of the bathroom, and Fergie was waiting, tall and looking prettier than a ten-pound box of thousand-dollar bills. Her smile this time was the one with the wry twist to one corner of her mouth.

"I'd be glad if you'd stay and keep an eye on the other two," Al said. "I won't be gone long. I know I don't have the right to ask, but I'm asking."

"I don't know what you can possibly expect to find out with just a little poking."

"Right now, do you have a good clear sense of what's going on here?"

"I don't have any sense at all. There's nothing to make sense of so far except a series of unexplained and possibly unrelated incidents."

"I don't have anything like the beginning of a handle on this either, and you know me."

"Yeah. Curiosity is eating at you to your bones, isn't it? But didn't Clayton tell you to butt out?"

"That's just his way. He knows how to egg me on."

"I don't think he was kidding. I wasn't sure we were going to make it out of that last episode. Are you sure leaving the house is safe? Or should we all be leaving and heading as far away as we can get?"

"I'm leaving my gun and the ammo in my bag. In case you need it. I'm just telling you so you know where to go for it if that need arises."

"Noted."

"Since I'm all toughed up, do you want a spanking before I go? Or to kiss a furry guy?"

She reached out to his shoulders and spun him so he was facing the bedroom doorway. "I've kissed a furry guy before. Not always the thrill you'd think. Just go if you're going to go, but get back quickly. Okay?"

He'd taken only a couple steps when her voice lowered. "Just remember one thing, Al. The last time Jaime helped you, he was hanging you out as bait. Do you really trust the guy?"

Al shrugged, trying to make it casual. He didn't want to stay and debate the point because he wasn't entirely sure himself.

Maury sat on the living room couch. He got to his feet as Al entered the room. Just the two of them, alone for the moment.

"A lot of ladies like to run up the pirate flag and slip to the dark side. I think you could make one of them happy, Al."

"Yeah, that's what I was going for, the bad-boy look."

"Mission accomplished."

Al stopped. He looked into his brother's eyes in a way he hadn't in a long time. "You know, Maury. It was screwy how it all happened, but I'm glad to have you around again. There were times I thought I was having a pretty good time living alone, but it had its lonely moments. I know I give you a hard time about your addiction to chasing women, but I have to confess something. I've had a close call or two myself."

"Do tell."

"Once I came within an ace of kissing the postal lady."

"Get your ass out of here."

"No, really. Most of the time she'd leave the mail out in the box, but when I got packages, she'd drive up to the door. She got a kick out of the deer, and we talked about them. Her name was Allison, and she was married and had kids and thought the deer had become my surrogate children."

"She's not wrong."

"Anyway, we were on the porch talking, and she took off her sunglasses. We were standing close. She had these terrific hazel eyes, and I caught myself looking at her lips then starting to lean forward."

"Did she lean back?"

"No, she didn't. Her eyes looked willing, but I started thinking about it. A married woman. That's not like me, not like me at all. I think she was disappointed when I didn't follow through."

"Do you think?"

"In the long run, I felt good about not starting something

I shouldn't. I mean there were a couple dozen cold showers before I got to that point. But in the end, I was glad."

"Oh, grasshopper, you have so much to learn."

"Yeah? Well, I'm not going to learn it from you. Take care of the ladies for me, will you? I'll be back as soon as I can."

He started to walk past. Maury rushed to him and gave him an enthusiastic hug.

"What was that about?" Al said when Maury let go.

"Who knows when I'll get to hug a biker again without getting my lights knocked out? Now take care of yourself. Okay?"

Maury turned away as Al went to the front door, wondering if he hadn't detected a little quiver in his brother's voice just then.

Outside, Jaime was backing the Harley down a ramp from the horse trailer. His vehicle was the usual black SUV.

Bonnie stood watching. She turned when Al came out the door. "Well, don't you look downright dashing in the light of day."

Al looked up. The sky was a solid grey bruised by black clouds here and there. It didn't look like an inviting day to be on the road at all.

"I still think you'd ride better with some serious boobs pressed against your back," she said.

"Probably so, Bonnie, but then I might not want to get off."

"Oh, you'd get off all right."

"Hey, Al, she's a real firecracker, no?" Jaime said.

"She's a firecracker, yes." He turned to her. "Now be good. Don't tie Maury up again. . . unless he needs it."

"Oh, Al. I'm gonna miss you." She rushed up to him and squeezed. She started to move her face toward his then stopped. She spun and rushed toward the front door. Al thought he heard her choking back a sob.

"You've got yourself quite a household there, Al," Jaime said. He put the bike on its kickstand and slid the ramp back into place then closed the horse trailer doors. "Now, in and out of a couple of places, and be all ears. Let me know if you get the slightest quiver of anything solid that I can use. Okay?"

Al nodded. They shook hands, and Jaime got into his SUV. Al slipped on a pair of yellow-lensed shooting glasses, fired up the cycle, and followed the trailer out the lane to the road.

Jaime turned right, and Al veered to the left, the long way back toward Fuzzy's.

He opened the bike up until he hit a steady sixty and was enjoying the feel of the road so close beneath him, the way trees felt closer and more real as they whizzed by. Easy to see why so many people got a kick out of riding their bikes from one end of Texas to the other.

The first time another biker passed going the other direction, Al nearly forgot. The man's hand came off his handlebar, and he held it out in a low wave.

Al's hand snapped out too, arm down, with his fingers in a peace sign. Jaime had felt that sign would give the least offense to any possible gang members.

Used to be the Harley riders didn't do the wave, but nowadays they did. Jaime claimed it was only the BMW riders who remained above all that. But Al had found them to be as outgoing and friendly as any other hobby riders. Go figure.

The sky was darkening, with a heavy hint of weather. Al had just the leather jacket, jeans, and boots he wore. He hadn't packed anything for rain. More than the weather, he found the ominous sky depressing.

He found himself thinking of a time he'd been driving one of the sheriff's department cruisers along Nameless Road. He'd just passed the Nameless Valley Ranch and the Nameless convenience store and had begun to feel the usual twinge of existentialism brought on by such heavy-handed silliness as a stretch of the county that had just decided not to name anything. Up ahead there was a field, a pasture that looked pretty played out. The past few times Al had driven by, an older palomino horse, probably put out to pasture, had stood along the fence facing the road with its neck stretched out over the fence. It stood still, looking off far away. Perhaps, Al figured, it was trying to remember if it had a name. But this time the horse wasn't at its usual spot. Al missed it being there. Then, at the far end of the field, in the corner, the horse stood in a stand of mesquite trees and agarita bushes. At his side stood a shaggy brown-and-white goat with medium-sized curving horns crowded close. They both looked off together, and for the first time, Al thought the palomino looked happy, pleased to have a friend, even if it was just a goat. It made Al feel good. Could be he was reading a lot into it, but that's the way thoughts work out on a stretch of back highway called Nameless Road.

Up ahead, the lights in the neon sign above Fuzzy's glowed in the rapidly dimming and weather-darkening sky. Al pulled into the parking lot, felt and heard the crunch of gravel. He parked the bike. Well, this was it. He headed for the door.

CHAPTER TWELVE

A L WALKED INSIDE WITH THE confidence of a seasoned biker used to popping into biker bars at nearly noon on a Sunday. He glanced around. Nothing had changed. Pool table off to the left, not being used. He smiled to himself and walked to the bar. Four guys with their jackets hanging off the backs of their chairs sat at a table, each with a longneck beer in front of him. Two old-timers sat at the far end of the bar with half-full bottles and empty shot glasses in front of them. A man rose from behind the bar, where he'd been shoving bottles into an ice trough not all that different from the one out in the open-air men's room.

"What'll ya have?"

Good thing this wasn't Peggy's shift. He watched the bartender's eyes sweep his gear, take in that he didn't appear to be with any gang. A usual and practiced glance probably motivated by the need to head off any trouble before it started.

Al ordered a Shiner Bock, paid for it, and carried it over to the pool table. The rack of cues ran along the wall just inside the front door. He went through them and eyeballed a couple for straightness. He picked out a seventeen-ounce cue with a freshly replaced tip, though its black paint trim was worn off almost all the way to the butt. It had a tiny bend to it, but it was straighter than anything else in the rack. He could work with a predictable bend. He racked the balls and broke, quietly getting the feel of a game he'd once enjoyed. Peeling a ball out of the pack, he ran it down the rail. Banked a shot to a side pocket. The light stick was just right for the three-quarter-sized table.

He took a sip of beer and looked up to see a pot-bellied biker watching him. Big fellow, probably over three hundred, maybe three-fifty, some of it still muscle. Most of the gangs were hiding their tats better these days, but this guy was old school enough for Al to make out a Texas Syndicate tat on an upper arm about the size of one of Al's thighs.

"You've played a bit," the man said, his voice like sandpaper on concrete.

"Out of practice, really," Al said. "I used to play. But who has the time anymore? Just saw the empty table and thought, 'What the hell.'"

"You up to a game?"

"Sure."

"I'm Rogelio," the biker said. He grabbed the nearest cue off the rack and didn't look at it. "Play for a beer okay?" His English wasn't perfect, but he'd spotted Al for a gringo.

"Couter," Al said. It was the name of a felon he'd put away some thirty years ago. It had been a while since he'd even thought of Couter, who may well be coming up for parole soon. "A beer's fine, unless you want to go higher."

"Let's stay with a beer until I see if you're still shooting the spots off them," Rogelio said.

While they were in their first game, the door swung open and a young man in black leather pants and a white T-shirt came in. He saw the other three Texas Syndicate members at their table and went over to sit down with them. Al glanced quickly at the boy's face then looked away. It was Roger Franklin, the preacher's son. He didn't look like he'd been to church. He chattered with the men at the table and was up like a shot to go to the bar when they wanted another round. He carried the beers back to the table, grasping them by their long necks, grinning like he was already a member of their group and not just someone wishing to be so bad he could taste it. He didn't look sad at the moment, although his best friend would be buried that week. Al went back to his game with Rogelio and let it have his full concentration, though he could hear the men laughing loudly at the far table.

After playing for only half an hour, Al had won the two beers now standing on the nearest table. They were beading up with sweat and getting warmer by the second as he ran the last four striped balls off the table and slid the eight ball into the far corner. It was all coming back to him, the sweet crack of one ball on another, the geometry of the game. And that was just with straight shooting. He was careful not to use a masse shot or anything the least bit fancy that might give away the hours he'd spent years ago in stretches of his wasted youth. To be fair, his opponent was a smasher at open balls with little at all in the way of finesse. Al looked up, and Rogelio had his stick in his hands and, from the bulging veins in his forehead and arms, looked ready to break his cue in half. It was a hefty twenty-two-ounce stick, but Al wouldn't have bet on the stick. The hint of angry red suddenly drained from Rogelio's face, and he put his cue down on the felt surface. "See ya," he said and started for the door.

Six men had just entered. They looked around as they went up to the bar to take stools. The three men at the table got up too, and they headed toward the door. One of them tossed a few bills on the table and didn't look back as he stepped lively to the door and out it. Roger still stood facing the bar. He turned around with four beers in his hands and saw the empty table. He glanced at the men who'd sat down on either side of him. One of the men took a beer from Roger's hands. Three of the others did as well. Al could see a bit of the capitol building peeking out from the neck of the shirt of the man at the end of the bar nearest him, who called out to Roger, "You'd better buy a couple more *cervezas*. We're real thirsty here."

"*Si. Mas cervezas*," another said.

Roger's face washed white enough it nearly matched his T-shirt. He turned slowly back toward the bar. The bartender had started to reach under the counter when the men had crossed the room, but one of them shook his head, and that was enough to make the bartender stop. He stared at Roger as he reached down and got two more beers out of the cooler. The Tango bikers didn't seem to care what they drank. They did seem to enjoy the floor show, a frightened young man who had been cozy with an opposing gang.

When Roger took out his wallet, the biker on his right took it away. He tugged out all the bills, shoved them into his own pocket, and dropped the empty wallet onto the bar. "How do you plan to pay for the beers now, kid?"

Al took in the bartender, who didn't look like he was going to do anything. Al put his pool stick down on the table and picked up the heavier cue Rogelio had been using.

The biker on the far end, who stood nearest Al, called out, "Hey, Ramon. Cut the kid some slack. You'd probably get him pregnant or something."

Ramon turned to glare at his friend. Al was looking at the biker who'd yelled. He'd limped as he came in, and Al placed him as the one he'd shot in the knee. Guy was doing pretty good, so maybe Al had missed the knee cap. Too bad.

Ramon turned back to Roger, said something low to him in Spanish. Roger shook his head. Ramon grabbed Roger's upper arm. The boy struggled but couldn't pull himself loose. Al stepped away from the pool table. The bright fluorescent light that hung over it was behind him now.

"I think you'd better let the boy go," Al said. "And when they do, kid, have the sense to go for the door. Pronto."

A couple of the other bikers had been talking low, but now all conversation in the bar stopped. Every head swung toward Al, who stood there, not a particularly tall man, nor a big one, with a mere pool cue in one hand. Even the bartender stared, his mouth dropping open slightly. The Tango Blast men slowly slid off their stools and stood. Roger had his head bent forward, peering intently. He stayed where he was, even though Ramon had let go of his arm.

"Hey, that guy's a cop! He was with the sheriff's department people!" Roger shouted as loud as he could in the still room.

If he'd waved a red flag in a room full of bulls, he couldn't have gotten a more dramatic and immediate reaction.

The biker on the end lunged toward Al, clearly forgetting he had a game leg. When his initial step slowed him to a lurch, Al reversed the cue until he held it like a bat. He gave a big, looping, upward swing that swept all the way from behind his shoulders. With all his weight and a little waist and legs behind it, the blow ended with the thick end smacking the biker square in his crotch. The biker's eyes opened wide then snapped shut in pain. He started to fall forward, but Al gave him a shove back. The biker knocked down the two guys behind him, who had been trying to surge around him. All three fell to the floor in a tangle. The fourth biker started around the other side of the pile.

Al lifted his cue. The thin end had broken off from the force he'd used on the limping biker. Fine. He grabbed what was left of the thick part by its narrower end, a better club anyway, and rushed the biker coming at him. Al swung toward the man's head. The biker twisted and ducked, leaving exposed his hip and a long wallet attached by a length of thick chain to the man's belt. Al grabbed the wallet and tugged. As soon as the biker realized his wallet was gone, he grabbed for it. Al flipped the chain around the man's wrist and pulled tight. As the guy toppled forward, Al swung hard, catching him right on the temple. He saw the man's eyes go blank as he fell. The man behind him struggling to rise tripped over his falling friend.

Al grabbed Roger's wrist and tugged him toward the front door. The little twit tugged back, trying to resist. Go figure. Al was saving him, and he was fighting back. So Al tugged harder, nearly yanking the kid off his feet.

With Roger fighting, twisting, and trying to get away, Al fought off the couple of bikers who'd scrambled back to their feet, swinging left and right, connecting with heads and extended arms and smashing shins, until the bikers were in a writhing pile on the floor. He yanked Roger through the front door. As soon as they were through, he pushed Roger away, went to one of the Harleys parked in a row, and wheeled it in a rush up to the front door. He toppled it over and jammed it against the door.

Give this to the stupid kid, he went over to the bike and tried to tug it away from the door to let out the bikers who had been giving him a hard time. Al was already on his bike and had it running.

"If I were you, I'd be making tracks, getting the hell out of here," he told the little idiot, who only kept tugging at the fallen bike.

The front door was opening in little surges, an inch

at a time, as several of those inside threw their bodies against it.

"Hey!" one of them yelled from outside. He must have figured out to come out the men's room and climb over that fence.

Al saw him with one leg over the top of the fence. The kid was still tugging at the bike that blocked the door, trying to help. *Well, you can only do what you can do,* he told himself. He gave his bike some gas and tore out of the parking lot in a spray of gravel.

A quarter of a mile up the road, he was just cresting the hill when he looked back and saw what looked like the whole pack of bikers coming his way as fast as their bikes could take them. And their bikes did seem faster than his.

Heriberto lowered the field glasses and watched those Tangoes pull the bike away from the door, hop on their bikes, and head off after the little independent dude. He'd have bet money on them Tangoes any other day, but he liked the cut of the new guy's jib. He was thinking well enough to be a *Mexikanemi*, and that was saying something. Heriberto pulled out his notepad again and reached for his pen.

His wife and three kids thought of him as a businessman, and they were right. He had picked up methodology and thoroughness in the marines. As for the ruthless edge that made him trouble to traitors in the ranks or the competition, well, he'd picked that up on his own.

He sat up high on the hill across the road from Fuzzy's. He, or one of his men, had taken turns watching, and today had been rich with insights. First the four Texas Syndicate dudes had rolled in then that independent solo dude. After that was the boy in the T-shirt, who still stood outside the bar looking down the road. Next came the six Tangoes. The four Syndicates exited pronto. He'd expected the Tangoes to mop it up pretty good with the independent, but he'd been wrong. So had they. Interesting. Very interesting.

The new guy had walked with a slight swagger, like one of the *Mexikanemi* who Heriberto knew with a Special Forces background. Esteban Moreno. It was better than even money that the Tangoes would catch the little dude within a mile or two of the bar. It wouldn't go so well for him then, whatever his background. Oh, well.

Heriberto finished making notes and tucked the notepad away. El Chapo wanted Heriberto to handle it, he'd said, and Heriberto would, but in his own way. He'd seen the way the *jefe* had been looking at him. El Chapo felt threatened. Well, he should. It was all going to go down, just the way El Chapo wanted, and Heriberto would make it happen. But that would give him a pretty good alibi too, wouldn't it. Shouldn't overlook that in a well-made plan.

He worked his way back through the trees, put the field glasses away on his chopper, and climbed on. He went back out the way he'd come in, out the empty cul-de-sac of a development that was still filling in. No houses on this loop yet, though the infrastructure was in place. Underground phone and electric lines. Water lines. He'd spent a few summers hanging sheet rock, so he could tell about how far along they were. Not quite done, though, so it was a good spot to keep an eye on things. The houses were popping up all over the development, and soon it would be a gated community to keep people just like him out. That was fine with him. He wouldn't need this spot much longer, not much longer at all.

CHAPTER THIRTEEN

A L LOOKED BACK IN HIS rearview mirror and saw they were gaining. He'd have been okay except for that brickhead of a kid and Al's own tendency to step in and back the downtrodden. In this case, one not smart enough to know when he was being trodden down.

Bikers liked this two-lane ranch road because it was hilly with lots of curves—more interesting for a Sunday ride. It had been a while since Al had been on a motorcycle and even longer since he'd had one open all the way. It took all the concentration he had to maneuver the curves, leaning into them and accelerating out of them. Each glance into the mirror showed the bikers gaining on him. They must spend time with their machines, keeping them in tip-top tune, and they certainly rode a helluva lot more than Al. The road was pretty clear, with only an occasional pickup going past in the other direction. He hit a straight stretch and opened the throttle all the way. So did they, and they were getting more out of their machines.

He rocketed past a bait store on the right and caught the glitter of three black SUVs snugged up close to the building. At least it wasn't a patrol car waiting to give him a ticket. On second thought, a patrol car would have been welcome if it meant interfering with a chase that was almost certainly destined to turn out badly for him.

As soon as he was past, the string of three black

vehicles pulled out onto the road, forming a blockade. He could see men in black SWAT gear pouring out of the vehicles and swarming to the other side. He imagined the bikers were braking for all they were worth. Relief flooded through him but was as quickly replaced by white-hot anger. That damned Jaime Avila. He'd used Al as bait once again. Al squeezed the handlebar grips tight and let the emotion wash through him. It began to trickle away until it was only red, then faintly pink. Finally cold, clear logic returned. He was calm again, as quickly as the rage had come. He'd been the one to ask to borrow a bike after all, to nose around because he wanted to know more about what was going on. Jaime had gone along for his own reasons, whatever they were, though they probably tied in somewhere. That was part of what he needed to untangle. For the first time, pieces started to fit together for Al. He could make a glimmer of logical sense out of what had been a confused muddle before. But he needed to check a thing or two. Where was the nearest library? Oh, hell. It was Sunday. None of them would be open. *Think, man, think.*

Ah, Dougie Stanton, and chances were he'd be home. Dougie was a reporter for half a dozen small newspapers that existed by selling ads to smaller communities. They needed good enterprise reporting to make the papers worth reading when they arrived free at residents' doors, waited in boxes outside restaurants, or were visited in digital form on the internet. That didn't mean Dougie wasn't good. He was one of the best, or at least had been before he'd fallen down the stairs of life sideways. The small-scale freebie rags were fortunate to have him, and he needed them these days as much as they needed him. The other handy thing about Dougie was that he lived right near where Al was tooling along, now at a reduced and saner pace.

Al made a left turn at a brown sign indicating a boat ramp. The road took him past a clutter of rustic cabins, double-wides, and an old collapsed motel. He swung past the ramp onto a skinny road that led along the shore to a spot where the road widened into a parking lot beside the defunct Catfish Barge. It had closed a few years ago. Maybe its hard-to-find location or its not-so-exotic surroundings had done it in, though Al could recall weaving his way here back in the day for deep-fried catfish with hush puppies or crispy, brown homemade fries. Now it was the residence of Dougie Stanton. And there was the happy journalist himself.

Dougie stood leaning against the rail of what had once been the front door to the restaurant, just on the other side of a short wooden bridge from the shore to the barge. The water boiled beneath him as Dougie tore bits from a loaf of bread and tossed them to the surface. He looked up and saw Al park the bike and put it on its kickstand.

"The place isn't open!" he yelled. "Can't you tell? Sign's down. Hasn't been open in years."

"Dougie, it's me. Al Quinn." Al tugged off his yellow glasses and waved them over his head.

Dougie stooped, his head stretched forward, his eyes squinting. All of this, on his six-foot-six frame, made him seem like a blue heron looking for small fish along the shoreline.

As Al got closer, Dougie said, "What the hell's happened to you, Al? Let yourself go to hell in a handbasket?"

That was rich coming from Dougie. Here was a guy with half of a no-filter cigarette hanging from his lip, about three days of stubble on his face, and greying hair tugged back into a foot-long ponytail. His waist looked no bigger around than one of Al's arms, though he wasn't naturally skinny like Pudge. His build had developed from an all-beer and cigarette diet that had gotten far enough along for him to break bones in his frequent falls. First thing Saturday morning he'd open a beer and light a cigarette and maintain that pace through the weekend—and every workday evening. The result? Malnutrition. Fellow could have been knocking on the Pulitzer's door but instead he'd bounced from the *Chicago Tribune* to the *Austin American Statesman* and on to gathering items and enterprise stories for a handful of free advertising papers.

He wore jeans that were almost thin enough to see through, dirty sneakers, and a T-shirt that might have been white once. He went back to tossing bits of bread into the water. As Al approached, he could see the pink rubbery mouths of carp thrust above the water, opening and closing in eagerness. In their rush to get the bits of bread, they pushed each other aside and down as wave on wave of them slid on top of each other, hungry mouths opening and shutting, grabbing air when there was no bread.

"It's an apt metaphor for the kind of news I toss to the hoi polloi these days. Don't you think?" Dougie bent forward and peered up at Al from beneath shaggy eyebrows that could stand a trimming. "Do you recall what Dorothy Parker said to Claire Booth Luce when Claire held the door open for Dorothy and said, 'Age before beauty'?"

Al had heard the anecdote. Out of politeness he let Dougie finish it.

"Dorothy walked on through and said, 'Pearls before swine.' That pretty well covers my journalistic situation as well."

When Al was all the way up to him, Dougie's eyes brightened. "Well, I'll be damned." He bent even closer to peer at Al. "You're working something, aren't you?" He stared at Al's chin. He held the bag of bread in his left hand, wet his right thumb on his greyish tongue, and reached for the tattoo on Al's neck.

Al backed up a step.

"Ha," Dougie said, lowering the hand. "You *are* working something, aren't you? Does it have anything to do with the four broadcast network trucks that all showed up at that organic farm, The Three Sisters?"

"If it did, you know I couldn't talk to you about it."

"Get out of town. Everyone knows you're retired. So, why the getup? Spill."

"Look, I just want to borrow your computer for a minute or two. Okay?"

"Okay. Sure. But we've got to have some kind of deal, Al." Dougie's eyes sparkled like a couple of lit-up pinwheels beneath his straggly grey eyebrows.

"You'd have to sit on this until I give you a thumbs-up, Dougie."

"What if you get shot, or killed, or something?"

"Then you can consider that a thumbs-up."

"Sweet." He realized what he'd said and almost took it back. But Dougie's eagerness won out in the end. "Aw, come on in."

Al followed the swaying ponytail inside. When he'd last been to the Catfish Barge, it had had a big open dining area with a kitchen at the far end. The tables and chairs were long gone, leaving an open hardwood floor. At the far end, a bare queen-sized mattress lay on the floor with a mess of sheets at one end and a piled-high ashtray by the two lifeless, flat pillows. The only other piece of furniture was a card table holding a laptop. No printer. Just a line running to the phone jack so Dougie could connect with the world out there.

Al realized he was holding his breath, so he let out air and breathed in a combination of ashtray and tired, stale sweat. Not really a Hallmark card sort of moment and somewhat further curdled by his happy memory of smelling deep-fried catfish and hush puppies in this setting.

He pulled out the folding chair at the computer and sat. Dougie hovered behind him, acting busy, tamping one end of a pack of Camels and then starting to tear off the cellophane wrapper.

The computer was already on the internet. Al went to the browser and typed in "Carl Franklin." He got quite a few. He had to scroll down and then click to the next page before he found the local preacher, and it was a mention of him doing a funeral. Another later listing mentioned the church and congregation. The man didn't have a very big digital footprint.

Al felt warm breath on his left ear and went back to holding his own after the first whiff of Dougie.

"Odd choice of people to research," Dougie said, his voice trying very hard, but failing, to conceal growing interest. "I do believe I have a card to play now."

Al turned in the chair and looked at Dougie, who, to his credit, took a couple of steps back and busied himself lighting a cigarette. A tremor showed in his fingers now.

"Okay, your turn to spill. But remember our deal."

"Rats." Dougie let out a stream of smoke from both nostrils.

"Well?"

"Some time ago I did a small piece on Carl Franklin. Lost in the spilled cornucopia of the many insights from my pen through the years. I certainly don't have a clipping, though Carl might."

"Can you cut to the chase?"

133

"It wasn't what you could call a scoop, though the next piece I do on him may be. But Carl once took a trip to Dimmit County."

"And? It's pretty flat as a story so far."

"What's Dimmit County known for?" Before Al could even try to answer, Dougie leaped ahead. "It's one of three counties in the absolute heart of the 'Golden Triangle,' that's Webb, La Salle, and Dimmit. Of all the Boone-and-Crockett-scoring deer shot in Texas each year, in all two hundred fifty-four counties, thirty-six percent come from those three counties. They're the core of the seven counties that produce fifty percent of all Boone-and-Crockett-scoring antlers of deer shot in Texas. None come from this county, by the way."

"What's the point of this ramble?" Al was starting to itch beneath the makeup stubble, and he grew eager to get back to the house and check on the others.

"Carl's big feat was to shoot a 'non-typical' fifteen-point buck. By itself, it was barely an item or photo opportunity. But add the fact that he's a preacher, and you have something. Turns out he was an army sharpshooter before he followed the path that led him to the pulpit. But he still likes to hunt. Makes a good oxymoron, no? Stir in the facts that someone was shooting at a couple of deputies and Carl's church is next door to the organic farm, and I'm smelling a real sizzler of a story here, Al. I've got to thank you."

"Save your thanks for later. Remember our deal."

"Can't I even write it up if you have to bring him in, as, say, a person of interest?"

"It would be public then, and you can sort that out with the sheriff. But spike the cannon for now. Okay, Dougie?"

Dougie nodded. But Al could already see him mentally pecking away at the story he would start as soon as Al was gone, so Al decided to accommodate him by leaving. "Gotta go. Thanks for the use of your machine, and even more for the background on Carl."

Dougie was already easing toward his computer as Al crossed the room, and he doubted if Dougie saw him leave.

Outside, in the parking lot, standing beside his bike, he punched in a number on his cell phone. Clayton answered.

"Yeah? What is it?"

"Thought I'd give you time to get home from church. But I have a lead on who your sniper at the farm might be. Turns out the preacher next door, Carl Franklin, was an army sharpshooter and hunts deer. His son, Roger, was best friends with Darin, and Roger has been hanging out at Fuzzy's, looks like a biker gang wannabe."

"Al, I thought I gave you pretty clear instructions to stay clear of this and to get your people over to Skinny's house."

"They're there, and safe. This other stuff practically fell in my lap."

"Sure it did." The line went silent, and Al could imagine Clayton putting the next steps into order in his mind. "I'll get the paperwork stirring and bring the Franklins in. You're okay for desk-jockey work at the office, so you can sit in, maybe contribute. But no sidearms or badge. You're unofficial, just a fly on the wall. You hear me?"

"Gotcha. Just give me a call before the questioning begins."

The line clicked, and that was that. Al put the phone back in his pocket and climbed back on the motorcycle. He already knew how fast it could go. Now he could stay within the speed limits and get back to the safe house in time for something to eat and, hope upon hope, a nap. He wasn't getting any younger.

CHAPTER FOURTEEN

AL TURNED THE HARLEY INTO the lane and eased up toward the house. He checked in all directions and could see no sign of anyone. The nearest house was a quarter mile away, and a copse of trees stood midway between the properties.

As soon as the engine slowed to an idle, he heard a gunshot. *Bam!* Then another. *Bam!* No time for the kickstand. He switched the motor off and lowered the bike to the ground on its side. He took off in a run around the corner of the house toward the back, the direction from which he'd heard the shots.

Bonnie and Maury stood close together. They swung around as Al came panting around the back corner. Maury held Al's Sig in one hand. He lowered it until it pointed at the ground. "What?"

"I'm teaching him to shoot, just like my dad did for me." Bonnie grinned as she watched the look of alarm and concern ease from Al's face. "You were sure Johnny on the spot to our defense, though. How did you plan to take on people with guns when you're unarmed?"

"You haven't used up all the ammo, have you? I only grabbed the one box." Al bent forward, hands on his knees, until he caught his breath.

"We've been careful. I'm just trying to get him the basics. I grew up with the point-and-shoot method and got pretty handy, as you may recall."

A row of sticks and one can stood at the base of a small rise. Bonnie took the pistol from Maury. She spun and fired. The can sailed into the air and clattered as it rattled up and over the hill.

She really could shoot. The one time they'd had to count on her, she'd been armed with a chief's special with a three-inch barrel, and she'd been darn close with it, enough so he'd been able to back her up.

"You don't have to sell me," Al said. "I've seen you in action. But have you considered what the neighbors might think?"

"Well, no." Bonnie glanced around. "No one's said anything yet."

"Al used to be quick like you, Bonnie," Maury said.

"Note the 'used to be,' if you will," Al said.

Maury grinned. "We had a Dalmatian named Pebbles. We could put a piece of cheese on her nose, and she'd sit until we said 'go.' Then she'd flip the cheese and grab it. Al used to snatch the cheese out of the air before she could gobble it. Just about surprised the spots off her. She'd look around. 'Where did the cheese go?' Then Al would open his hand."

"Are you still that fast, Al?" Bonnie tilted her head and narrowed her eyes at him.

"Oh, I have flashes now and again. Now, let's get inside. I want to get this blasted makeup off and, if there's any justice in the world, sneak in a short nap."

"So, everything went smooth," Maury said. "Did you learn anything?"

"Not what you'd think." Al waved off any other questions and went around to the front to park the bike properly.

Al's eyes slit open to the sound of knuckles rapping on

wood. The bedroom door opened, and Fergie stuck her head in.

"You left your cell phone out here, and you have a call."

He felt something warm and naked pressed against his back. He spun, his eyes snapping all the way open. Bonnie lay with her head on the other pillow, the coverlet pulled up to her chin and a grin on her face that nearly touched each ear.

"Why did you let her get in bed with me?" Al turned back to Fergie.

"She says it helps you sleep." Fergie's mouth was twisted up at the corner, somewhere between smile and smirk.

"What were you thinking?" Al asked her.

"Hey, I get different stories," Fergie said. "Who am I to believe?"

Al looked back to Bonnie, who seemed to have way more dimples than usual as she grinned.

"Humpf." She snuggled closer. "We had a girl in high school the boys called 'Tammy the trampoline.' They finally shortened it to just 'Tramp.' But I'm not her." Bonnie yanked the coverlet off the bed and wrapped it around herself, but not before Al had seen way more than he'd wished to. Still, as she walked across to the bathroom, with the back of the cover hanging open, he wasn't able to take his eyes off her swaying round derriere.

When the bathroom door closed, he looked back to Fergie. Her grin was darn near demonic.

"What?" he asked.

She walked over and handed him the phone then went back to lean on the wall with her arms folded.

"A little privacy?"

She shook her head, still grinning.

He grimaced and lifted the cell phone. "Yeah?"

"Jaime here."

"Hey, I've got a bone to pick with you." Al felt the warm flush of anger sweep through him.

"Before you go off halfcocked, Al, you weren't in any way supposed to be bait. We were just handy in case you needed backup. And it turns out you did. You're welcome."

"Well, thanks then. I think." There was nothing like anger flooding him only to wash back out. About as much fun as when the bathtub leaks. "What about those Tango Blast guys? Did you get anything from them?"

"Other than that they were mighty ticked off that some squirt of a guy they now think is working with us kicked their asses? No. We had to turn them loose. Before you ask, it's the cartels we're going after. Remember? And we didn't get squat that was new from these guys. Kudos, by the way, on dusting these guys in the bar. But they would have caught you on the road, Al. Do you know why?"

Al waited.

"Because you're a turtle, Al. You know that now, don't you? Watch your back, and be careful."

"Maybe I'm a snapping turtle."

"You'll be snapping at air with these guys."

"We'll see." Al hung up.

"My, my. Tango Blast again," Fergie said. "You do like to poke the hive, don't you?"

"I didn't find anything out at all about Bart," he said. "But I did manage to find a lead I need to follow. How long did I sleep?"

"Oh, at least an hour."

"No wonder I feel so rested." He thought he heard his back creak when he stretched his arms. "You didn't let anything happen in here, did you? I mean with Bonnie. I don't want to lose my amateur status."

"Oh, honey, you lost that long ago." Fergie looked a half step away from giggling out loud.

The surreal feel of his current personal life made him think of Dougie. It had been easy enough for him to look askance at the way Dougie lived. But there were more parallels than differences to the way Al lived himself, or had envisioned himself living. He fed deer. Dougie fed carp. Neither of them had made room for people in their lives. Al's presently crowded life had happened all on its own, whether for a reason or just some comedic sense of karma. But he knew that without these people in his life, he might be another Dougie himself. Maybe not drinking, but sitting around playing chess by himself and moping.

Before he'd had time to dwell on that, the house phone rang. Fergie stayed where she was, leaning against the wall. Al raised one eyebrow but picked up the phone and glanced at the caller ID. Clayton. He answered. "What is it, sir?"

"We've brought Carl Franklin in but haven't found his son. You're still a desk jockey, but I'll okay you being on hand when Wayon questions him, if you like."

"I'm on my way."

Al hung up and looked toward Fergie.

"I'd better drive you there," she said. "One of Jaime's men came and picked up the bike while you were doing whatever it was you were doing with Bonnie."

He waited for her to leave the room until it was clear she had no intention of doing so. She smiled and shrugged.

He suppressed a low growl and pushed the covers off, got out of bed naked, and climbed into his clothes while she watched. At least she didn't throw dollar bills or anything, though she did chuckle.

Jesus came limping into the Tango Blast's rented warehouse. "What you got for smashed *cojones*, Rolando?"

"I ain't gonna wrap them, I'll tell you that. Take a couple aspirin, wash them down with tequila, and don't cross your legs."

Alejandro and Lance came in, dragging the kid, Roger Franklin, who twisted and kicked. Lance backhanded him across the cheek, and he settled some.

"Feisty one, ain't he?" Ramon said.

"Let us talk to him first," Juan said. "He's got a lot he's dying to tell us. He just doesn't know it yet. Like who's his gringo cop pal." Juan patted the leather Kydex sheath at his side. It held a Ka-bar knife and had an extra pocket for a carborundum. He took out both and began to hone the blade against the stone, making a slow hiss of steel against rock. His was a military Ka-bar with a seven-inch blade and an edge he could already shave with. Yet he sharpened it some more.

"He's not my friend. I'm a biker, just like you!" Roger tugged and twisted at the hands that held him. His voice had gone up an octave, making him sound more youth choirboy than biker.

"You were trying to point toward us, get the law onto us, and get us even more involved. Why?" Juan's words were slow and careful, but the pace of his honing the knife picked up into a raspy, eager rhythm.

"I didn't."

"The note you put on the old lady's corpse?"

"I-I . . ." Roger shook his head. His eyes stayed fixed on the blade rubbing across the sharpening stone.

"We know you put it there then took it back. Why?"

Roger sighed. His eyes left the knife blade and fixed on Juan's unblinking dark eyes. "Dad made me. Said it was stupid and had my fingerprints and maybe DNA on it. That it might tie me to something I had no part of."

"Why did you put it there in the first place?"

"They didn't know about it. I did it on my own. . . to help them."

"Who's they?"

"I can't say. Won't say."

"I wouldn't be so sure about that, kid."

Alejandro and Lance dragged Roger over to a pile of wooden automatic rifle crates. The two men holding him stretched him across the side of the crates with his back to the wood. His eyes opened wider, and the smell of fear emanated from him. They held him by the wrists, and though he could kick, he didn't when Juan stepped forward. The tip of Juan's knife flickered in a sweeping slash. His left hand came away with the sleeve of Roger's T-shirt. Juan rested the top of his knife's blade on a rippled patch of blurred skin on Roger's upper arm. The dim outline of a capital *S* entwining a capital *T* still showed. "What's this, then? Are you down with the Texas Syndicate?"

Roger glanced down, his eyes stuck on the knife's blade. "It was. . . it was going to be a tattoo I was getting. I'd only gotten started with it. My dad made me get it lasered off. He's. . . he's a preacher."

"Tell us about the cop," Jesus grumbled. He held a bottle of Jose Cuervo and took a sip from it. "We wanna know all about him, even if you have to make stuff up."

The others crowded closer. The tip of Juan's knife pressed into Roger's skin, and a red line of blood beads rose along his pale upper arm as Juan let the blade coast downward. Then he pressed harder, and the skin split open as the tip neared Roger's elbow. The sides of flesh at the open wound peeled back, and blood began to ooze and fill the cut. Some ran down to Roger's elbow and dripped to the warehouse floor. Roger's eyes opened even wider. He stared at the widening spot of red.

Juan grinned, his eyes glittering and the gap where he'd lost a canine tooth in a bar fight showing as a square black hole in his smile. He lifted his knife until the tip touched Roger's other arm. He started the blade down the same slow path he'd taken on the first arm.

Roger began to cry, and through the weeping and choking sobs, he talked, and talked, and talked.

CHAPTER FIFTEEN

WAYON AND CLAYTON STOOD ON this side of the one-way glass, waiting. Al closed the door behind him and moved over to stand beside Clayton. He looked inside the room where Carl Franklin sat on a steel chair, his feet under the steel table. Carl seemed to be praying.

"Well, what's it going to be, Al? Do you want to be bad cop or good cop?" Wayon asked.

"Why don't we surprise him and both be good cops?"

"Only you would think of that, Al." Wayon glanced toward Clayton.

"Just get with it," Clayton said. "Forensics is already on the way to the house with a warrant. Judge was reluctant, him being a preacher and all, until I mentioned Carl allegedly shooting at two cops. Then he couldn't sign fast enough."

Al followed Wayon. He knew he had his own interrogation style and that Wayon had his, that almost every investigator has his or her own technique. Most were some spin-off of the Reid method, while others were more original. This was going to be different than some situations, but with Wayon's personality, he would still have to be wary of coercing a confession. That rarely turned out well once it hit the courtroom.

When Wayon and Al walked into the room, Carl looked

up at them. Neither said anything until they'd each pulled out a metal chair on the hard floor, the legs making the usual racket, and sat down slowly, facing him.

Wayon looked wound a little tight to Al, but he let him take the lead.

Wayon bent forward to lean close to Carl. "Does my face look familiar? Ever see it through a scope?"

"I don't know what you're talking about."

"Come on. A man of the cloth? Isn't that one of the seven deadly sins? It at least breaks one of the Ten Commandments." Wayon glared, stayed close.

Carl did not react, except to ease his head back a half inch to regain some of his personal space.

Al noticed Wayon had skipped right over the part where he asked non-threatening questions to establish Carl's baseline reactions. Carl, on the other hand, was relaxed and talking, so he had no grasp of the basic steps to avoid confessing during a police interrogation that many guilty or hardened subjects knew: Remain silent. Imagine the words "I invoke my right to remain silent" painted on the wall and stare at them throughout the interrogation. Momentarily break your silence to ask for counsel. Cultivate hatred for your interrogator so you don't fall into traps and start talking.

Wayon waited a few more ticks then said, "We've got a warrant and are going through your house right now. You'd better tell us the combination to the gun safe so we don't have to blow it open."

"I'd rather hear how you convinced a judge to allow a witch hunt on a clergyman and veteran of the armed forces." Carl managed an indignant look, though it was nothing Al would have bought into across a poker table.

"You see, that armed forces thing is part of the problem, that and you being a sharpshooter," Wayon said.

"It's just the next step up from marksman."

"Would you rather the word 'sniper'?" Wayon asked.

"I still don't. . ."

"Oh, come off it!" Wayon slapped the table hard with his open hand. "It was *me* you were shooting at," he shouted. "I want to know why."

"If I had been shooting at you," Carl said, far more calmly than Al expected, "you wouldn't be here."

"Not if you were just creating a diversion so your son could retrieve a note he probably shouldn't have written."

"Shouldn't I have a lawyer present?"

"You can if you think we're charging you with anything," Wayon said. "What was the note about?"

Carl crossed his arms and stared back.

"Do you know where Roger is?" Wayon asked.

Carl said nothing. His eyes shifted away from Wayon to stare at something behind him.

The "give him a hot foot of stress" approach didn't seem to be working for Wayon. At least he had only tried to cause discomfort, confusion, and insecurity and hadn't resorted to invading Carl's personal space, not allowing Carl to speak, fast-pitching contrasting alternatives, and positioning confession as the only means of escape. Most of those brainwash approaches had gone out in the days of beatings with a rubber hose, even though Wayon did have a propensity toward playing the bad cop.

Al cleared his throat. Wayon glanced toward him then leaned back in his chair.

"Look, I know," Al said. "It's difficult raising kids these days, so many new things to tempt them. The biker life can seem sexy and exciting to someone that age. We're just trying to locate Roger so he doesn't get into trouble. More trouble. Can you help us?"

Carl looked like he was going to stay with the stonewall

approach. But he lowered his hands to the table and said, "Someone said something horribly cruel to Clarisse and me once. Over nothing too. I'd asked the congregation to rise and move closer to the front. Some of them resented that, I guess. I thought it would make us cozier, more of a family. Some thought I was being a control freak. Anyway, one couple got up and left in a quick-stepping snit. Clarisse and I went to visit with them at their home and got the wife to come back, but the husband said right to our faces, 'I hope your children are terrible disappointments to you!' Well, we only had Roger, but he's been a joy—a trial at times—but on the whole, a joy. Clarisse, as you know, is no longer with us. She's in heaven."

"Did Roger ever indicate that *he* might think you are, well, a control freak?" Wayon asked.

"Of course not. Well, every kid thinks that now and again of his parents, but we'd ironed all that out."

There was a tap on the door, two quick pops of a knuckle.

Al nodded. He slid his chair back with a metal rasp and stood. Wayon stood too. They went out of the room.

Clayton stood waiting for them outside the door. Al didn't care much for his expression. He looked like he'd just swallowed a hairball.

"What happened?" Al said.

"We just found the kid," Clayton said. "What's left of him."

"Where?" Wayon asked. "Should we go there?"

"I've already got the site sealed off and the forensics team on the way. They know the way. It's back on the farm."

"Oh, no." Al glanced back toward the interrogation room. He couldn't see Carl from there. "Dead?"

"Very. One of the other younger workers, young black

girl named Betty, who's now half a tick from a nervous breakdown, found him on the scarecrow cross. Same place as before."

"Are you kidding me?" Wayon asked.

"It gets worse."

"How?"

"It looks like he wasn't dead when he was strung up. But he was castrated and bled out while he hung there."

"Holy crap." Wayon glanced toward the room where they'd left Carl.

Clayton said, "You'd just as well leave that part out. He's probably going to want to talk now, but someone's gonna have to break it to him."

"I'll do it," Al said. "I've been good cop so far."

Al headed into the room. Carl looked up at him, expectant.

"We've found your son."

Carl's eyes opened wider.

Al shook his head.

Carl's shoulders dropped, and his face fell into his hands.

"We're sorry for your loss. We're looking into it."

He came back out barely a minute later. Carl needed time to digest the news.

Al and Wayon headed back toward the room fifteen minutes later. Clayton had stayed to watch Carl through the one-way glass. Wayon carried two cardboard coffee cups. He handed one to Clayton. Al carried two as well. He followed Wayon back into the room. They sat down across from Carl, whose face was still in his hands. Al slid the extra cup of coffee in front of Carl.

Feliciana and her cute-as-a-dozen-buttons daughter

Mariposa were allowed to operate a corner stand in the sheriff's department lunchroom next to where vending machines lined one wall. They made breakfast tacos and always had wonderful-smelling tamales and enchiladas for lunch. Their peppy salsa was homemade from fresh ingredients every day. They also made some of the best coffee Al had ever tasted. So far, as expected, they were kicking the vending machines' butts for lunchtime revenue. The smell that drifted up from Al's cup was intoxicating. But it might as well have been vitriol for all Carl's expression let on when his head lifted.

"Do either of you have children?" he said. The words came squeezed out of a red face wet with tears.

"No," Wayon said. "But we're sorry for your loss."

Al didn't even try. He just shook his head.

Carl put his hands around the cup of coffee and drew it toward him. He didn't try to open it, but the warmth seemed to comfort him. He stayed that way, head lowered again, and Al suspected he might be silently praying.

When his face lifted again, Carl said, "Roger came to me and said he'd done a stupid thing. He said he'd wanted to throw attention away from something or someone, or toward something else. I couldn't tell what he meant, or even if he was acting on his own. He'd put a note on a dead woman, and the note had his fingerprints on it. I was reluctant, at first, thought the best thing to do was stay clear, but eventually I realized he hadn't done anything wrong himself, had only shown poor judgment. So I finally agreed I'd create a diversion so he could get the note. No one was to get hurt. That was part of our deal."

"What did the note mean?" Wayon asked.

"I have no idea. I can only guess it had something to do with bikers, pointing to one bunch or the other of them. Tell you the truth, I can't tell any of them apart. He so wanted to be one, no matter what I said, maybe. . . maybe *because* of what I said. Seems every preacher's son must rebel. I know that, knew that, but. . ."

"But you don't really know what the note meant?" Wayon asked.

"I just want my son back." Carl's voice quivered then broke and went all the way to choking sobs. Wayon and Al looked at each other. They got up again and went out of the room.

———————

Rogelio Perez, Jorge Torres, Anthony Espinosa, and Adrian "Beaver" Martinez each held a corner of the twitching, jerking, fifty-inch, olive-drab, army canvas duffel bag. It took all four of them to carry the bag into the stone-walled room. The kicks from inside could be knees, elbows, or feet. The positioning of the kicks suggested that whoever was inside was larger than fifty inches.

Bart sat over on a corner of what had been his desk, a stout oak dining table with legs as thick as a piano's. Julián Zapata Garza opened a leather kit with a row of pockets that held dental tools, scalpels, picks, and a variety of blades. He eyed them with the pride of a father for children. Bart had seen him turn the most reluctant tight-lipped prisoner into someone singing like he was in the tryouts for that Mormon choir.

The four of them lowered the bag. Bart nodded to Julián, who took out a scalpel and stepped close to the throbbing bag.

"You'd better hold still, or you're liable to get cut," Bart said to the bag.

Julián bent close and with one slash of a scalpel opened a slit two-thirds the length of the bag. An arm and leg shoved out, and a bleeding slit on the forearm showed that the person inside hadn't listened to Bart.

A head stuck out, long hair tousled and eyes open wide.

"You should listen to me, Larry," Bart said. "Everything will go better if you do."

The others got Larry the rest of the way out of the bag. In spite of his struggles, there were enough of them to move him over to the empty captain's chair that went with the desk. Jorge took a silver roll of duct tape from the desk. Limb by limb he fixed Larry to the chair while the others held him.

Bart looked around the room. Each wall was solid stone, the upper corners rounded. It was his favorite room in the place, and not just because it had taken the longest to build. It was cool in the hottest days of summer and never colder than fifty-five degrees in the winter. With the steel door in its steel frame closed and dead-bolted, he felt he could fend off the world. He felt safe, a whole lot safer than ol' Larry was going to feel. Bart was going to miss this room most of all. He sighed.

"Now, Larry. Let's have a talk." Bart leaned forward on his corner of the desk and rested his hands on his knees.

"What the hell do you want? You've got no right. I'm one of your best customers." Larry took in a couple of the tattoos. "These guys are Texas Syndicate. What the hell are you doing with these assholes?"

"Really, Larry. Your diplomacy skills are deplorable."

"Hey, I'm not with any gang. I'm just a customer, and a darned good one. Didn't I just hand you five large?"

"The thing is, Larry, I don't have that anymore. Not your fault. Well, maybe some of it's your fault. You were the last person I saw before someone doing a drive-by started tossing pills my way that weren't meant to do me any good. A coincidence? I don't think so. But what the hell? I'm nothing if not fair. The thing you have to remember is, I'm trying to maintain a low profile here. You must know that. Suddenly my profile's not so low. Why don't you explain yourself?"

"I had nothing to do with that. I was getting on my bike when the truck went by. When they started shooting, I went the other way."

"Didn't even think to come back and see if I was okay? You had your righteous weed and you didn't even fret about the future of your source?"

"I don't stay anywhere where there's shooting." The blood ran off his forearm to form a small puddle on the stone floor.

"Did you know this used to be my office?" Bart asked. He waved a hand at the solid limestone walls, the steel door that was the only way out. "None of my stuff is still here because I'm moving out, wrapping up. One more crop, then zip. I'm gone."

"Why are you telling me this?"

"To give you inspiration, Larry. Be inspired to tell the truth. I'm going to leave Julián in here with you, and you'd be surprised. People start out being as tight lipped as deep-water clams. But you know what? Before Julián is done, why, you're liable to be downright chatty."

"Why? I've done nothing."

"If that's the case, then you'll have a clear conscience. I hear that's a good way to go. Now, the rest of you. *Vámonos.* Let's go. We've all got work to do."

CHAPTER SIXTEEN

AL STEPPED OUT THE FRONT door of the sheriff's
department building. A cool clean breeze swept
down the street and brushed across his face, but
it did little to erase how he felt or what he'd seen.

He looked up and down the street and didn't see any
bikers—or trucks full of gang members either, for that
matter. It could be trucks, he reminded himself. He was
never all the way comfortable with the edge that paranoia
brings, but if there was ever a time for it, this was it.

Fergie sat in her car in the visitor's row of parking
spaces.

When he slid into the passenger seat, those large eyes
of hers turned toward him.

"You are the very picture of patience," he said.

"I've had a fair number of things to consider."

"Such as?"

"Why are the media vans forming up by the building?
And why were they crowded so close behind the meat
wagon that just rolled in?"

"Well, whatever we thought was going to hit the fan is
hitting it pretty good just now. Roger's dead, murdered
and hung on the same scarecrow cross. Castrated. Bled
out. His dad, Carl, is talking at last but really doesn't
have much to say."

"So you still don't have anything close to a clear idea
about what's really going on, do you?"

"Nope. It just gets deeper and more tangled."

"What's your usual approach when that happens?"

"I think of it as the aircraft carrier technique."

"How's that work?"

"Only one plane can land at a time. One plane in, one plane out. I have to clear the deck and focus on one thing at a time, no matter what and how much other confusion and chatter is going on."

"Sounds like a luxury I never had when I was a city detective."

"It's just a methodology, an approach that gives me the sense of untangling things long enough to see that one tiny thing that brings everything else into focus."

"So, what next then?"

"All roads lead back to the farm, Fergie. All the heavy-handed steering seems to be pushing us there. We just have to find out why."

"I think we're going to need to tool up," she said.

"Guns?"

She nodded.

"We could knock off a local drug dealer for his guns. I've seen that done in any number of movies."

Her eyes widened. She said nothing.

"But that's old hat. I suggest we go to a sushi bar I know that has a mean squid salad and the best green tea I've ever tasted."

"Sushi? That's your answer?"

He hated to see those violet eyes of hers framed in a frown like that. "I'm a little congested from Bonnie's cooking, to tell the truth. A light lunch will be cleansing."

"Really? You're not kidding? Sushi is your answer?"

"Give it a chance. I just need to swing by my bank for a sec."

"Pricey place?"

"Can be. You never know."

She drove him to his bank and waited while he went inside. He came out, waved to her as he walked by the car, and ducked into a pharmacy next door. He came back out of it carrying a gift-wrapped package.

"Should I ask, or just say, 'What the hell?' We should be rounding up what we need."

"All in due time, Fergie. First, that light lunch. Okay?"

She followed his directions until they pulled into the lot of a restaurant, which, according to the red-and-green neon sign, was The Flying Dragon.

"This doesn't look like a sushi bar. It's more like a Chinese restaurant."

"Vietnamese, actually. And sushi isn't on the menu. You have to ask for it. But what you get is first rate."

"I suppose there's a story here somewhere."

Al didn't reach for his door handle. He stared off for a moment before turning to Fergie. "Back when I was still with Abbie. . ."

"Before Maury got tangled up in that personal mess of yours that crashed and burned?"

"Yeah, the end of my marriage. The only one I ever had. Old news." Though Al had flinched. "Maury and I are trying to work past it. Anyway, Abbie and I used to come here a lot. It was our favorite Asian place. We got to know the owner quite well. A fellow who likes to be called Gyp Sing. I never did know his real name. I got to know him in a few other ways too, but for Abbie, it was just a great place to eat."

"Does this story ever have a point?"

"One Christmas season, Abbie baked cookies—chocolate chip and oatmeal raisin, as I recall—and put some in a box, gift-wrapped it, and brought it with us to the restaurant. When Gyp came to the table, she gave him the package. His face collapsed. It was like we'd killed one of his children. Then he stood straight again, forced a smile, took the present, and hurried off to the kitchen. He came back a few minutes later, with a genuine smile. He carried a package. He'd used the same wrapping paper and bow Abbie had used, but inside was a box of a thousand bags of restaurant-quality tea. It had been something he could grab and give back. It would have shamed him if he didn't have a gift for us."

Fergie grinned. "Abbie didn't even know she'd accidentally kicked sand in his face, did she?"

"She figured it out. We hadn't meant for him to lose face. But we were glad he was able to figure something out without having to commit hari-kari. Seppuku? Whatever you call it."

"That's Japanese, isn't it?"

"And something only samurai would do, but Abbie didn't know that. She regretted putting him in that position, for potential dishonor. But it worked out well in the end. Gyp was an even closer friend after that."

"Is he still around? That must have been some time ago."

"Let's hope." Al picked up the package and opened his door.

Inside, they were met at the hostess station by a pretty young girl in jeans and a white blouse. Al muttered something low to her, and she ushered them to a table beneath a large tank of goldfish.

They sat down while the girl scurried off.

"What was that you said to the girl when we came in?" Fergie asked.

"Just 'goldfish.' Oh, and 'tea.' It's all that needed to be said."

"Are you saying you speak Vietnamese?"

"Just enough of a tiny smidgeon to get me in more trouble than not. Once I bought three pounds of lychee nuts for five bucks in New York's Chinatown when I'd only wanted a sample. I gave the whole lot to a guy in Washington Square who was begging for food and who really probably would have preferred a bottle of Mad Dog twenty-twenty."

A different waitress, this one in a black skirt with the white blouse, brought a pot of tea, two cups without handles, and menus along with a small pad and pencil.

When she'd gone, Al pulled the pad close and started writing.

Fergie bent across the table to look. "Oh, my lord. You're writing in Vietnamese, aren't you?"

"Not very well. What do you want? I'm having a squid salad and sashimi."

She opened her menu, saw they'd been brought the Vietnamese menus, then closed it. "I'll have what you're having."

Their waitress brought them each chopsticks, a small squid salad mixed with seaweed, and a larger plate each of sashimi and pickled ginger, as well as a shrimp and spearmint spring roll.

"Nothing like a warm meal," Fergie said. She picked up her chopsticks.

"You've always got the tea." Al didn't reach for his chopsticks because a small man with buzzed-short white hair, a black silk shirt, and black pants was approaching their table. As he neared, Al stood and gave him a nod, a slight bow with hands together and thumbs somewhat outstretched.

Gyp returned the nod as he stopped by their table.

Still standing, Al said, "This is Fergie."

Gyp gave her a nod. He turned to Al. "Where Abbie?"

157

"Long gone, I'm afraid."

"Al. You a playboy."

"So it must seem," Al said. He picked up the gift-wrapped box and handed it to Gyp, whose eyes opened wide.

He blinked then spun and headed off toward the kitchen, clutching the package to his chest.

"You did it again," Fergie said.

"This time on purpose, a reenactment." He picked up his chopsticks and started in on his squid salad, which was every bit as good as he remembered.

Fergie had taken a bite of her spring roll and spooned on some of the sambal chili garlic sauce. Her eyes watered. She raised a napkin to dab at them. "Stuff kind of sneaks up on you," she said.

Twenty-five minutes later, when they were at the tail end of their meal, Gyp came back with a slightly larger box gift-wrapped in the same paper. He put it down beside Al's plate and smiled. Then he turned to Fergie. "Missy like?"

"Yes, the food is quite good. The tears are from joy."

"That is very fine. I not like to discommode you." He winked at Al then turned and ambled off toward the kitchen, checking in at other tables as he went.

"He went to college in California," Al explained. "The rest is part act and part a bit of fun for him. He's the one who was teaching me the smattering of Vietnamese, just in case I get deported there someday."

When they got back into the car, Al handed her the package to put in the back seat.

"It's heavier now."

"Yeah," he agreed. "Now we're ready for business."

"What is your pal, some sort of gun runner?"

"Not even close. I asked for what we needed, and he sent out for it. So don't be pointing him out to any of your friends on the force. He was just doing me a favor, and it beats me having to go all kung fu Christmas on a room full of drug dealers just to get what we needed."

"Where to now, then?"

"I'd like to get a quick look at some of that farm in the daylight and come back for another peek at night. That okay with you?"

"Sure."

"Just for chuckles, let's park in the church parking lot on the property next to the farm and hike over. I suspect the front of the farm is crawling with media vans and perhaps some of Clayton's men."

"Gotcha."

The light meal and hearty spices were still square-dancing around inside Al's stomach by the time Fergie drove up to the church and parked in the far back left corner of its asphalt parking lot, nearest the farm. The spices might explain the warm glow on Fergie's face, a spot of pink on each cheekbone.

He opened the package and took out two Glocks. He handed her the Glock 19 and kept the 17 for himself. He opened one of the two boxes of 9mm ammo, popped his clip, and started loading his piece. He left the chamber empty for now. She did the same, with practiced hands that finished the task at the same time he did.

"Why don't you tell me what you know, Al?"

"Can't."

"Because?"

"I don't know anything for sure yet. I just have a few ideas."

"You could share those."

"Could, but I won't. It'll be best if you keep a clear mind."

"What if something happens to you?"

"If I get killed, I guess you can start where I did, with darned little to go on and most of that a tangled knot."

Fergie sighed and jacked a shell into the chamber of her gun, then she switched on the safety.

Up close like this, and in the bright of daylight, he realized once more that her eyes weren't really violet as he sometimes thought, but a deep, deep cobalt blue with little flecks of sparkling red. Not bloodshot but with radiant beams of scarlet among the blue. He needed that just now, at this precise second, the realization that he didn't know her as well or as thoroughly as he'd thought after being acquainted for nearly a lifetime. He found himself leaning closer but shook off where he was going with that thought.

Al slid the box of ammo, gift wrapping, and empty box under his seat and put the gun at the small of his back. Old habit. Fergie carried hers in her hand at her side, for now. They got out of the car and started off into the thick green of mountain cedar, live oaks, and all manner of prickly shrubs and cactus. Al slipped into the lead so he could keep an eye open for snakes and pick the path of least resistance. Fergie seemed glad to let him, especially when a young mesquite bush made a snatch at him with its stickers and clung to his jeans. She stepped out and around it.

Al kept a close eye on the forest floor and the vegetation they passed. He saw only the slightest indication that anyone had been through this way. Someone was being careful. But the way wasn't pristine. There was no reason for anyone to come this way at all. The ground was littered with loose rocks, and the holes beneath the lower edges of some of the larger stones looked ideal for snakes. The growth was thick enough to be impassable in places, and they had to weave to get through at all. Birds chirped, and a couple of squirrels and a lizard scampered, but other than that, they were as alone as two people can get. None of the people tromping around down nearer the farmhouse had come up this far, unless Gladys had in her wanderings.

He watched Fergie edge away from a stand of prickly pear cactus that looked particularly snaky. Al enjoyed a nice hike through the woods, particularly when using one of the established trails strewn with wood chips or light gravel packed into a path. This was nothing like that. It was what seasoned hikers call "off trail" or orienteering, and he hadn't even brought along a compass. He knew he could get turned around, so he kept track of where the sun had been when they'd entered the woods and factored in the time of day. Still, he paused now and then to rethink exactly where they were, or at least where he thought they were. In his mind's eye he could see the layout of the farm, with the crops and worked land down where the soil was rich, furrowed, and flat. The other side of the farm sloped up in a rapid climb to the adjacent park where Carl Franklin had parked. This side was much the same, only rougher, less open. In open fields, he'd recently seen live oak trees with their bottoms eaten up as high as cows could reach, what ranchers called "goated." Here most of the big trees had skirts of limbs that draped down all the way to the ground, and those were matted into thick stands of other thorny plants. He picked his way with care through the unorchestrated maze of it, all the time trying to keep track of their bearings.

He suddenly stopped in his tracks and held up a hand. Fergie eased up closer and leaned in to whisper, "What?"

"Let's hang here a minute or two," he whispered back, so close to her his lips brushed her ear.

He held a finger to his lips and signed for her to follow.

He eased over until his back was to the bole of a pecan tree that was thick enough to be hundreds of years old.

She leaned against the tree beside him, looked the way he was looking. She bent closer and whispered, "What are we looking at?"

He pointed.

She peered and peered then finally saw it. She straightened and smiled. A brown wire ran from the ground up the trunk of a tree twenty feet away. High in the limbs, the outline of a small antenna stood out against the sky. It's what Al had seen, and unless he'd been looking specifically for something like it, he never would have.

Fergie leaned close. "So maybe Gladys wasn't seeing things. Men might've been in the tree installing that. What about the men coming out of the ground?"

Al held his finger to his lips again and pointed to the likely spot, an open green patch where a collection of bunch grass formed a mounded clump.

They leaned against the tree and stayed where they were for another forty-five minutes. Al finally nudged Fergie, and they started back the way they'd come.

As they stepped out of the edge of the woods at the parking lot, theirs was the only car. He looked back to where they'd been and said, "We'll have to come back at night. They must move in and out then."

"So you believe Gladys now. Who do we tell?" she asked.

"No one for now." They crossed the parking lot, keeping an eye out all the way. "It's all supposition and conjecture. It's possible she did see something and told Darin. He might've even told Roger. But all that's without a thread of any kind of proof. That's not the kind of limb I'm comfortable crawling out onto just yet."

"But we still have more to go on than anyone else just now, don't we?"

"Only a few wispy threads. I'll feel better when I have my hands on the rope."

"You are one careful turtle, Al." She took out her keys and unlocked the car's doors.

"It's how I have come to live to snap another day."

She frowned, and he grinned back at her. They both got into the car.

CHAPTER SEVENTEEN

FERGIE REACHED ACROSS HIM, OPENED the glove box, and put in her Glock. While she had it open, he took his gun out from inside his belt at the small of his back and put it in the glove box too. She started the car and backed out of their parking spot while Al dug out his cell phone and punched in Bonnie's number.

"That's funny," he said after a minute. "She almost always answers."

"Call Maury."

"No phone yet. He hasn't needed one with Bonnie there. I don't like this. I'm getting a very bad feeling."

Fergie stepped on the gas, and they surged down the church drive toward the road.

Just before they got to the road, a white Toyota shot in front of them and came to an abrupt stop. Fergie hit the brakes hard, and they slid until they were within inches of the white car.

The first agent tumbled out of the passenger side, and the other had to climb out that side too, since his door was blocked. Al could see the bold yellow "DEA" on their blue jackets. "Now what the hell?"

Fergie shifted to park but left the motor running.

The two agents split up, and one came to Fergie's side of the car and the other to Al's. Fergie lowered both windows all the way. Both men walked with a swagger Al hadn't seen since the days of those western movies made in Italy.

"Luis Bracknall," the agent on Fergie's side said. He displayed his ID.

"Richard Blue." The agent on Al's side flashed his ID then put it away and bent forward so Al couldn't miss the Beretta 92FS hanging butt forward in a leather Galco shoulder holster. He was close enough for Al to read the "Galco" on the brown side of the holster.

"Where are you two going in such a hurry?" Luis asked. He leaned closer to Fergie. Both the agents were sweeping the back seat and floorboards with restless eyes.

"We're on private church property," Al said. "Why do you ask?"

Luis gave Al an irritated squint, as if he was angry Fergie hadn't answered.

Al didn't like the smell of this at all. Ambition and impatience were dripping off these two, always a bad combo for agents who looked to be still in their late twenties. He was thinking of fourteen-year-old Ashley Villarreal of San Antonio, who'd died three days after being shot in the head by a DEA agent while driving away from her home. Or the DEA agent in Kansas who'd flown into road rage after a fender-bender and beat the other driver so badly the man won more than $800,000 in damages from the agency. As well as the DEA agents who'd gone after a suspected drug dealer and gotten the wrong house, traumatizing an innocent Sterling Heights family, or the DEA agents who'd beaten up a disc jockey in Hyannis. Sure, those were just isolated cases that made the agency look bad, but none of the DEA agents Al had met while with the sheriff's department had possessed the blatant cockiness he was seeing here.

"We just got to this area and are getting up to speed,

looking for anything suspicious," Richard said. "And you flying around like a bat out of hell struck us as suspicious."

"You don't have anything like probable cause," Al said.

"What are you? Some kind of armchair cop?" Richard asked.

"We have over twenty-five years of law enforcement experience," Al said. "Each. Her with the city. Me with the county. You doubt us? Here, I'll just call the sheriff and let you talk to him."

Al reached for his phone.

"Hey!" Luis stepped back and reached for his gun in its belt holster. "You going for a gun?"

"Cell phone," Al said and brought it out with two fingers.

Luis and Richard exchanged glances. Al couldn't make anything from the looks. Maybe a touch of disappointment. Boy, these two were sure spoiling for a fight.

"Do you mind if we take a look in the trunk?" Luis asked.

"Okay. But that's it," Fergie said. "Anything else, and you need a warrant." She popped the trunk.

Luis walked back and took a look inside. Richard stayed bent over by Al, keeping a close eye on them. Luis came back to Fergie's window. "Okay. That's clean, I guess."

"Close the trunk," she said.

Luis shook his head. "You want it closed, close it yourself."

Fergie threw her door open, and Luis had to leap back a step to keep from getting hit by it. As she went by him, he gave her a thumping smack on the back of her jeans.

Fergie spun, grabbed his crotch as hard as she could, and twisted with all she had.

Luis screamed and dropped to his knees. When he looked up, Fergie was holding his gun in her hand.

Richard had frozen in place when his partner screamed,

and Al's hand had darted out and pulled the Beretta free from its holster. He had thumbed the safety off by the time Richard looked down to see the barrel of his own gun pointing at him.

Fergie slammed her trunk shut and started back to the open driver's side door. Luis was standing but still held a hand to his crotch. "You're threatening a federal officer," he said, but his voice didn't have quite the punch it'd had before.

"Yeah, and you just assaulted a police officer," Al said.

"Give us our weapons back, and we'll talk," Richard said.

"You'll get in your car and back it the fuck out of the way," Al said, "and we'll leave your pieces behind when we leave. And we don't expect to be followed either. Understood?"

The agents traded looks again, only this time their glares held little confidence or joy. Richard went to their car and backed it up. Luis stayed where he was, hand still covering his damaged goods.

The gun Fergie held was aimed at Luis's crotch, a detail he seemed fixed upon. "Tell him to turn off the engine and toss the keys out the window," she said.

Luis conveyed the instructions in a loud voice that quivered more from suppressed anger than fear.

When the keys sailed out the window, Fergie shifted into gear and eased past the unmarked car. Al emptied the chamber of the Berretta and thumbed all the shells out of the clip. He left it jacked open in a stovepipe jam. Fergie handed Al the Smith & Wesson 39-2 she'd taken from Luis. He emptied it too. The road was clear both ways. Al put the shells in his side pocket and dropped the guns and clips out his window. Fergie turned out onto the road and hit the gas.

Al looked back to see Luis running, albeit with a limp, toward the guns.

"Well, I don't think we made any friends there," Al said.

"I fear we might be in a shit pot full of trouble. But one problem at a time. Let's get back to the house and check on Maury and Bonnie."

Al tried Bonnie's number again. Still no answer.

Fergie pressed her foot down harder on the accelerator. She glanced back in her mirror a couple of times, but the agents weren't doing anything more stupid.

"What do you think that was about?" she asked.

"I imagine Clayton had the saddlebags from Fuzzy's sent to the crime lab. Chances are they scored a hit on some pretty strong stuff, perhaps some of that domestically cultivated cannabis with that much higher tetra-hydrocannabinol level you mentioned, the kind that might bring 5 G a brick. That might have lit up their lights if they're part of the Domestic Cannabis Eradication/Suppression Program."

"So these DEA guys leaped at the chance to swoop in to turn this into their bust? Well, I don't have any problem with that if it takes Bart down. But I don't know if they have the smarts to get the best of Bart."

Al nodded. He was thinking about Bonnie and Maury. He probably shouldn't have left them alone, safe house or not. Still, who could possibly know about the safe house, except Clayton and Jaime?

"By the way, that was some pretty fast handiwork getting Richard's piece like that," Fergie said. "Quite a nifty grab for a turtle."

"I have my days. To give credit where it's due, though, he was a tad distracted by you scrambling his partner's eggs. Guys are sensitive that way."

"So I've heard." She gave him a quick grin.

"I thought that was *my* go-to move."

"It's everybody's go-to move when dealing with men. Bear that in mind."

"Oh."

He had nothing else to say the rest of the way back across the county to the safe house.

———◆———

"We going to talk about it?"

"No." Luis was bent over, had just found a clip. It belonged to Richard's Beretta. He held it up. "Here."

"Come on. I don't ever want to go through that again. Are we going to do anything about it?" Richard saw a glitter of blued steel in the tangled vines of a buffalo gourd plant. He rushed a step and lifted Luis's clip. Both clips were empty, but he had a box of ammo in his pack in the truck. Luis did as well.

"Look, I'm the one should be pissed, Blue. She had me by the hacky sack. Remember? Not you."

"Okay, then. We just dust ourselves off and go high gear on our other lead. Unless you want to call this in and pursue wherever that takes us?"

"As far as I'm concerned, it never happened. Unless we get the chance to straighten it out ourselves later. Hear?"

"In a very personal way," Richard agreed. "And you have a bit more payback coming than me, way I see it."

"I swear to you that as soon as it's convenient I'm gonna square myself with that bitch. And if my balls ever bounce back, I'm gonna have my grandchildren take care of her grandchildren."

"I don't know. She didn't look all that young. She might already have grandchildren."

"You're not helping," Luis said.

"I'm just saying."

"You're not the one was in that vise grip of a claw. I

mean, she was squeezing and twisting with everything she had."

"I could see that from her expression. Yours was something worth seeing too."

"Is that what you were doing, watching me while that old turd of a cop took your piece away?"

"I can see why you didn't want to call this in. I'm on board with that. Nothing good can come from us sharing what just went on."

"Let's eighty-six that kind of talk for now. Okay?"

Luis popped the trunk and got his box of ammo out of his bag. Richard loaded his gun, took the extra clip out of his bag, and put it in his side pocket.

Neither said a word as they headed into town. It had been an unlucky morning. Maybe the afternoon would shape up with more promise. There was that activity at the warehouse they'd heard about. A good tip from a reliable source.

They sat quiet in their seats all the way through the city traffic that had formed maddening tangles in places. But they kept calm, actually growing more confident and sure by the time they got through at last. Place was right up ahead. Richard glanced toward Luis, who grinned back at him. It looked like a quite live and active lead as soon as they got there. This was much more like it.

A truck was backed up to the loading dock, and they could see men going to and from the truck's open back doors with dollies and a forklift.

Luis grinned and stared ahead.

"Call it in?" Richard asked.

"Let's make sure first. In case they're loading stoves or something." He eased the car back into a parking slot. They both checked their guns again. Outside the car, they moved forward carefully, hugging the wall as they did.

Jesus Vasquez, his hurt leg up on the stool beside him, sat at a table facing four laptops displaying feeds from cameras monitoring the exterior of the warehouse. He took his job seriously.

Juan came up behind him and said in Spanish, "We'll be ready to roll in an hour. You okay, or you want someone to spell you?"

Jesus didn't turn around. Instead, he said, "Hey, take a look at this. You see these two guys? Can you believe this?"

"I sure do. They look like all kinds of not right," Juan said. He gave a low whistle. The two visitors wore blue jackets with the bold yellow "DEA" on the front.

"Any others with them?" Juan asked.

"Nada."

Two of the other Tango Blast members came up to them, rushing past Lance, who wheeled a forklift with a stack of wooden automatic rifle boxes on the front toward the open truck. Juan signaled for him to keep going but to keep his eyes open. It wouldn't do for the noise inside the warehouse to stop suddenly.

Juan signed for the other two men to take the far side. He slipped around until he was hidden just behind the opening to the dock.

The forklift, its front empty, headed back to get another load. Juan knew the two guys would wait until Lance's back was turned. He counted to himself, "One tortilla, two tortilla. . ."

The agents burst inside the doorway, guns up and ready, one slightly ahead of the other. Juan flowed along in the shadow of the second one and was behind him, knife up and beneath his chin, in an instant. He swept the length of the blade across the man's neck and stepped back as the blood sprayed and the gun dropped to the floor. The sound of the gun hitting cement made the lead man turn in time to see his partner crumpling to the floor, blood everywhere. The sight made him pause just long enough. Juan reversed the knife in his hand and thought for half a second about chest or neck but threw to the man's stomach instead. The agent's eyes popped open wide. He dropped to his knees, his gun falling out of his hand. He stared down at the knife handle sticking out of his stomach.

"Better get to him fast, Rolando. See if we got any time or if we need to get the hell out of here," Juan yelled. "Jesus, keep an eye out. Ramon, help me drag this one out of the way, and let's put something down, some cardboard or something, or we gonna have blood everywhere."

As they came up the lane, Al could see that the front door stood open. Not a good sign. He'd seen a lot of action in his days in the department, but this gave him a rush of adrenaline and fear that had his heart pounding hard by the time Fergie stopped and he could throw his door open.

"Maury! Bonnie!" Al ran to the house, and once inside, he rushed to the kitchen, past dining chairs that had been knocked back from the table and lay on the floor. A few dishes rested in the sink, half through being rinsed off. He ran to the bedroom, checked the bathroom. Fergie was coming in from the back when he returned to the living room.

"Nothing out there," she said.

"They've been grabbed. But who?"

"As far as I know, only one person knew of the safe house outside Clayton."

"Jaime Avila." Al pulled out his cell phone and started

punching in the number. It rang a couple of times, then a recording came on that said the party wasn't receiving calls. Al hung up and stared at Fergie. "Where the hell do you suppose he is?"

"Take it easy, Al. Think."

"Think?" he shouted. "What do you think I'm trying to do?" He kicked the end of the couch.

"Couch probably had it coming," Fergie said.

Al took several deep breaths and forced his fingers to unclench. "Okay. Let's try this." He dug out his cell phone again and punched in a number.

"Hey, it's me. Yeah, I'm lying low, just as you ordered. I was wondering, do you know where Jaime is? Okay. I understand." He hung up. "Clayton either doesn't know or won't say. I got the impression Jaime's up to something but not on Clayton's turf. That probably means city. Do you want to try?"

"I wondered why you didn't tell him Maury and Bonnie are missing. Then I realized that would mean admitting you weren't staying here, where Clayton wanted you." Fergie punched in a number on her phone. She lowered her voice and walked to the far side of the room, stood looking out over the open fields surrounding the safe house while she talked. She hung up and turned to Al.

"Protecting your sources?" he asked.

She ignored that. "Something's going down, all right. In town. A city SWAT team has just scrambled, and Jaime's bunch is involved somehow."

"Let's go!" His insides fluttered with urgency, rage, and helplessness at not being able to do anything. Then he felt enraged about *that*. Al glanced around on the way out. Nothing here he could do much about either. He didn't bother locking the door as he went out.

CHAPTER EIGHTEEN

THE THREE MEN HAD GATHERED close to each other outside a convenience store. Heriberto, who sat on the lowered tailgate of his pickup, kept his unblinking eyes on El Chapo. He strived to look deferential and eager, but not too eager. This was the moment for which he had been waiting.

In his left hand, El Chapo held a bag of *chicharones*. He took one of the crispy pork rinds out and popped it in his mouth. He tilted his head a quarter inch, chewed, and looked up at his second in command.

"Heriberto, you know I want you to head this operation. You did all the scouting. Of course you lead." El Chapo thumped him on the thigh with his open hand. "You okay with that? Viejito here can stay with me as *segundo* while you're away. That means you'll be *jefe* on this job. All right?"

Benito "Viejito" Huerta stood on the other side of El Chapo with one hip leaning against the side of the truck. He grinned and bent closer like one of the apostles at the Last Supper. He'd been a *Mexikanemi* soldier for eight years, and this was the highest honor he'd ever been paid.

Heriberto looked as relaxed as he dared and shared a slow smile.

"Look, you don' wanna do it, I can get Viejito here to do it," El Chapo said.

"*No problemo.* I'll do it." Heriberto didn't want to seem too reluctant.

"Okay, then."

"Sure thing. I may lead this one time, but you're still always the *jefe.*" Heriberto raised the red can of Tecate beer he held and took a sip.

"This is a big thing I'm asking of you, Heriberto. Don' you let me down."

"You can count on me."

———◆———

Fergie pulled her car into a parking space at least two blocks from the warehouse. It was as close as she could get. As Al got out on his side, he could see the two large black vans, one ICE and the other the city's SWAT team. Cruisers with lights on and flashing blocked off the street at the end of the block. A KVUE news truck with satellite dish on top was just pulling up, another media van was already there and setting up, and a small crowd milled outside the yellow tape a crime scene crew was still stringing up. Al spotted the unmarked car of the local agent in charge for the FBI.

Al got to the edge of the yellow tape and was half a tick from ducking under it in his rush to confront Jaime. Then he saw the car. The white Toyota was parked close to the back wall of the warehouse, around the corner from its loading dock. He glanced to Fergie. She stared at it too.

"I have a bad feeling about this," she said.

The pumping in Al's chest slowed—the anger, confusion, and eagerness to do something sank down to his socks like warm sand. He waited and watched as the different players went through their drills. The city's SWAT team came back out and climbed into their vehicle. That van was backing up to leave when the ICE crew came out.

Al saw Jaime walking at their rear, the only one of them not in full gear. He peeled off to talk to a small huddle of two FBI special agents and the local agent in charge. They were joined by a man in a suit who didn't need to be wearing one of the DEA jackets for Al to know who he was. He was Cal Maxwell, the head of the DEA field office in Austin that worked out of the Houston Division. He didn't look happy. In fact, he looked like he'd just swallowed something very sour.

Jaime was talking and glanced up in Al's direction. He finished what he was saying, excused himself, and walked over to Al and Fergie. "What brings you two here?"

"Maury and Bonnie are gone," Al said. "We think they've been snatched."

"And you think I'm the only one who knows where the safe house was, right?"

"Well. . ."

"Thing is, Al, I haven't told a soul. You've got to remember any attack didn't come to you two until Bart was threatened. Then it was instantaneous. Maybe you should focus on where Bart is. As for myself, I've been busy. You can rule out the Tangoes too. Looks like they just moved a ton of stuff out of what's now a pretty empty warehouse."

"What about the two DEA guys?" Fergie asked.

Jaime's head snapped toward her, and his eyes narrowed.

"That's their undercover car, is all," she said. "Seems like it's parked in a bad place."

"Well, they aren't going to need it anymore." Jaime looked toward the car then the warehouse. "Way I hear it, they got a hot lead. Maxwell says the tip came from a local cop, though they didn't say who. They didn't wait for backup. You should always wait for backup. After. . . well, what happened in there, Tangoes must've been already loading a semi and got busy and finished loading it before they took off. Some Bandido bikes and jackets got left behind, though."

Al could guess at what Jaime was remembering from in there. Probably wasn't pretty. Al hadn't much cared for Richard and Luis, but they were on the same side, and he wouldn't wish what had happened to them on anyone, no matter how brash. They should have waited for backup, but he could recall a time or two when he'd done the same thing, rushed ahead in his eagerness. That had been a few years ago, though still within memory.

Jaime turned back to Al. "I understand you being upset. I'll keep my eyes and ears open, let you know if I hear anything at all about your brother and Bonnie. Be a shame to lose that bouncy gal. Your brother's a nut job, but he's still your brother. Is there anything else? I gotta get going now that DEA is here to claim their own."

"These guys weren't local, were they?" Al asked.

"Nope. They just came through, supposedly working on something else. Happens all the time. Why do you ask?"

Al shook his head. "Just a thought. Look, I need to ask a favor."

"Now what?" Jaime's head moved back half an inch.

"Do you have any night vision goggles? I just need a short loan."

"Really?"

"Yeah. Just going to try a little night fishing."

Jaime's mouth opened then closed. "Probably better I don't know. The short answer is no. Yes, I do have a few sets over in that big black ICE truck. But no, I'm not going to loan them to you, Al. You know why? Because you're a turtle. Remember? I know you're upset about Maury. Leave this to us, and Clayton, and anyone else.

Go home and hibernate, like a good turtle should. Okay?" He winked. Then he turned and headed toward his SUV.

Al didn't say anything all the way back to Fergie's car. They slid in. She sat there a moment.

"Your friend was a little dismissive. How's that feel, Al?"

Before he could respond, his phone sounded that he'd just gotten a text message. The caller ID said the call was coming from Bonnie's phone, but he had a hunch she hadn't typed it. The message hit him like a punch low to the stomach. It read, "Stay home and do nothing for two days and you'll get them back."

He showed it to Fergie.

"We've *got* to call Clayton," she said. "This is big, really, really big."

"Why? He would tell me to do pretty much the same thing. Just like Jaime. I'm the turtle, remember?" Al felt angry, frustrated, and impotent all at the same time.

"Well, we've got to do something."

"You're right about that."

"What then, if it's not to tell Clayton?"

"We have only vague hunches, and if I share those with Clayton, he'll have every reason to dismiss them. Even if he acted, it might well get Maury and Bonnie killed in the bargain."

"What, then?"

"Just let me think!" he snapped. He took a few deep breaths. "Sorry."

He waved a hand for her to start the car. She glared back at him, finally relaxed enough to reach for the key.

As soon as she'd started the engine, Al turned on the radio and reset it to an FM station.

"Do you mind?" he asked.

"Kinda late to be asking. But no."

Classical music filled the car. He goosed the volume a bit.

"What. . .?"

He held up a hand. "I just need to think a bit. The music helps. Ah, Rachmaninov's *Rhapsody on a Theme of Paganini*. Perfect." He leaned back in his seat with his eyes closed.

"Where to?"

"Just drive around, or go someplace and park."

"It's a little late in life to be parking with the likes of you."

"Wait." His eyes snapped open, and he looked toward her. "I know." He gave her an address on South Lamar. "After this, we look for a motel. Now, for a few moments, quiet please."

He leaned his head back again and closed his eyes.

He stayed that way until the crunch of gravel beneath the wheels announced Fergie had turned into a parking lot. His eyes flew open. The sign read Rudy's Railyard – Pawn Shop and Military Paraphernalia.

"Let me give you a couple of footnotes before we go in," Al said. "First of all, there's no Rudy. Instead there's a fellow named Irving Dagrell, small fellow, no known priors. Nothing that ever got proven, anyway. By 'military paraphernalia' he means surplus. In particular, he specializes in the kind of stuff private detectives use when doing their nosing around on the down low—cameras, sound taps, and, yes, night vision goggles. Mind you, none of it is illegal, at least in the form he sells it, but how the stuff is used is up to the buyer. I heard about Irving when I was working an abuse case that had hints of pedophilia. A tip led me to this little weasel of a human being."

"Why weasel?"

"He's a clever fellow, and nothing in the pedophile line

led directly to him. We couldn't pin anything on him. Yet, while we're talking, chewing the fat about this and that, Irving freely admits to me that he spends his free time traveling to Mexico, the Philippines, and faraway spots like Bangkok. Want to know why?"

"I get a hint where this is going."

"Yep. Irving tells me, to my face, that the reason for his trips is that those are the places where he can buy the favors of tiny eleven- and twelve-year-old girls. He tells me, with this note of pride, 'At least I don't have a thing for little boys.' He smiles, and I see his eyes fade because he's drifting off to some wistful memory that would make most people lose their lunch."

"He's a perv, a pedophile, Al. And you didn't arrest him?"

"For what? In this country he's clean as a bag of new whistles. He's just telling me so I know he's smarter than our whole system. He's never going to get caught or be made to register wherever he goes or lives."

"Why did you tell me this?"

"So you'll go easy on him if you sense any of this on your own."

"Oh, I'll go easy on him, all right." She got out of the car. Her fists were clenching and unclenching.

Al watched her and grinned to himself, eager to see how this would go.

They opened the door and went inside. Merchandise lined the walls in the bright colors of the faded dreams of other people. Appliances, guitars, amps, sporting goods, and lawn equipment all provided a wide variety of opportunity for anyone wanting pre-owned goods. Only one other customer stood in the store, a long-haired young man in a tiny, dark, porkpie hat. He had a case open and held up what looked—from where Al stood—like a Les Paul guitar. The man turned, saw them, and put the guitar back in its case. He took the case with him as he headed for the front door, going around the other side of a center gondola display of knives and jewelry in glass cases.

The man at the back by the cash register frowned. There are people who can smell cop, and he was one of them. As Al walked back through the store, Irving recognized him, his eyes flicking to the back as if measuring a way out or thinking of something he needed to hide back there. His hand swept up to rub at a head that had a really good start on male pattern baldness. Only a few wisps of hair remained in the tonsure that was shaping up, and Irving rubbed at those hard enough they might fall out soon.

"You're up," Al said to Fergie out of the side of his mouth.

She seemed okay with that. She went behind the counter and stood next to Irving, who stood a foot shorter than her. He had to look up at her.

"Small hands, small feet," she said. "That may be part of the reason, Al, but it's still no excuse."

"Hey," Irving said. "What you guys want? I still got rights, you know."

"Really? Why do you think that? Because you're such an outstanding citizen and all?"

"I'm. . . I'm. . . Tell her, Al. I've. . . I've cooperated in the past."

"I like the way you just assume I'm in law enforcement and not some leader of a women's rights group, or something like that." Fergie stepped closer, and Irving's head had to tilt farther back to look up at her. She was in his space, eyes squinting hard and nostrils flaring. "You see, first of all, I'm not short and tiny, like you like, and I'm not, well, young. So I'm outside your comfort zone. Way outside it. More like your archetypal bad dream."

"Al. Al! Help me out here. What is it you guys want?" Just as a bully is often a coward inside, someone like Irving, drawn to petite younger women as he was, appeared to have an inherent fear of towering women his own age, especially when they looked like they really wanted to punch him one in the beezer.

"There you go," Al said. "The thing is, we'd like to borrow a couple of night goggle sets. That is, if you don't mind?"

Irving was the type of fellow able to make logical deductions in his head quick—nanosecond quick. He reached for a set of keys in a baseball-sized bundle that hung from his belt. He did so without taking his eyes off Fergie. Al gave her credit. She looked just about ready to bite. Irving was feeling through the keys, had to look down for a second to find what he wanted. When he did, he held the key, still attached to the whole ball of other keys, out to Al. "Here. Case is over by the long guns." He looked back up at Fergie, the way a bird will when hypnotized by a snake. Fergie might have disputed that, argued that Irving was the snake.

Al went over to the case, undid a lock that held two sliding pieces of glass together, a lock that wouldn't begin to stop a burglar who meant business. Al reached inside and took out two of the three night goggle sets sitting there. One was the Yukon 25025 1 x 24mm Night-Vision Tracker Goggles with the hands-free head-gear unit. Exactly what he wanted. The other set was the Night Owl Tactical Series G1 Night Vision Goggles. Equally good, perhaps better. Certainly worth a hundred or two more, and Irving had priced them accordingly. Al left behind the Spy Net Real Tech Night Vision Infrared Stealth Binoculars, which might be fine for peeking into a neighbor's home but were nothing compared to the other two.

"There we go," Al said. He nodded to Fergie, who came back around the counter and joined him. "Thanks, Irving."

"Hey, take care of those, and bring them back," Irving yelled. They made their way back to the front of the store. "I don't suppose you'd consider a rental fee or anything? Something where the county pays?"

Fergie looked back at Irving, who apparently had decided he'd said all he was going to.

Outside, the sun had heated up Fergie's car until the door handles were just short of painful to touch. They got back into the car, and Al put the two night goggle sets under his seat on the passenger side.

"Was that approach necessary?" Fergie asked as she put the key in and started the car. The AC blasted them with a lukewarm rush that quickly cooled as the system struggled to get the interior back to a bearable temperature.

"No, but you'll have to admit it was more fun."

"It was. It was, indeed, Al. Now, what do you need those for?" Fergie adjusted the mirror without looking toward him.

"You'll see." He was watching out his window for bikers, and he almost missed the fellow in the truck who did a double-take at them.

"Quick. We've been spotted. They're at two o'clock but are slowing."

Give Fergie credit. She took a quick glance at the truck, its driver easing off on the gas so he and his passenger could have a better look at them, and jerked the steering wheel left, enduring the honk of a driver irritated at being cut off.

He left the driving to Fergie, a seasoned city cop who'd been in on her share of heated pursuits, although usually from the other side. She caught a yellow light in a screech of tires onto Sixth Street and beat out an SUV seeking to change lanes. The truck behind them had to run a red light amid a quick flurry of exasperated honking.

Sixth Street is Austin's version of New Orleans's Bourbon Street. By night it was one nightspot after another stretching along both sides, with milling people moving about from one to another. By day it was still a crowded street, which is what Fergie had been after.

She worked her way into the left lane of the one-way street and twisted the wheel to jerk into the small parking lot for Hut's Hamburgers. A car was starting to back out. She whooshed past it, but it kept coming as if it hadn't seen her. Al opened the glove box, took out both guns, and glanced back. The truck pursuing them screeched to a loud stop on the other side of the car. Fergie bounced over a small hump into the adjacent lot for Frank & Angie's Pizzeria.

Al could see some arm-waving going on behind them, but they were rocketing along on Fifth Street far enough away that he couldn't hear anything.

First chance she got, Fergie turned into an alley and went along behind a row of businesses. She worked her way around until they were heading down South Lamar at a far statelier pace. Al kept an eye on the traffic behind them, but they'd lost the truck.

"Who do you suppose that was?" she asked. She wasn't even breathing hard. His own pulse was throbbing along vigorously enough.

"If one group has Maury and Bonnie, that leaves two other groups out there. I just don't know who put them wise to us."

"It is worrisome."

Al watched in all directions for anyone else who might

have an unfriendly curiosity. "We'd better find a cheap motel and get some rest. It could be a long night."

"Nothing we can do right now?" Fergie glanced his way.

"No. I wish we could. It kills me not to be able to do anything fast, but what I have in mind only works at night. We have to wait, like it or not."

"Separate rooms, though." She pulled out into traffic.

"Of course. I really do just want to sleep." That was only partly true. What he really wanted was to go barreling off after Maury and Bonnie. But his years of experience told him that rushing would do more harm than good. They'd wait.

She glanced his way. He kept his eyes on the road. "Sure you do," she said.

"How about this place?" He nodded toward an independent place called Cactus Flower Motel. It was neither exotic nor a dump, because neither of them could handle one of the really cheapo motels. This one gave them a hope for quiet rooms at the back since they needed to sleep by day and leave after it got dark. Plus, it was close enough to a pharmacy that they could walk over and buy a couple of toothbrushes, since they were traveling light.

Fergie parked at the far end of the lot, where she was out of sight. Al came out of the office with the two room keys and walked to the car. She motioned to him, and he got back inside, handed her a key to one of the rooms. He could see she had a question.

"Why back to the farm?"

"It all comes back to the note from the kid."

"Roger?"

"Yeah, him."

"Why?"

"He thought he was saying something of significance, maybe pointing away from the logical suspects, the gang he had aspirations to join, the Texas Syndicate. He might've been saying to be sure and check the *Mexikanemi* and Tango Blast too. It's the way a kid like that might think it through. Tango Blast seemed to be trying to draw attention *toward* the farm. Roger would be trying to steer that focus *away* from the farm, probably toward Tango Blast. They're some of the people we should be worried about. But I'm more anxious about the ones we haven't heard from at all, the *Mexikanemi*. It's already a crowded picture, and that third gang shoe hasn't dropped yet." As Al said it, the whole thing sounded nearly capable of being logically pat. Then why didn't it make sense to him yet? Not a single hard clue, really. Just a lot of wild thoughts galloping around every which way.

"Then you believe there was something to what Roger was trying to convey?"

"Maybe. Maybe not. Misguided as the young sprat was, he was trying to accomplish something, even if he went about it bass ackward."

"Do you know what he had in mind?"

"Not yet."

"You've dealt with these gangs before, as have I. How do you keep them apart in your mind so they don't all blur together and become part of the same big bunch?" she asked.

"The trick is to think of each as a temporary personality and then seek the tensions where they don't get along. There are just the basic three around Austin. Houston is ten times as complex. Here the Texas Syndicate is leery because Tango Blast is growing, fast. The *Mexikanemi* is old school, the Mexican mafia. They used to collect ten percent, their dime, from other gangs and anyone doing any serious trafficking through their area. Now they're getting pushed around too. That can't make their local *generalissimo*, Joaquin Zambada "El Chapo" Arellano happy. None of them get along with each other. The tension between them amounts to a temporary tolerance at best. It's what helps define them, same as with the cartels. They're all somewhat like military businesses, which is why it's so hard to combat them. Add to that that the agencies we have up against them—ICE, the DEA, and the FBI—don't get along together so well, nor do they share all they should. That's what tripped up those two DEA agents. They came in under everybody's radar and just started poking around on their own. Couple of mavericks. Not the best idea, as it turned out."

"You're right. It's a tangled mess."

"Maybe a nap will add some clarity. See you." He got out and headed for his room, which was on the upper floor, quite a ways from hers.

Inside his room he looked around. It wasn't bad, but it wasn't the Plaza either. Two beds, a small coffee maker, a television he wasn't going to turn on, and a bathroom. At sixty dollars a pop for each room, it seemed steep for a short nap. He could have saved some if they'd used the same room, even if that meant separate beds. Fergie was throwing up a pretty clear deflector shield, though, and for the time being it was just as easy to respect it, given all they had going on.

He sat down on the end of the bed, thinking the same thing he'd thought earlier. What he really wanted to do was rush out there to the Three Sisters farm right away. He knew Maury and Bonnie were in real danger, if that's even where they were. But to go out there in daylight wouldn't help them. Maybe just get himself and Fergie killed.

He kicked off his boots and stretched out on the bed, too restless to fall right to sleep. There had been a time when he could pop off in a second. Not anymore.

He got thinking about something Jaime had asked him once. Jaime had said, "When you were detective for the sheriff's department, did you ever get approached by any of the gangs tied to the cartels, offered any money to look the other way?"

"Of course," he'd said.

"But you never went that way, even though there is a massive amount of money involved?"

"You know I didn't."

"Yes, I do," Jaime had said.

Now Al wondered why Jaime had bothered to ask at all. Probably no real reason, except that Jaime liked things right out on the table when he could get them that way, which wasn't always.

Al glanced toward the closed curtains. Two layers of thick curtains pulled tight, with some kind of matching rubbery lining. Yet he could see a tiny bit of light coming in around the edges. He set his mind for three hours and closed his eyes. Didn't think he'd be able to sleep at all for a while. Three hours later, his eyes popped open. Time to get moving.

CHAPTER NINETEEN

THE MEN HOLDING HER WITH rough hands and a tight grip pushed Bonnie then let go of her. She stumbled forward a few steps but managed to stay upright. Low center of gravity, she figured. A curse, and a blessing. Maury wasn't so lucky. Shoved from behind, he stumbled forward almost to her, his twig-like arms and brindle stick legs tangling as he staggered. He fell in a heap onto the cement floor before she could catch him. She crouched and bent over him, checking him over, untying him like a loose knot. These men had been big and rough, and Maury was, well, not. He was nothing like his brother, who seemed made of pure flint. That's one thing she liked about Al. Her ex-husband had been a hard body too. Only thing was, though, he was hardheaded to go along with it.

Whether Maury's years of womanizing had taken a toll, or whether he'd just been weaker in the first place and that had led to his Lothario days, she couldn't tell. But she'd been a nurse, and tending to people like him was what she did. She helped him up from the stone floor. As she did, she looked around. Bare stone walls, a wooden chair, and wooden table. A lone light bulb in a bigger-than-usual fixture at the center of the stone ceiling lit the room. A pair of wires ran from it across the ceiling to the doorframe. She'd already grasped the reality of their situation. What she saw made her shudder.

Maury dusted himself off and felt for any bruises. "I don't suppose we're going to get anything like an attorney or a phone call out?"

"I'd bet against either. That's with the law, and these guys sure aren't law." Bonnie moved closer to the door. She had to concentrate to keep her voice from quivering. *Best not to alarm him.* "It looks like we're in a room of solid rock and sealed in behind a locked steel-on-steel door. This doesn't look good. Not good at all." She saw a dark-brown spot on the floor, knew by the color and shape it had been a pool of blood. She didn't mention that to Maury.

"And no private bathroom or shower, either," he added.

"Worse, they got my—well, Al's—gun, before I could plug a single one of them. I'd hate to shoot it in this room, anyway. I doubt it would do much to that door, and the bullet would bounce around in here like a BB."

Maury sat down on the chair. Bonnie went to the table and lifted a corner. With one hand, she tried to unscrew a leg. She lowered the table and tried to twist the leg again with both hands. "Legs are glued into place. Thought I might have a club I could use."

She looked around the room. It was the perfect prison—solid Texas limestone all around them. "Al and Fergie probably know we're missing by now. I'll bet they're worried sick."

"Tell you the truth?" Maury stared down at the brown spot, must have figured it out. "I'm more than a little worried myself."

<hr />

Fergie drove past the front of the farm. Al watched in all directions for any sign of gangs. He felt wide-eyed alert, as much from growing paranoia as from the brief rest. All the media vans were gone. The new hot scoop had moved into town where the two agents had been brutally killed. A lone sheriff's department cruiser sat near the sign at the front entrance. It sat within sight of where the two bodies on the scarecrow had been found—now a double crime scene, still surrounded by fluttering yellow tape.

She eased up the church drive. The two DEA agents wouldn't be here, they knew that, but they wanted no surprises. The church lot was empty. She started to park the car in the same spot at the back of the church parking lot.

Al said, "Let's put it way on the other side, behind some bushes, if possible. I'm thinking anyone else may come in this way too."

"You're still playing some kind of chess game in your head, Al. When are you going to let me in on what moves you think will happen next? Or are you still on the permutations?"

"You'll be the first to know. Right after I know anything for certain."

She switched off the dome light, and they got out. They had their Glocks, hers shoved inside her belt in front and his behind his back. Each of them had a handful of spare shells in a side jeans pocket. The guns hadn't come with spare clips. Al handed her one of the sets of night vision goggles. They didn't put them on yet. A mercury vapor light lit most of the parking lot nearest the church, a white, wooden, two-story building with the usual steeple. It looked like it couldn't house a congregation of more than maybe two hundred.

They stayed on the far, dim side of the parking lot, where they could dart off into the thick vegetation if any other vehicles arrived. Al eyed the thicket, a real tangle of chaparral, one he didn't want to leap into unless he absolutely had to. He could hear occasional rustlings as they went past—probably raccoons, possums, or armadillos. Too late for snakes, lizards, and such, though scorpions might be moving around.

They had almost made it all the way to where they'd parked the last time when a set of headlights started up the church lane. Another pair of lights was coming along behind that. Al nudged Fergie toward the thicket.

"You first, lamb chop," she said, switching places. She gave Al a shove.

Al pushed into a tight cluster of yaupon, each sapling fourteen or fifteen feet high. So far, so good. No stickers. He lifted his night vision goggles to his head, settled them into place, tightened the strap, and flipped the switch on as soon as they were in place—just in time to see a waist-high stand of prickly pear cactus. He veered left, skirting the mound of cactus stickers, and saw the bole of a large tree to his left and a blurred tangle of plants to his right. His eyes were still adjusting to the view through the night goggles when a sweep of headlight beams swung past, temporarily blinding him. At the same time, Fergie came up behind him and nudged. He opted for the known rather than the unknown and pushed forward to press himself snug against the back of the tree, away from the lights. Felt like pecan bark. The crunch of fallen pecan shells under Fergie's feet as she came up to crowd in beside him confirmed that. A second set of headlights swung across the empty lot, and that vehicle pulled in to park beside the other. Al was glad they'd left Fergie's car way over on the other side of the lot.

He heard the vehicles' doors slam. Al was already scouting the quickest way ahead through the thick growth, but then he thought again. He eased around to the far side of the pecan tree's trunk and pushed back out to the parking lot. Fergie was right behind him. They turned off their night goggles, flipped them up, and hugging the outside edge of the parking lot, they rushed around to where the two twenty-six-foot Penske rental trucks had parked. As they slipped by the trucks, Al tapped on the backs. Empty for now. They were both poised and ready to take on a load, at least fourteen hundred cubic feet worth each. He pulled his night goggles back down into place and headed into the woods.

Anxious, Al moved faster than he should have. A stick broke beneath his foot. He slowed to a halt. Just as well. One of the men had stopped and fallen behind while he watered a tree. Fergie came up beside Al and touched his arm to let him know she was there. He wondered what the gang member would think if he knew a lady cop was watching his nature call.

The man zipped up, turned on a small flashlight, and hurried to catch up with the others. They all headed toward where Al had spotted the antenna in a tree. The cluster of lights ahead grew closer together then began to disappear. One by one the men climbed down inside an open trapdoor where Al had seen the tight grouping of bunch grass when they'd scouted the area earlier.

He and Fergie crouched down and waited until the last of the men had climbed inside and the trapdoor had closed. Above them a sliver of a rustler's moon barely lit the sky, but to Al, through his goggles, it beamed at them like a spotlight.

Fergie punched Al low in the ribs. "We did it. We found where they're going. That poor old lady was right. People *were* coming and going in and out of the ground."

Al didn't let himself feel too elated. The rough patch was just about to begin. They had to get inside and see if they could find Maury and Bonnie, if they were there at all. Good hunch; no guarantee. The place might well be filled with armed gang members just looking for a playful diversion.

"Let's roll." He took off in a run for the trapdoor, with her right beside him.

Before they got there, she tugged him to the side. "Wait," she whispered. "What if we could find the power source, shut it down, go in with these glasses. We'd be the only ones who could see."

"Wouldn't work."

"Why?"

"First of all, we don't know where their power source is coming in. And even if we could find it and cut it off, we'd be in total darkness down there. Night vision goggles don't work in total darkness."

"Oh."

"Let's leave the goggles up here where we can get them if we need them on the way out." He found a bush a few feet away where he could tuck his goggles out of sight. She added hers and followed him back to the trapdoor.

"You're really confident about this, are you?"

"No sense looking at it from the other side just now. If we don't get out, it won't matter to us what happens to them." He knew he sounded more confident than he felt. He didn't want to bring up their real chances of getting back out at all.

With that thought rolling around in his mind like a loose bearing, Al felt around, found the edge, and lifted the trapdoor enough to peer inside. The initial stretch was a wooden ladder with flat steps descending ten feet down into a dark shaft to a lit square below. He started to climb in. Her hand shot out and grabbed him by the upper arm. It was quite a grip, and he could only imagine how that claw hold had felt to the DEA agent.

"Are you sure about this?"

"Of course not," he said.

"Yet you choose to take the risk?"

"I don't have a choice. Maury might be down there, and Bonnie. They may not be, but I think they are. It's the only way I can see it."

"You could call Clayton. Get help?"

"And tell him I have a rough idea, a suspicion that Maury is down here? Or have the department, the DEA, and who knows who else come pouring in here to make the bust, only to get Maury and Bonnie killed in the process? You know how these situations go."

"Yes. Yes, I do."

Her hand eased its grip, and he started down the wooden steps.

The bottom opened into a doorway-sized hole he could walk through. He waited until Fergie was all the way down and beside him. When she turned around, she saw what he'd been staring at. The room was a wide hallway of a cave. Rows of grow lights had been strung above what was now a solid wall of chest-high green marijuana plants that covered half the open space. The rest of the room, to the right, was filled with stretched lines from which drying plants hung.

The area around Austin is riddled with caves that formed when the limestone rocks were deposited about one hundred million years ago when a warm, shallow sea covered central Texas. That, no doubt, was the origin of this cavern, too. But when someone had discovered it, they hadn't thought tourist attraction. Instead, they'd thought, "Ah. Marijuana farm." From what Al could see, the area looked as big as two football fields.

Now Al understood the urgency. With marijuana being legalized in state after state, these guys had to hustle to get this crop out there while it still held the charm of being illegal. Come down here a year or two from now, and he might find them growing poppies for opium.

He could hear voices. At least two men worked on the far end of the room, pulling down dried plants from the hanging lines. Al did the math in his head for what looked like a major harvest. That explained the waiting trucks. He could hear the sound of a trash compactor coming from the next cave room, probably packing the bricks of processed weed to be sold. The smell of the dry plants seemed stronger than the green growing smell, all of which filled the cave with a heavy fecund odor.

Al waved for Fergie to stay low, and they started to their left toward a door he'd seen near the far end of the cave. Beams, ropes, and pulleys were piled along the wall beside the shaft they'd just come down. Looked like a hoist would be set up above ground to get the product up the shaft when that time came, all under cover of darkness.

Some men must have needed to come and go as they took care of the plants, watering them and such. That probably accounted for the people Gladys had seen emerging out of the ground.

As they got closer to where the cave narrowed before opening into the next large chamber, Al could see more drying plants ahead. This was a huge operation. Years ago, Al had heard of an underground marijuana farm near Nashville that had been big enough to grow a hundred pounds of marijuana every eight weeks, yielding at least six crops a year. It had brought in millions, and this operation was every bit as big, possibly much bigger. That would be millions upon millions of dollars' worth, all underneath property owned by three little old ladies who couldn't possibly keep an eye on all their land. Gladys, though, must have stumbled onto something that made her suspicious. Her sisters may have doubted her, and maybe her son did too, but that might have changed after her death. So the son had had to go too.

Al and Fergie passed an open area, a side pocket where a half dozen cots crowded one wall and an open-air bathroom and multi-head shower ran along the back. Not much privacy, but a place to crash for some of the workers. Al could feel as much as hear the low hum of machine noise that probably came from generators. He recalled that the hidden underground marijuana farm near Nashville had been discovered when the local power company had noticed anomalies in the area. Tracing their lines, they'd found where some had been spliced to tap power directly without paying for it. Someone here at this location had headed off that possibility, possibly tapping power from the farm now and then but largely sustaining what they needed on their own. They would need to bring in fuel. The builders had probably needed to drill a well too. All quite doable, and the returns had to mean serious money. An operation this size, and with marijuana of this quality, had to make a dent in the market of what was being shipped into the states from Mexico, as well. That wouldn't make the cartels happy. They were businesses, after all. More pieces of the puzzle were falling into place for Al.

He heard voices coming their way. Al spun and grabbed Fergie, held her hand, and pulled her back to the room with the cots. A large pile of loose camouflage canvas and brown army blankets had been piled against the opposing stone wall. He pulled her down, and they covered themselves with the blankets. They both held still while the voices grew louder, passed, and went on toward the shaft with the trapdoor, perhaps to start setting up the hoist.

Al waited longer than may have been necessary. He nudged Fergie, and they climbed out from under their cover.

"Whew," Fergie said. "I don't think whoever was under those blankets was overusing the shower."

Al leaned out and didn't see anyone except the two men on the far side who were still busy taking down the dried plants. He ducked low and started out to their left toward the door he'd seen. It was dark brown, almost burgundy. When he got closer, he could see that it was a steel door in a steel frame. The best news was that he could see the silver gleam of a key in the lock. He looked around again, and Fergie crowded close. He turned the key, heard the rasp of the deadbolt, and swung the door open. Maury sat on the end of a table. He said, "Don't!"

Al glanced to his right. Bonnie held a chair and looked ready to swing it down on Al's head.

"It was gonna be a gamble," she said, lowering the chair. "But we figured we were gonna die anyways."

"You can tell us all about it later. Let's get out of here as quickly as we can." Al looked them both over. Maury had a skinned patch of pink on one cheekbone, and he was rubbing an elbow, but otherwise they seemed to be in one piece. "Are you okay to run? We have just one objective now, and that's to get us all out of here. There may be some shooting, and we might all have to hightail it pretty fast. You up to that?"

"Never more so," Bonnie said.

Maury sighed. "If you're sure there's no other way to do this."

"We checked, Maury. No elevator. Just the one way out we know of," Fergie said.

"Can't you call for help on your cell phones?"

"Not from inside a stone cave," she said. "That'd be a stretch for the best tower, even if it was sitting over our heads."

Maury sighed. "Let's do this thing, then."

CHAPTER TWENTY

"STAY CLOSE TOGETHER," AL SAID. "Fergie, do you want to be on point?"

She nodded.

"Then I'll bring up the rear." He turned to Maury and Bonnie. "We just know the one way in or out, and we think there may be a crew setting up a hoist there. Could be an issue. There are a couple of guys in the cave chamber just outside who were taking down the dried plants. We need to keep them in mind and stay as quiet as possible. Okay?"

Maury nodded. Bonnie glanced at the gun at Fergie's waist and knew about the one at the small of Al's back but said nothing. A self-professed crack shot like her had to have an itchy palm to get her own hand on a gun. She nodded.

Al eased the door open, looked each way, and went outside in a crouch. The others all ducked low and followed. As soon as they were all out, Al let Fergie ease to the front and start back the way they'd come in. He looked across the wide cave chamber for the guys harvesting on the other side. They were out of sight, though he could hear them talking.

Ahead of him, Maury stuck close behind Fergie. Bonnie stayed alert, checking in all directions. Al considered the motley crew of them. After their one intimate fling he'd thought might turn into something, Fergie had apparently decided to keep to herself. Al didn't know why, nor did he blame it on anything he'd done. Bonnie just looked eager to get her hands on a gun and start popping some of the opposition. He grew aware he was evaluating them, the way he would fellow troops heading into a battle, studying their body language, their movements. Even Maury looked alert, eager, and hopeful. He was keeping up and fit right in. Al realized he'd never been prouder of Maury. Sometimes it felt easy to think of Maury as the product of an intervention, since they'd had to wean him away from his woman chasing. It was coming back to Al slowly that this was the brother he'd grown up with and now cared for as much as anyone could after twenty years of not speaking. He didn't know if this evaluative moment came from them being together on the very edge of death, nor did he care. He savored the good he could in the moment and braced himself for whatever lay ahead.

Fergie held up a hand. They slowed. Al watched her scan the empty sleeping quarters. Neither Bonnie nor Maury indicated a need to use the limited restroom facilities, so Fergie ducked low and hugged the still-growing marijuana plants as they forged on.

A sudden huge crash of wooden beams and metal froze them. Stopped in place like statues, they heard loud laughter. They relaxed. The unflinching brightness of the grow lights bothered Al. There were few shadows. The closer they got to the exit shaft, the slower they went, hugging the plants as the sound of voices got louder.

Al was doing some math in his head. These guys were Texas Syndicate, every one of them he'd seen so far. The last report he'd seen had said there were about thirty-eight hundred members in Texas. He didn't have an exact number for Austin and Travis County, but he guessed no more than two or three hundred. That compared with about four hundred Tango Blast members in the same area, out of the six to eight thousand of them in the state. The Texas Mexican Mafia, *Mexikanemi*, had five thousand in the state and maybe about the same number locally as the Texas Syndicate. So, how many of the Texas Syndicate gang could be down here? A hundred? He didn't like those odds at all.

He liked them worse when they got near the shaft he and Fergie had used to come in. Fergie slowed and waved Al forward. He eased up beside her until he could see what she was seeing. He counted nearly twenty men setting up the hoist. Others pushed carts of the bricks that could be hauled in their canvas baskets up to the top. It was the long way to go about it, but they had the manpower, and this way maintained more secrecy. The marijuana cave near Nashville had used a large hydraulic door at the back of the garage of the house on the property. A truck could back into the garage and get loaded. With no building close, this bunch had improvised. They'd probably found, or knew about, the caves and had expanded them to their use. The property above was nearly useless, so there was little chance of people roaming about. It had been a good spot. But they seemed eager to load as much of it as they could, as quickly as they could.

The text message Al had gotten about staying away for two days added to that sense of urgency. That was the gang's window. Probably half of that. It looked like they were going to try to clear the place to the walls tonight. With all the recent gang activities nearby, he wasn't surprised. It was starting to look like some competing group was trying to bring attention to this operation and close it down. If it was pinching the business of the cartels, that didn't surprise him either.

He leaned close enough to Fergie that his lips were once again touching her ear. "Too many here," he whispered.

She nodded then shrugged.

He leaned close again, whispered, "Place like this has to have one or two escape routes. They always do. We just have to find one and not get spotted while getting to it."

They turned, with Fergie in the lead again, and started back the way they'd come.

———◆———

Heriberto led the caravan, driving the same white pickup they'd used to plink at that bad cop at Fuzzy's. Someone should have given them a medal for trying. When word had come all the way up from the Gulf cartel to shut him down, El Chapo had been slow to act. But not Heriberto. He'd talked it over with Viejito. El Chapo had once been as ruthless as any of them in his day, had killed, maimed. But now he liked to eat, and to play with his grandchildren. He no longer enjoyed the screams from the villages. You lose that, you lose your edge. You have to enjoy the screams from the villages, the weeping of women, and the despair of the young.

Seven trucks and more than forty motorcycles headed up the highway. The turn into the church lot was just ahead. Heriberto took out his cell phone and hit the number.

"*Ahora*," he said and closed the phone. Soon there would be a whole new order.

———◆———

Joaquin Zambada "El Chapo" Arellano, *jefe* of the Austin cell of the *Mexikanemi* for almost twenty years, sat in a folding lawn chair Viejito had positioned just right for him, high on the hill above Fuzzy's, the same spot from which Heriberto and his men had been observing, taking notes.

"Who was that?" El Chapo asked. He kept the binoculars up to his eyes, watching.

"Heriberto. It won't be long now." Viejito reached into his pocket, felt for the wooden handles. He drew out the garrote, two pieces of wood cut from a broom handle with a G string from a guitar tied to the middle of each piece. *We gonna make beautiful music, El Chapo,* he thought and stepped up behind the lawn chair. He had forty pounds of sodium hydroxide lye in the back of his truck. Heriberto had already sneaked a mini backhoe excavator up here and had a five-foot-deep hole waiting, covered by a tarp.

Viejito formed a loop with the wire and dropped it over El Chapo's head. He leaned back and pulled with all his strength. The field glasses fell to the grass, the chair toppled, and El Chapo grabbed at the wire with fingers that soon bled. His legs kicked steadily then more slowly and finally stopped. Viejito gave it another full minute then relaxed.

He took out his cell phone. When Heriberto answered, Viejito said, "It is done. *Finito.*"

"*Bueno.*" Heriberto hung up.

Now for the grueling chore of dragging El Chapo to the hole. He might have to roll him some of the way. But no matter. He had just shot up in the ranks as a new favorite son of the Gulf cartel, their left hand of God in America. Today might just end up being worth more than a million dollars to him. *And let's face it,* he thought, *the man was past it.*

⊰◇⊱

They eased past the sleeping quarters once more and weren't quite to the room Maury and Bonnie had been locked inside when Fergie held up an abrupt hand. She spun and headed back, crowding them all into the sleeping room. They pressed up against the stone wall. Al could feel the cold of the rock that seemed to be sucking at his body heat. He heard the click of boots on the limestone floor, the sound of wheels rolling.

The cart rolled past, one man with what looked like an AK-47 slung over his shoulder pulling the cart from the front. Tattoos covered his shaved bald head. The second man, younger and with long black hair, carried a Heckler & Kock MP5 with a banana clip in his right hand and pushed the cart with his left. That was a sweetheart of a gun. Al wondered for a second why they were all so heavily armed, as if they were expecting trouble.

The second guy glanced back and saw the four of them pressed tight against the wall. Before he could shout, Al leaped at him, grabbing a handful of long black hair in his left hand and pushing as hard as he could with his right palm on the man's chin. The snap was loud enough the man up front spun around. When he saw Al, he let go of the cart and started to yank the AK-47 clear from his shoulder.

As the man Al let go fell, Al snatched the gun from his hands and rushed forward, swinging it as he did. The barrel end slammed into the side of the bald man's head before he had the gun all the way clear. His knees buckled, and he crumpled straight to the stone floor, his head hitting with another hard crack.

"Oh, my lord, Al. Did I just see what I think I did?" Maury said.

Al held a finger to his lips. He grabbed the collar of the man nearest him. He dragged the body toward the pile of blankets and tarps where they'd hid earlier. Fergie didn't wait to be told. She went to the other fallen man, and

Bonnie rushed to help. They dragged him in the direction Al had gone.

Maury stood there until Al pointed toward the cart with the end of the H & K. He waved to his right. Maury caught on and started shoving on the cart, didn't stop until he was fifty feet farther along. Al, Bonnie, and Fergie were waiting by the time he turned around. He hurried back to them.

Al was giving Bonnie his Glock as Maury came up to them. Fergie held the AK-47. She handed it to Al, who flipped the selector switch to automatic fire and handed it to Maury. Al kept the H & K, just the sort of thing for this kind of situation. None of them spoke. Fergie started off again, and they followed. Maury clutched his weapon like some junior Rambo, and if the situation hadn't been so tense, Al might have chuckled to himself. Maury's hands still trembled, as if he'd been the one to just finish off two men. He kept glancing back toward Al with an expression that was hard to figure—a little awe and, yes, more than a touch of fear.

Where the cave narrowed before opening to the next large chamber, Fergie paused and waved for Al to come take the lead. He peered around the corner. This room would be tougher. Most of the hanging plants had been taken down. Two men on the far right were processing and packaging on a long metal table beside what looked like a trash compactor. Bricks were piled to their right. Two more men were approaching with another canvas cart on wheels that looked like it might have been stolen from a post office. Probably a federal offense, but that was the least of this lot's worries. More than a million dollars' worth, maybe even two or three, of some pretty potent marijuana was being loaded and about to roll out to all parts of America. Not for the first time, he reasoned that getting it out on the streets before the damned stuff became legalized everywhere may well have been part of their haste.

What caught Al's eye was a steel ladder mounted on the wall halfway up the chamber on the left, on the far side of where the men worked. *Escape route,* he thought. Had to be.

Only a couple rows of the hanging dried plants still remained on this side, and a pair of men were working at the far end of the chamber, getting those down.

Al signaled the others to follow and took off, staying as low as he could. He watched the men across the far side of the chamber. The noise of the compactor probably drowned out everything else for them. He shot forward, went in spurts, fast then slow. Fast again. Keeping an eye out all the while. Every time he slowed, Bonnie or Maury bumped into him. He didn't glance back to see who it was. All his focus and concentration was fixed on what loomed ahead.

When he was beside the ladder, he looked up while the others caught up and crowded around. He signaled Fergie close. She leaned in so he could whisper in her ear. "We'll go in dashes. You first. Open that trapdoor and get out of sight as quick as you can. I'll have the others follow when I'm sure no eyes are watching."

She nodded.

Fergie got her feet planted to run. She watched Al. He checked on the two men far at the end of the lines of dried plants then took in the crew on the far side of the chamber. He turned back to her and nodded.

She shot across the open space, scampered up the round steel rungs of the ladder, and pushed inside the trapdoor, easing it back into place. She was out of sight. It had taken just a few seconds.

He waved Bonnie close and whispered in her ear, "Like

that when I give the sign." Al checked again, and when he was sure no one had responded to Fergie's dash, he gave Bonnie a nod. She moved pretty fast for a roundish girl, but she was young.

Al was already calculating what to do if someone sounded an alarm. He and Maury would both have to dash, and he would have to lay down cover. He hoped it wouldn't come to that. A quiet exit would be so much better.

The trapdoor lowered back into place, and Bonnie was gone. Maury slung the AK-47 over his shoulder and looked at Al, maybe with a touch of apology for not being in better shape. When Al checked and nodded, Maury took off. He made nowhere near Fergie or Bonnie's time, but he did better than Al had expected. He paused only once halfway up the ladder, where anyone in the cave could see him, as he caught his breath. Long seconds stretched out while Al scanned the room and wished Maury would please, please move faster. At last, after what seemed a lifetime to Al, Maury clambered the rest of the way up the ladder. When Maury slipped up through the trapdoor at last, Al realized he'd been holding his breath and let it out.

No alarm. He checked once more and took off himself. He held the H & K in his right hand, and it clicked briefly as he raced up the ladder, a tiny metallic clang. But he checked around, and no heads turned toward him. Then he was through the trapdoor and let it close behind him.

He wasn't outside, as he'd hoped. This was a long shaft with a steel ladder attached to one wall. The ladder was the same as the one that had led up to it. It was dark in the shaft.

"Up here," Fergie whispered. "We were just waiting to make sure you made it."

"I'm fine." He started upward, trying to remember how long the shaft they'd come in through had been. He got his answer when he bumped into Maury's foot.

"Okay. Go on out," Al whispered.

"I'm trying. It feels stuck," Fergie said. "You might have to come up and knock it open."

Al started to work out how he was going to crawl over the others and get up there. The damn thing should have been easy to open if this was an escape route.

Maury pressed to one side. Al squeezed past him. Bonnie was next, and she was the kind of soft bundle that was harder to get to one side. That, or she pressed against him on purpose. Fergie moved to the right so Al could put his shoulder to the upper trap door. Should pop right open. But it didn't. He tried again.

"Getting older, Al?" Fergie asked.

That gave him the incentive he needed. He moved his feet up a rung and pushed his shoulder hard against the door until it finally began to give. He took a breath and used both hands.

Then the door swung open. First he saw the lighter night sky. Then a beam of light speared down at them. Al pushed out with his arms to see past the others. Not good. There was Bart's face, and he was pointing the double barrels of a 12-gauge shotgun down at them.

"Now, isn't this nice," he said. "You're all going to pass your weapons up to me and then slowly back down the ladder, or I'm going to open fire. And I've got to tell you, in this kind of space, that's going to make a real mess."

They had no choice. Al passed up the H & K, and the others did the same with their guns. Al could hear Bart speaking into something. Must be a small walkie-talkie, because a cell phone sure wouldn't work.

When Al opened the trapdoor and started back down the ladder in the light of that cave chamber, a ring of gang members had formed below him. They all held weapons. Not good. Not good at all.

CHAPTER TWENTY-ONE

ART WALKED CLOSE BEHIND THEM with the shotgun, a 12-gauge Rossi Overland short-barrel—a stubby little thing, with only two barrels, two hammers, and two shells inside. Al knew both hammers were back. Bart had been right when he'd said the gun would have made a helluva mess of them in the tight confines of the escape route shaft. Several of Bart's men also crowded close to escort Al and the other three back to the cell.

Work went on all around them, men still moving mounds of the marijuana bricks to where they were being lifted above ground. Some of them glanced toward the small caravan of prisoners headed back toward the cell, but they showed only minor interest and a little amusement—a petty interruption in the bigger scheme of reaping a huge profit in which they had a share.

The key was still in the cell door. Bart swung the door open, glanced around inside, and saw nothing, so he waved them in. Maury looked gutted and dragged his feet, but Al thought Bonnie and Fergie did a good job of not showing how he was sure they felt—defeated. They'd been so close to getting away.

"Now, back to work, everyone," Bart said to his men as he swung the steel door shut from the outside, leaving the four of them alone again.

Al heard the key twist. Bart didn't remove it from the

lock, but that didn't matter. There was no way to get to it. None of that pushing the key out of the lock with a paperclip and catching it on a paper and pulling it back inside. The door was too tight, and they didn't have paper or a paperclip. They had nothing.

"Well, isn't this a fine kettle of fish," Bonnie said. She and Fergie went over to lean on the side of the table. Maury eased himself down into the chair. He stared straight ahead at nothing.

Al glanced around. Not much to see except solid limestone.

Fergie looked around at the stone walls as well. "I have to admit that you helped me find Bart, and we probably have enough on him now to really give Internal Affairs a plateful. If we ever get out of here." She was going to say more but glanced at Maury, then Bonnie, and stopped.

"That's Al, the guy who never gave up that time with the blue boat," Bonnie said. "He gets there in the end."

"You wouldn't feel as good if you'd heard how that story ended," Al said.

Bonnie pushed herself up onto the table to sit. She looked toward Al. "He's in prison now. Right?"

"Should be. That's not how it came out once the case had rolled through the wheels of local justice." Al tasted something bad in his mouth as he said it. "Jim Bob Grady was ordered to pay a $1,500 fine and had to serve only one hundred days in county jail, not prison. He also got a ten-year probation. He pled guilty, mind you. The charge should have been manslaughter. He admitted in his statement that he saw two people in the water in the moments after the crash but that he abandoned them and left the lake. He admitted burying the blue boat and its trailer and to having been at the helm in the early-morning hours when the boat struck the boys' boat head on. But the prosecutors said they felt that the plea bargain to an official charge of failure to render assistance after a collision involving serious injury or death was the best resolution to the case because of the amount of time that had elapsed since the accident occurred. You should have seen the family members of that dead boy in the courtroom. Their faces fell about fifty feet."

"Holy crap in a bucket," Bonnie said.

"Yep. Justice isn't always all you hope it might be."

"I'd show some justice to this gang if I could just get hold of a gun again, even that pepper spray Bart was carrying." Bonnie glared at the door. "I'd give them something they'd understand."

"I'm still getting over seeing what Al did to those two guys with the cart. Unbelievable. What do you suppose Bart will say when he finds them?" Maury asked.

"With these guys it's like a war and they're in the military," Fergie said. "They expect to take casualties. It's part of the picture. Those left get more reward. That's all."

"Al?" Maury asked.

"Yeah?"

"What do you think is going to happen next? I mean to us."

Al didn't want to answer that. He still thought of Maury as fragile and didn't want to voice what they all knew.

"It's not good, sweetie," Bonnie said. "Let's just try to think of something else for a spell."

Al leaned against the cold stone wall, could feel vibrations and occasional thumps and banging, probably the process of getting that much product out of the cave and up and into the trucks. They were making progress out there and had to be close to done. He grew restless at not being able to do a damned thing. The helplessness gnawed at him. He pushed himself away from the wall and examined every edge of the door, rattled the knob. The dead bolt was flush enough the door didn't budge. He looked at every corner and seam of the stone, tapped in places, found it all solid and unmovable rock. It was only a matter of time. Had it been just him in the shaft when Bart opened the top, he might have fired away. As it was, that would have risked the others. Yet where were they now? They were all going to die. There wasn't much doubt in his mind. He went over every inch of the room again. Still nothing.

He didn't dare look at the others. This was as low as he'd allowed himself to get.

The moments stretched on and on—long, dead, and far too thoughtful moments. For a second he thought he either heard or felt something different. Then he was sure. Al heard a thump, then another. Shots. Maybe a small explosion or two. He was sure of it. What was going on out there with them trapped in here? He went to the door and pressed his ear against it, could hear shouts, more shooting—some single shots, some automatic weapons fire. He couldn't make a clear sense of it. First the shooting came from one direction, then another. For a brief second, hope fluttered up into his chest. A rescue? Or fighting among themselves? He couldn't tell. The moments ticked by as if stretched out like some Japanese Noh play, where each action takes place in exaggerated slowness. He stayed with his ear pressed against the door, listening to each scrap of noise until he thought he heard the click of boot falls coming to the door.

At first, he doubted what he was hearing. Then the key turned in the lock, and he stepped back. The door swung open. There stood Wayon Gallard.

"Ah, there you are," Wayon said. He smiled.

"Wayon, thank heaven." Al started for the door.

"Not so fast," Wayon said. He lifted his right hand, held a gun pointed right at Al. "You still haven't figured it out, have you?"

Al stopped, staring at Wayon.

Wayon closed the door behind him, put the key in, and locked it with his left hand, all without taking his eyes off of Al.

"Well, hell, Wayon." Al shook his head.

"Starting to connect the dots, are you?"

Al nodded. "Yeah, I guess everything *is* starting to make more sense now. Almost everything. Bart never asked if I was on my own, or if the department was coming in right on my heels. He didn't have to. You could tell him. By the way, who just burst in to attack Bart's Texas Syndicate people, the *Mexikanemi* or Tango Blast?"

"The Tangoes."

"That's what I figured."

"I doubt you're quite as on top of things—even now—as you think. Always the clever dick, top detective and all that. What did you think is really going on here?" There was no quiver to the gun Wayon held pointed at Al.

Al glanced to the others. He knew his expression showed concern for the others, a vulnerability that Wayon seemed to be enjoying. Al took a deep breath. "I think what made this case an unusually tangled mess was that it changed what it was all about in midstream. The way I had it figured at first was that the cartels behind the *Mexikanemi* and the Tango Blast gang both saw Bart and his Texas Syndicate connection as unwelcome competition, that the two gangs were charged by their cartel ties to shut him down, to eliminate a source of product that didn't have to go through them. The only sense I could make of hanging those bodies on the scarecrow was trying to draw attention to Bart, to expose whatever his operation was and let the cops do the rest. That's what comes from trying to make sense of what that screwed-up kid got himself killed for trying to communicate."

Wayon looked smug in a way Al had never known he had in him. "That boy was desperate to be accepted by the Texas Syndicate. He'd done a few errands for Bart and thought an act of bravery might look big in their eyes. I can't say what made him decide to declare there were three gangs that were players in what was going on and not just one or two. Just how kids think, I guess. His dad almost erased the boy's foolishness in time. Almost."

"I don't imagine you minded Roger being a little harebrained since you knew all along what was going on."

"His fumbled attempt at communicating sure kept you running around in circles until Bart and his pals could make their final harvest before the hammer falls."

Al nodded. "Putting aside that you are one of Bart's pals as well. The moment I saw you pull that gun, I knew what was at stake here since the cartels work in millions, even billions. Enough to afford you."

"You really think you have it figured out at last?" The gun Wayon held still didn't waver a bit.

"Hell, it's real estate rule number one all over again," Al said. "Location, location, location. Marijuana is practically passé as an illegal product. In the states where it isn't already legalized, the medical varieties are becoming more available. The law is even looking the other way. It's just a matter of time before anyone can get what they want at the corner drugstore."

Wayon grinned. "Then what is the plum here?"

"A location like this, a hidden farm, could be turned to where the real money is, growing poppies. The level of ruthlessness I've seen so far should have told me this was about more than pot." Al looked to the others, who didn't seem cheered by any of this, then turned back to Wayon.

"I'm guessing Bart still thinks you're on his side. But you're not, are you?"

"What makes you think that?"

"You're not eager to run out of here to escape, nor do you seem worried about it when you do leave, so you're probably friends with the Tangoes out there as well. Working both sides of that fence, eh?"

"Oh, Al. Being right always mattered so much to you, no matter what." Wayon was irked. His mouth pressed tight. Then he smiled. "Maybe you don't know it, but you're looking at the only millionaire deputy in the department. How's that make you feel? But I guess that sort of thing is outside your moral compass, eh? You'd rather just figure out what's going on, enjoy the puzzle. But you've only got part of it. How're you doing on solving the murders, then? Did you make any progress there?"

Al eased forward a half step. He let a bit of awe creep into his voice. "Don't tell me you know all about that when I got nowhere."

Wayon's grin was the kind the British might call smarmy—oily, sly, and smug.

"Come on. What's it matter? Who killed Gladys and Darin?" Al sounded so befuddled he almost convinced himself. Al glanced toward Fergie. She stood frozen in place, perhaps counting her last moments of life.

Wayon smirked. "I doubt it matters now. Bart killed the woman himself, found her staring at him when he came up out of the ground. Went to hush her, and she was so fragile he thought what the hell and just twisted her neck like a chicken's. He figured she'd already told her kid, so he dumped her body in one of the farm's fields. Then he borrowed a boat and took care of the kid on the lake. I doubt forensics found anything at all pointing to Bart. His clean-up skills are quite practiced."

"How'd her body get on the scarecrow, then?"

"The *Mexikanemi* did that. Had to be them. They apparently were watching the area closely with the hunch there was a big weed-growing facility close. Got the body where Bart had left it after he killed her and put it on the scarecrow. They no doubt thought stirring us up might make us slip and show them the way."

It didn't seem like Bart to leave a body lying around where it could be found, but only a few minutes later he was stealing a boat and running over Darin. He had been working a pretty hurried schedule.

"And Roger? Did the Tangoes squeeze all they could out of him then kill him and put him on the cross? That must've been before they had you all the way signed on. Otherwise, you could have told them what they wanted to know."

Wayon's smug smile grew. Al could feel Fergie, Bonnie, and Maury all wanting to say something, even scream. But, bless them, they kept still.

Wayon nodded. "When I was first talking with the Tangoes about our arrangement, I ran into a fellow who had a bum leg and a couple of smashed maracas, all courtesy of you. A guy named Jesus Vasquez."

"We've met. Man doesn't know pool room courtesy." Al inched closer.

"I heard how you gave him a lesson in manners. He said a Tango named Juan Madrigal did the preacher's kid, Roger. Juan is also the one who decided to add Roger's body to the scarecrow, just to mess with everyone's minds, the *Mexikanemi* especially."

Al gained another half step when Wayon glanced at the others. Al said, "Here I thought those Tango Blast fellows must have mistaken my white truck for the one some *Mexikanemi* dudes were driving when they did the drive-by shooting at Bart. But it was you who sent the Tango Blast after Fergie and me, wasn't it? It sure stirred up the whole mess to a new level of confusion. Just about did us in as well."

"Must bug the great detective to be so far out of the loop on everything, right?" Wayon said. His grin was just short of hysteric glee.

"What's your plan now? Will we four all wind up being casualties of the fray?"

"Nothing delights me more than telling you how you're wrong once again, Al. You see that oversized box holding the light bulb over your head?"

Al kept his eyes locked on Wayon's.

"It holds six sticks of dynamite all set and wired to go off. I watched Bart flip the switch that starts the timer, and it's ticking. It's backed by a twelve-volt battery in case the power goes out. Won't do you any good to cut the wire. That'll just set it off. He set it up that way when he thought he might have to get rid of all his records quick someday. Gotta hand it to Bart on that. He's knows what he's doing there."

Al risked a quick glance up. This was no bluff. The housing for the single bulb, painted the same color as the steel door, was way too big, enough to house any blasting cap needed and six eight-inch sticks of dynamite, something Bart would have had around when he was shaping the cave to his needs. Having a device like that ready to instantly eliminate any files when this had been his office probably had made sense to him. Though Bart had cleared out anything like data by now, a charge like that was nothing Al wanted to witness from inside the room. A stick of dynamite of the type used to blast rock, unlike

TNT or military dynamite, contained nitroglycerin soaked into an absorbent substance like sawdust, powdered shells, clay, or wood pulp. Al knew, from a distant-past case where a despondent farmer, Bruce Lyles, had ended his days by sitting on a stump and detonating a stick of dynamite under it, that the explosive power of a single stick was around 7.5 mega joules per kilogram. They had found some bits of the no-longer-sad Bruce at the far corners of what was going to be his wheat field. Al figured that six sticks in this confined space would do far, far worse damage.

Wayon looked like he was trying hard not to break into laughter at the look on Al's face. "Much as I'd like to stay, I'm gonna have to say good-bye. I think you know what six sticks will do, Al. All of your insides will be jelly. I don't have to do a thing. All that's on Bart's head. The good news for you four is that it'll be fast. You just won't know when it'll go. Maybe you have ten more minutes here, but maybe it's five. I guess you'll get to figure it out when I'm long gone."

"You know," Al said. He stood only a couple steps away from Wayon and moved closer. "People think they know you when you feed deer. You said as much yourself."

Wayon grinned, his confidence and cockiness as high as Al had ever seen it. "And you take in every other stray and mutt that comes along." His eyes swept Maury, Bonnie, and even Fergie. "You've got a big heart. I'll give you that."

"Folks assume that should make me soft. They're wrong." Al felt his anger boiling into a rage.

"How so?"

Al's hand moved as fast as he'd ever thrown a punch, coming up with the heel of his palm to Wayon's nose, smashing the nose upward and the cartilage behind it up into Wayon's brain. Wayon never got the second and a half it would have taken him to think, respond, and pull the trigger. If he'd trained as hard as he should have, been as ready as he needed to be, had any idea how much speed Al could generate by channeling his anger, and not taken Al for granted, he might have still been alive. The deputy's eyes fixed, went blank, and closed. He was probably already dead before his body crumpled to the floor. Al caught Wayon's gun as it fell from the corpse's hand on the way down.

"I suppose that's going to lead to more paperwork," Al said. He tossed the gun to Bonnie. "Check him for anything else we can use," he told her.

"Al! Holy crap. I can't believe. . ." Maury started to say.

"It's going to have to wait," Al said. He went to the table Fergie had hopped off of and smashed it against the back stone wall, again and again. He felt a familiar white-hot anger flowing through every inch of him. He flipped the table, grabbed a leg, wrenched it back and forth until it popped free—a metal screw and bolt sticking from one end and bits of shattered wood still clinging to that. He held the leg by the small end, as a club.

"Sometimes you have to play chess. Other times you need to upset the board. Today's shaping up into one of those 'don't play nice' days. Let's get out of here," he said.

Whatever was in his voice and narrowed eyes zipped the lips of the other three. They gave him space as he went to the door, opened it, and charged through it.

CHAPTER TWENTY-TWO

A L BURST OUT OF THE door and stayed low. He looked both ways at the noisy chaos around them. One of the Tango Blast members stood just to the right, his back to Al and shooting an automatic weapon at someone running down the middle of the growing marijuana plants. Bits of leaves flew through the air at the sound of each shot sizzling through. Al gripped the table leg with whitened knuckles and aimed for the cheap seats with a swing that darn near lifted the man's head off his shoulders.

Bonnie and Fergie glanced toward each other. Al picked up the man's gun, an AK-47, and tossed it to Fergie.

Another man came running toward them from their left. Bonnie spun and fired Wayon's gun. The guy tumbled into a heap, his feet still going, and then stopped for good. It didn't matter which gang he was with. Everyone was a target now.

Maury ran to the body, came back with what looked like the same kind of Heckler & Kock MP5 with a banana clip Al had held earlier. Maury handed it over to Al. "It's that gun you liked," he said.

"Thanks." Al tossed the bloody table leg aside.

The fighting seemed sporadic and unplanned. Al kept them in a tight group for the moment, knowing they might need to spread out soon. A man jumped up from the middle of the plants and started to lift a gun toward them. Bonnie whirled and fired. The guy flew backward.

"Better go get his gun," she said to Maury.

"I'm glad you're on our side, Bonnie," Al said.

"Me too," Fergie agreed.

Maury came back with a shotgun and a handful of extra shells, which he shoved into one pocket. The gun was nothing fancy, a 12-gauge Ithaca Model 37, the kind police used as a riot gun. He seemed quite proud of it. The only time he'd ever had to shoot in their defense, he had done well with an automatic shotgun, and he'd become familiar with Fergie's Winchester Model 12, a similar pump shotgun. All he had to do was point it in the right general direction and pull the trigger. How hard is that? He smiled.

They all had weapons now. That was something. But a real circus was going on. Shots sounded from both directions. Al considered going back toward their original shaft until the shooting from that direction suddenly went berserk. It sounded like someone had dropped a box of firecrackers into the fireplace, only louder, more intense, and deadlier.

He waved them the other way, toward the ladder route where Bart had cut off their escape. It was the only other way out he knew.

A huge *crump!* came from behind them, followed by the sound of rocks flying and a metal door slamming all the way across the cavern. Al figured that was the cell they'd been in. It measured the bare margin by which they'd gotten away.

Men from the left were rushing toward the action to the right. Then some of them came running back the other way. Other gang members had dropped all harvesting and packaging activities to join the melee by taking potshots at opposing members. It was hard, even for them, to know who to shoot at.

Al edged into the next cave chamber. For a moment it seemed calmer than the one he'd just left. An abandoned canvas cart full of marijuana bricks blocked their way. Al straightened it out and began to wheel it along. Might come in handy as cover. A shot whizzed over his head.

"Get down behind this cart," he called back to the others.

Maury crouched down right away, then Bonnie beside him, her head just over the upper edge, watching for a clear shot at anyone. It was harder for Fergie, tall as she was, but she got down as best she could. They started the cart moving. At a sudden flurry of shooting, Al ran across the short open space to join them. It made for a tight crowd. Wild shots were crossing the cavern in at least three directions, some ricocheting off the stone walls. It made an ungodly racket. There was no way all of them knew exactly at whom they were shooting. Men popped up, fired, and dove back to look all around themselves. Al rose enough to push the cart and keep it moving toward the escape route. The others stayed low, behind the cart's cover, and shuffled along, bumping into each other but gaining ground toward that ladder that led up and out of the cave.

A blast that sounded like a grenade came from the room behind them. Al pushed the cart faster and kept his eyes peeled for anyone coming toward them. Maury, Bonnie, and Fergie waddled faster, like eager ducks, but kept up. Another cart full of the bricks stretched across the path in front of them, only a dozen feet from the steel ladder going up the wall. Al tried to ram the cart, knock it out of the way. But the two carts jammed together with Bonnie,

Maury, and Fergie pinned between the two, the stone wall at their backs.

A sudden wave of gang members surged through the cavern opening to their right, the one they'd just passed through. These were from a different gang altogether. They'd been careful to wear their colors. *Mexikanemi.* Just fucking great! All three gangs were present now. The men to the left rallied. Texas Syndicate men gathered in one pocket along the same wall as Al. Tango Blast gang members formed in another good-sized clump along the other far wall. Al and the others were off to one side but right between the three warring gangs, and the only way out was a short dash away and up that exposed ladder. Bullets clipped bits off the wall. Other shots sprayed the remaining hanging dried plants into snowfalls of dry leaves. Al climbed over the nearer cart and got behind with the others. He kept his head up long enough to see the converging swarms of varied gangs coming toward them.

The *Mexikanemi* kept advancing from the right. The Tango Blast and Texas Syndicate groups started back toward them. Bullets began to thump into the shielding carts as groups on both sides drew closer. Maury crouched low, shoving the shotgun shells from his pocket into the gun. Bonnie got one clear shot, fired, and for once missed a man. It made her mad, and she fired twice more at where he'd dove.

"Pace yourself with the ammo," Al said. He was counting. He could see somewhere between sixty and eighty men in the cavern, from three groups that fiercely hated each other. They were as armed as they ever got, and they all kept coming toward where Al and the others were pinned down. A shot whizzed toward him and thunked into the cart. Al ducked back down beneath the cover. The others took turns popping up and having a look around. Al eased back up often enough to monitor their chances, which looked less and less good.

Fergie spotted Bart in the midst of the group sliding along the wall, coming their way. She yelled, "Bart!"

When Bart spun toward her, she fired. The shot went under his arm and into the belly of the man behind him.

Bart aimed and started firing a pistol. Perhaps it was even his department piece. He must have used up and discarded his sawed-off.

Fergie ducked low. Maury rose and fired three times into the crowd, taking out a Syndicate man each time. Bart kept firing, and Maury fell back behind the cart. Al saw blood starting to soak through Maury's shirt at the shoulder. Bonnie tore off a strip from the bottom of her blouse and knelt down next to Maury.

"Bonnie, I need you up here. You're our best shot. Let Fergie do it."

"Well, how come you never said I'm a good shot?" Fergie asked.

"We're going to need you too. But first patch up Maury. How bad is it?"

"Just grazed him. Well, maybe a bit deeper than that."

"That was good shooting, Maury," Al said.

"Not really. I was aiming for Bart."

The Syndicate group edged close enough that Al could clip a couple of them with the

H & K as they drew nearer. That caused them to veer to their left, out into the middle of the cavern, behind the cover of the hanging plants that still remained. They began to run.

The *Mexikanemi* picked up their pace from the right, and with a whole lot of firepower. It was like pinchers, squeezing tighter. Then the Tango Blast group rose in a wild wave and came across from the other side, shooting at Bart and the Syndicate men to the right, as well as at the *Mexikanemi* to their left. Some shots went straight ahead toward Al and the others crouching with him.

One big fellow Al was certain he had seen with the Tango Blast came charging like a bull toward Al and the others. Al wondered what emboldened him. Bonnie rose and squeezed off a shot that Al clearly saw hit the guy in the chest. The guy just jerked, as if stumbling, then kept coming. Al recalled the guy now. Juan. Fergie had shot him once, yet Al had seen him again. Must be wearing a vest.

"The head, Bonnie. Go for the head," Al yelled.

She shot again.

This time the guy's head snapped back, and he tumbled over in a flop.

Though the guy had only been a dozen feet away by the time she got him, Al doubted if one woman in a thousand could have made a shot like that. He was sure glad she was on his side.

They both had to duck back down when the pace of the shooting picked up in earnest.

The bullets came in a flurry, like steel hail, thumping into the carts and quite a few pinging off the stone wall behind them, showering down a fine dust of limestone powder. Bonnie, Fergie, Maury, and Al all had to duck low as the shooting got relentless and closer by the second. Al looked around at each of them. There were a few things he'd like to say to each of them, but it didn't seem likely he would get the chance. He pulled his clip, counted the remaining bullets—only two shots left—and put it back in place. A bullet came all the way through the cart, through his pants leg, and then screamed off the wall behind them. There was going to be a lot more of that, real soon. Maury, Fergie, and Bonnie each looked back at Al and then toward each other. The shooting around them had increased to a mad frenzy.

It was a hell of a thing, a gut-wrenching thing, to go through all they just had only to realize they were going to die. Words wouldn't come to Al, and none of them could have heard him if they had. They could read the realization and despair in each other's eyes. This was it. The final "it." They were as far down and as out of hope as they could get.

Crouched low as they were against the stone wall, Al heard an odd whining. It changed pitch, rising and falling. Then came a steady thumping, first far off then closer by the second. Helicopters? Then larger thumps—big explosions, he figured—came from either end of the cave. It started so suddenly he couldn't believe it, or trust his own hearing. He might have been imagining it, hoping too much. But it was still there. He understood, though Maury and Bonnie didn't yet. There was a chance, a slim but growing ray of a chance, that they might be saved. He dared take a deep breath.

With her thumb, Fergie wiped away a tear that had started down Al's cheek. She shook her head but shared as much of an uncertain smile as she could manage.

The trapdoor above the steel ladder burst open, and a rope fell through it. One after another, black figures slid down into the cave. From the right, behind the *Mexikanemi*, another wave of men in black swept into the cave. Off to the far left, same thing. Al could make out the clear letters on the outfits: ICE, DEA, and FBI. He'd never been gladder to see those black-clad guys come pouring in at such strength. Trained professional teams at the top of their game—swarming down, returning fire, sweeping in, taking control of the caves inch by inch. A warm glow surged up inside him and spread to his limbs.

He'd felt this way when the Navy SEAL team had slipped into Pakistan that time to finish off Osama bin Laden, and the feeling was far more intense now, since it was his life and the lives of those close to him that could be saved.

To see a couple of agents getting too eager and a bit ahead of themselves, the way Richard Blue and Luis Bracknall had, was one thing, an exception to the way things should work. Seeing the combined agencies swarm in and attack the gangs with everything they had was a whole other thing, a good thing, one that made him swell with pride to be a citizen of his country and a witness to doing things right as a team.

This was not a time to relax, though. Al nudged each of the others to be ready. They could as easily be shot by their rescuers, if they weren't careful. But now they had a chance. It was just dawning on the faces of the others, though it didn't wash away the fear still clear there.

CHAPTER TWENTY-THREE

S HOTS CONTINUED TO PING OFF the wall behind them
and shower limestone dust down on them. A flurry
of automatic rounds pounded into the carts that
barely sheltered them. Each shot sounded like it might
well punch all the way through. Maury's face was a white
mask of dust. He looked grim but clutched his shotgun,
ready. Fergie glanced toward Al, and the look was almost
tender.

The fighting hadn't slowed with the arrival of the various
crews of agency men. The shooting had instead increased
to a new fury of intensity. Even Bonnie, who seemed
always ready to squeeze off a round or two, huddled down
closer to the cave floor. They were down to their last few
rounds of ammo. She grinned at Al, yet it was a strained,
uncertain, wide-eyed grin. None of them knew for sure
that they would weather this.

Al heard a scuffle of running boots sliding to a stop
near them. He rose to peek in time to catch a Syndicate
member trying to pull the carts away from the wall and
hide behind them himself. The man's eyes widened in
surprise. He started to raise his Mac-10. Al snapped the
H & K up at the same time. It was going to be close.
Then the guy's head jerked back as a red dot appeared at
the base of his neck. The arm holding his gun lowered,
and his body crumpled.

"Freeze. Drop it!" Al's head turned. Three men in black with "FBI" on their chests formed a line, weapons all pointed at Al's chest. Al lowered the H & K, let it drop. He raised his hands. He looked down to the others. They put their weapons on the stone floor. Maury stood first, then Fergie and Bonnie. They raised their hands too.

One of the FBI team jerked the cart nearest them away from the wall. He yanked Al out first. He and another man wrestled Al to the floor. Not as easy as it sounded. Al was trying to cooperate, yet these men were full of desperate hard moves pounded into them during training. Seize control, subdue everyone, and straighten it out later.

Al ended up with his face pressed to the ground by a knee as the man on top of him spoke to someone Al couldn't see. Shots still rang out, but the frequency was slowing. Only a few pockets of resistance must have remained. Bonnie had ended up flattened out and facing Al.

"Did you know you're bleeding, Al?"

"Where?"

"A couple of places."

"Quiet, you two!" the guy on top of Al shouted.

They lay as still as they could while the FBI team cuffed each of them and slid them over until their backs were to the wall. Al had Fergie on one side and Maury on the other. One of the FBI team stood over them, talking into his mic.

Fergie looked worried. Then Al felt a warm trickle run down from the left side of his forehead, past his nose, on downward to drop off in a red dot onto his jeans.

Al still wasn't able to relax, and he doubted the others could either. But he felt the first few tingles of relief trying to course through him. All they had to do was wait, hope a stray shot didn't do in one or all of them.

Time seemed to crawl. The floor was cold, and Al was

tired, as tired as he had ever been. He felt like he'd spent far more energy and worry than he'd had stored up. He nodded, half ready to doze off, in spite of the sound of shots here and there and a great deal of shouting.

"Al?"

He looked up, and there stood Jaime, grinning like a fox in the chicken yard. Two of his men stood behind him. "Didn't I tell you, Al? A turtle. You're lucky to be alive. Darn lucky."

"Then why don't I feel lucky just now?"

Jaime nodded to the FBI agent, who stepped in close and unlocked their cuffs. He took them with him and went off.

"Most of the cave is contained," Jaime said. "What a helluva place. Who knew?" He bent down, and Al thought Jaime was going to help Al up, but he eased Bonnie to her feet first. The other men got Fergie and Maury upright. Jaime held out a hand, and Al tugged himself to his feet, wincing as he did.

"Well, maybe *you* knew, Al. First to figure it out anyway." Jaime's eyes swept the cavern they were in. "This'll be a plum for the DEA, one they need after losing a couple of men. Not much intel in the site for us. Though we might get something about cartel connections from a few of the gang survivors. Looks like the guy leading the *Mexikanemi* bunch here was a lieutenant, Heriberto Alonzo, an up-and-comer. He went down in a spray of heavy fire. We'll have to work up and down that ladder to find any connections. What a tangle at the moment, though. We've got everything but Hell's Angels down here." He grinned.

"But, hey, listen. I need to get you guys up to Clayton. He's topside," Jaime said. "His men and the troopers have secured the road and are setting up a medical tent. Looks like your little bunch here will want to look into that. You too, Al. Did you know you're bleeding? Then I've got to get back and play nice with the other groups for a while."

———⬦———

Al lay on his back on a gurney with two paramedics swabbing his wounds clean and taping him up enough to head into town. The inside of a white tent stretched out above Al's head, and the lights were bright. He was stable enough that they didn't seem worried about him. The ambulances and copters were screaming in and out, taking more serious cases away. Al had a through-and-through shot on the inside of his left thigh. It was just starting to throb. A few inches higher, and it would have been a bigger deal, at least to him. A bullet had apparently grazed his scalp and forehead too. They'd been pretty free with the scissors getting the wound open to where they could patch him, hair falling in moist, bloody clumps, and they'd ignored him when he'd asked for a little off the sides while they were at it.

"There you are."

Al would have recognized that bear-from-the-cave grumble anywhere. He started to sit up, but the paramedic pushed him back flat.

Clayton moved closer to stand towering over Al. "Stands to reason that when I tell you to butt out and act retired that I find you right here in the middle of this. If I told you to stay on the ground, I swear you would somehow learn to fly. Jaime tells me you're the one who kicked the hive. That so?"

"He had a lot more figured out than I did." Fergie came up to stand beside Clayton. She had a white bandage on her left temple and a white wrap around her upper right arm.

"And Bart?" Clayton asked Fergie.

"He was still down there the last I knew. Why? Didn't anyone get him?" She glanced in a direction Al guessed was where men were being brought out, ready to be hauled away.

"No one's come across him yet, and he had to have one or two more escape routes up his sleeve," Clayton said. "He's in the wind so far as I know."

"That's a shame," Fergie said. "But I have enough for IA now to get them off my back."

"Clayton," Al said. "I need to tell you about Wayon."

"Save it for your report, Al. I recall what a joy doing reports always was for you. They brought out what's left of Wayon's body already. Wasn't much. You get exploded inside a limestone box like that, your body is mostly soup. No way they're ever going to be able to establish cause of death. I'll want statements from Maury and Bonnie as well. I'm gonna need a ton of paper on this one."

"You think he was blown up down there on the department's behalf?" Al asked.

"Of course not. Wasn't even supposed to be there. But like as not he'll end up with a posthumous commendation. That's what usually happens to a bent sour grape like him these days." Clayton leaned closer, spoke in a whisper. "Turns out Wayon just opened an account in the Cayman Islands. Internal Affairs let me know they'd successfully tracked it barely an hour ago. You have to be discreet and clever to hide money that way. He was neither. But he was one very rich young man there for a day or two."

"Then you knew he'd gone over to the other side, that the little case he was looking into was going to spin into all this?" Al nodded toward where men were still going in and out of the exposed entrances to the cavern.

"I had only glimmers of hunches, Al. You ever see a lump under a carpet where you put your foot on it and it moves? No telling what it is until you finally herd it out from under the rug. This kind of thing"—Clayton waved a hand toward where the mess was still untangling—"can sweep a lot of people along with it. The money's too big to ignore for some."

"You never worried about me?"

"Never had to. I know you almost as well as you know yourself, Al. Now, you're gonna have to get off that gurney and give some of those waiting a chance to get patched up. I haven't seen anything like this in all my born days, or at least all my days of sheriffing."

"Before you go," Al said, "Wayon told us he'd gotten information on one murder out of a Tango Blast member named Jesus Vasquez. Jesus fingered a fellow Tango, Juan Madrigal, for killing Roger. Wayon also said Bart told him he did Gladys and Darin."

"Please tell me this Juan guy's still alive and can talk."

"I wish I could. But he was coming at us, and I watched Bonnie plug him. He'll be the one wearing a bulletproof vest, but the hole will be in his head."

"Oh, sweet gobs of grits. So I've got nothing?"

"Except all four of us hearing Wayon brag about getting the info out of Jesus and Bart. Will that do?"

"I guess it'll have to. It's nothing I can take into a courtroom, but it is what it is." Clayton sighed and turned away.

He lumbered off while the medics helped Al sit upright. He still felt a little dizzy and tired enough to weep openly. But relief was flooding all the way to his toes by now. Fergie put an arm through his and led him out of the bright lights in the tent, over to where Bonnie and Maury both sat on a small patch of trampled grass. They got to their feet when they saw Al. Maury's shirt had been cut away and his shoulder patched. Maury rushed to Al and gave him only the second hug Al could recall getting from him in decades. Bonnie waited until Maury let go. She rushed to Al and embraced him with the right balance of eagerness and care not to hurt him.

"You and Maury still have to go to the hospital," she said. "Gunshot wounds and all. There'll be reports."

"Clayton says he's going to want statements from you and Maury," Fergie told her. "The sheriff's department is going to want all they can on what happened to Wayon. It'd be nice to just hint he got blown up helping others, but Clayton already knows or suspects too much. So we'll have to stick pretty close to the truth."

"We know what happened to Wayon," Bonnie said. "Al happened to him."

"Just pick your words with care. Don't say anything you don't have to, but if the conversation gets that far, make sure they understand it was self-defense."

"But it was . . ." Bonnie started.

"Self-defense," Fergie repeated.

Fergie's car pulled up outside the hospital two days later. The sun was harshly bright to Al's eyes, and heat rose like a pizza oven from the sidewalk and the asphalt of the parking lot. Al stepped out of the spot of shade where he'd been waiting. His leg was wrapped tight and gave him only a twinge or two, so he was able to get around without a cane or crutches, just a slight limp. He climbed into the passenger seat and wouldn't be much of a detective if he didn't notice her bags were in the back seat. She glanced into her mirror and pulled out into the street.

"You aren't coming back to the house?" His thigh throbbed a little, and he was either getting a headache from the abrupt exposure to sun and heat or he was detoxing from the pain medicine they'd insisted on but he'd quit taking after the first day.

"I don't know."

"What don't you know?"

"If that's such a good idea. I'll have to think on it."

"You know you're welcome."

"Well, you've sure taken a bend with the wind, Al. Not too long back I'd have said you were reveling in your hermit's life."

"Bonnie and Maury are still there. I doubt one more would hurt. Things get hectic, I can always go fishing."

"You sure?"

"No. I'm not so sure about anything anymore. You'd think people our age would know what they want."

"That's not all of it. We all have plenty of baggage by now."

"Is it the way I took out some of those men?"

"That's something I won't soon forget."

"But under the circumstances?"

She looked away then had to concentrate on a pickup trying to pull out into traffic right in front of her.

He waited a couple of blocks. "Hey, I know I've wrestled with anger through the years, but generally I've gotten the best of it."

"Yeah, that's why you never killed Maury after what happened between him and Abbie."

"Just stayed away, didn't talk for twenty years. Never dated or married again either."

"Al, you can't think all that scar tissue inside you makes you more attractive."

"No. It just is what it is." He gave her a sideways glance. "I understand if you need some time."

"I do."

"Okay, then."

They were silent the rest of the way out to his place. He got out of the car and turned to lean back in. "Well, I'll see you around."

She just nodded, unable to speak. He closed the door, and she pulled away. He watched the car until it was out of sight.

He stood there, taking slow, deep breaths, his feet feeling like two broken boat anchors. Maury and Bonnie would be inside, waiting. Al didn't feel up to facing them, or anyone, just yet.

The leaves of a stand of yaupon rustled, and a brown head eased out, then another. Big eyes stared at him. The deer had found him. Life was going on around him whether he wanted it to or not. He sighed and limped toward the shed to get them a bucket of feed.

CHAPTER TWENTY-FOUR

HEAT LIGHTNING RIPPLED ACROSS THE morning horizon, haloing the over-large orange sun as it rose—reluctantly, it seemed to Al.

He sat in the front fishing chair and used the foot pedal to nudge his boat closer to the rocky point that projected from one side of the mouth of Cow Creek. The wind feathered toward him just light enough to cast a sheet of ripple across most of the lake's surface, except where lees along the shore showed as slick mirrors. The water along the rocky edge lay still enough Al could see the gentle weave of a swimming snake that hugged the shore fifty feet away. Only a smattering of clouds dotted and streaked the sky in places. It was a good day for fishing. Hell, it was a good day to be alive.

Though it had only been a week, he hardly felt a twinge at all when he moved his left thigh. He nudged the boat into position for a cast that would take his lure a couple yards past the point and then allow him to reel it in in a parallel path along the shore. He cast. The lure landed with a gentle plop. Perfect. He twitched the rod tip then began to reel the lure slowly back toward him. In his mind he could see it dropping along the face of the rock, past hiding holes and ambush spots where a bass might lurk. His phone rang.

He started to reach for his pocket when something hit

the lure hard enough to nearly yank the rod from his hand. He got both hands back on the rod and lifted the tip high, setting the hook. Oh, my. This was a real bucket mouth. The phone kept ringing. He cranked steadily, using the rod to lift and reel. He had his drag set all the way tight, and if a fish this size got its head to run on him, it could break off.

The minute he got it close to the boat and saw the size of the bass, it saw the boat and twisted in a surge of energy to dive straight down. He lifted up, and his rod bent until its tip nearly touched the side of the boat. Then he began to gain back line on the fish. His phone kept ringing. When he got it close this time, he swung the bass close to the boat and reached down to grab it by the lower lip, his thumb inside the fish's mouth. He lifted it out. Now that was a pretty fish. Five, maybe six pounds. He took the hook out of the bass's mouth, eased it back into the water, and watched it take off down into the deeper water in a flash of waving tail. If his friend Logan had caught a fish like that it would probably be a ten pounder by the time he was telling the tale back at the dock, and it would be pushing for a new state record by the time he was telling his wife that evening.

The phone was still ringing. Al rinsed his hands off in the water, rubbed them on his pants legs, and dug the phone out of his pocket.

"What do you want, Bonnie? You know I'm out fishing."

"It's your friend, Fergie. She's here for a visit. I know you haven't seen her but the one time since you got back from the hospital. She's here with her new boyfriend, and she'd like to see you."

"Really?"

"That's what she says."

"Okay." He hung up. Well, that was a shame. The day

had been shaping up to be one of those really fine days on the water.

Al sat for a minute in the chair and stared at the light chop of waves around him. How had he pictured his reclining, declining years? Like this? Not likely. Still, there were rare moments here and there where he thought it all might be going better than he'd expected, or deserved. As for those peaceful days of too much time spent alone, none came to mind. But the general sense and tone was one of being far from boring. He sighed and pushed himself up from the chair.

Bending forward, he lifted the electric motor up onto the bow and went back to fire up the big motor. He let it warm for just a minute then turned the boat and headed back toward the dock at his house. Only a couple of other boats were out on the lake, another reason he liked to fish on weekdays. That was the bonus of being retired, going out whenever he liked and not facing a crowd.

He tied up along his dock, bow and stern. No sense putting the boat up yet. He might get a chance to go back out. He took off his life vest and left it in the boat. He tossed his ball cap in too. His barber, Scottie, had just shaken his head and given him a buzz cut until everything had a chance to grow back evenly. "They sure made a mess of my handiwork," he'd said. "And I gotta tell you, this new part you're working on isn't gonna be easy to work with either."

"It's a bullet wound," Al had said.

"I know it is. I read the papers. Yet here you are alive and lucky to be getting your hair cut at all is the way I see it."

"I'm living the dream, Scottie," Al had said.

He walked up the sidewalk from the boat ramp to the back door. He smelled his hands. Yep, kind of fishy. He took a moment to step into the downstairs bathroom and wash them. There was just the one bed and a dresser down there. He called it the guest room. Maury stayed there. Either Maury or Bonnie had made the bed. Al went up the stairs two at a time. The words "new boyfriend" were just sinking in. Well, she'd made it pretty clear she didn't want to refresh what she'd had with Al. Power to her, though he hardly felt a big urge to know the guy.

At the top of the stairs the first thing he saw was the back of Maury's head. He was sitting in the chair. Bonnie and Fergie both sat on the couch, somewhat stiffly. As he stepped all the way into the living room, he followed their eyes, letting his head swing right. There stood Bart Haley, his back pressed tight against the wall so Al wouldn't see him until Al was all the way into the room. Bart held a gun, and it was now pointed at Al's middle. Al squinted and looked closer. That sure looked a lot like his Sig Sauer. Now, wouldn't that be a big laugh, to get shot with his own gun. Bart must have kept it when he'd grabbed Maury and Bonnie.

"Why don't you sit on the couch, Al, between the two ladies?" Bart waved the point of the gun.

Al slid past Maury and then Bonnie's knees. Bart stepped around and stood on the other side of the oak coffee table. Al had gotten the coffee table from the Amish Furniture store, and he'd been pretty proud of it at the time. Lovely smooth finish to the touch. He never thought it would be keeping him from rushing someone who clearly threatened his life, as well as the lives of Maury, Bonnie, and Fergie.

"I'm sorry, Al. I should have just let him shoot me at the motel instead of letting him force me to drive here." Fergie was looking at Al in a way he wished she'd looked at him earlier. So it goes.

"And you, Brainiac, when I say Fergie's 'boyfriend' you don't think something might be up?" Bonnie said. She gave Al a dig in his lower ribs with her elbow.

"How was I to know? You kept everything pretty short and cryptic in that call," Al said. "Fergie having a new boyfriend seemed credible enough to me."

"Hmpf," Fergie said.

"Women," Maury said. "Who can figure them out? And, when you do, you're always sorry."

"All of you, shut up! Just shut the fuck up!" Bart shouted. "I've waited a week for this. You ruined everything. One more fucking day, and I would have been so out of here."

"Nothing's stopping you," Fergie said. "You can still leave."

Bart's head snapped toward her. Al watched the hand that held the gun, the trigger finger in particular. Whether she knew it or not, Fergie had just come as close to dying as she ever had. But something was holding Bart back. Maybe he wanted to crow a bit. Little good that would do him. That wasn't going to get him his business, his money, or his badge back. It also told Al that Bart was pretty close to the edge. Any little thing might set him off. Good.

"No, I can't just leave. Peggy took off with everything we'd set aside," Bart said.

Al had to think for a moment about who Peggy was. Ah, the barmaid.

"What's this all supposed to prove?" Al said. "Does this mean you're smarter, or better? That you got away with murder and laughed at the law? Or does it just show you're mean and petty, that you're a vindictive little screw-up prone to blaming others for your deciding to cross the line into a life of crime it turns out you couldn't even manage well? You can kill an old woman and a boy yourself, but you have the gang members to do any real heavy lifting. Right?"

Bart's head jerked back an inch, as if he'd been slapped with a wet fish. The fingers on his gun hand whitened.

"Think about it, Bart. Even Peggy could spot a loser."

Al caught Fergie, Bonnie, and even Maury giving Al looks that said, "What the hell are you doing?"

"You swagger around like you're a big man on campus, but you're really just a boy bitch for a third-rate gang, one that may well be the loser in the current struggle. Probably will be, if there are any of them left. That must make you feel real special."

Al suspected that Bart had rehearsed a "feel-good" speech, one he very much wanted to get off his chest before emptying Al's gun into the four of them. Bart's face flushed pink beneath his tan, all the way to his temples. He was struggling with all he had not to just open up with the gun right then.

"The thing is, you have respect for no one. I mean no one." Al shot a quick glance to Maury. "And that's a two-way street. Why do we care how you redeem yourself in your own eyes? Just keep saying you're not a loser. We don't care. Not a rat's furry little ass."

Bart had been a guy who had spent years staying cool under duress. But he'd been pretty rattled the past few days, and Al was ladling it on quite thick. He watched Bart's eyes and knew the second he snapped. "The hell with it," Bart said, and his gun hand straightened, the barrel pointed right at Al's chest.

Maury, the only one with clear access to Bart, flew off his chair and dove into the back of Bart's knees.

Bart's knees bent forward, and his upper body crumpled backward, his gun arm rising toward the ceiling as he fired. The shot sent a shower of plaster and paint down toward the couch.

Al was already off the couch, leaping across the coffee table, with one foot on it. He grabbed the wrist of Bart's gun hand and twisted as he dove and rolled hard to his right. Another shot smacked into the wall, not far from where Maury's head had been while he was sitting.

Al's dive carried him and Bart to the floor, sprawling across Maury as they fell. Al kept his twist going until he had Bart's gun hand all the way up, pressed as high as he could get it up the middle of Bart's back. Bart squeezed off another shot that sent bits of his own hair into a flutter and the bullet into the ceiling. Al yanked upward as hard as he could and heard the loud snap as the arm broke. The gun fell from Bart's limp fingers. He screamed and fell over onto his side away from the arm that was still twisted behind his back.

Al got to his feet and helped Maury up. Bart was trying to get to his feet, in spite of being in quite a bit of pain. Al whirled and kicked Bart, the point of his boot hitting just below where Bart's ribs met in the middle. Al kicked again, catching Bart under the chin. Bart slammed back onto the floor, gasping and screaming. "You broke my fucking arm!"

"Yes, and I'm going to break the other one, just for fun, if you make another single move toward these people." Al was breathing hard as he picked up the gun, his own gun. He pointed it at Bart.

The others were staring at him, as if catching a rare glimpse inside the gates of hell.

"Call the sheriff, would you please, Bonnie?"

"Sure. Sure thing, Al."

"Thanks," Fergie said. "Thanks for saving us, again. I really. . . well, I should have. . ."

"Save it," Al suggested. "Maury here's the one you should be thanking. He's the one who did the real brave work. I just followed up with the close. I don't know about you guys, but I intend to buy him the biggest steak I can order, with all the trimmings."

Maury was beaming as much as Al had ever seen him. It warmed Al's heart. He had never been prouder of Maury, or of having him for a brother.

Bonnie closed her phone and was shoving it into her back pocket when the front door crashed in. Splintered wood and broken glass flew four feet into the front of the house. Two men dressed in the full dark-blue action gear of ICE burst in with weapons drawn. They swept the room and took in Bart on the floor. They lowered their weapons. The big blond guy with the buzz cut said, "Well, crap. I'm Campbell."

"What the. . .?" Al started to say.

The other guy, with darker Latino features, held up a hand. "Garcia."

Campbell was already on his cell phone. He turned to Garcia. "The boss says, 'I told you so.' Looks like we both have to pay up."

"Tell Jamie he owes me a fucking door!" Al yelled.

"Calm down. It wasn't supposed to get this far." Campbell put his cell phone back in his pocket. "Jaime heard your place wasn't being watched. He decided to fix that. We just got here to stake out the place. We'd barely started to set up the sound system and heard enough to realize the guy was already here. Hell, his bike wasn't out front. So we hustled right down. We were way up the hill."

Al knew the spot. A sniper had staked out the house from there once. He could picture them up there setting up their directional parabolic dish, with at least a three-band equalizer—nothing but the best for these guys—and aiming it toward his house. He wasn't sure how he felt about ICE agents listening in on every fart and squabble in his house. "I live out here where I do for the privacy. But I suppose that ship sailed a while ago. And it's just as well you were here in time to hear me goading Bart so you could come kick in my door after Bart had already been rendered a non-participant."

"You can beef about the door to Jaime." Campbell turned to Garcia. "Think we oughta cuff him?" He nodded toward Bart.

"Naw. He doesn't look ready for anything. He makes a move, we'll turn this old dude loose on him again."

"Why you guys and not the DEA?" Al said.

"Maxwell and his crew are swamped working that mother lode of a cave. We're on loan as a favor, and because Jaime likes you."

"Jaime told you two we'd be okay in here if Bart busted in?" Al said. "Then what's all this he's been pitching to me about being such a turtle?"

Campbell laughed. "Aw, he was just trying to piss you off. Looks like he succeeded. According to him, when you're pissed off, you're bottled lightning. He wasn't wrong."

Al felt some of the anger trickling out of him. He still felt pretty peppy inside, like he wouldn't mind biting someone.

"Hey, isn't anyone going to help me?" Bart had stayed on the floor when the new guys had burst in. He tried to use his good arm to get up.

Al stepped closer, put a foot on the side of Bart's head, and pressed down. The eyebrows of both agents rose.

"Okay, I admit it. I can be a sugar plum one minute and a raging tiger the next," Al said. "I begin to think that Jaime knows me pretty well. My flaw could be a liability to most people but an asset in his line of work. Still, it's a burden in a life spent trying to live in the proximity of more peace-loving people I try not to alarm. You understand?"

"Gotcha. You and Jaime might well be twins. Anyway, we need to take this guy to Jaime." Campbell's phone rang. He looked at the caller ID and answered quickly. He frowned. "Okay. We'll do it that way then."

He hung up, glanced toward Garcia, then to the bulge of a cell phone in Bonnie's pocket. He fixed his stare on Al. "The sheriff has already heard that Bart's here and wants to talk to him first. Apparently, your boss and the county will see that this guy gets to the hospital, *then* our boss can work out the details for talking with him along with the county, city, and the DEA folks at the hospital. Sheriff Clayton just had a chat with Jaime. Sounds like he's quite a convincing fellow, that sheriff. He's got the idea this guy's good for the two murders Clayton has open, and that puts Clayton at the head of the line. City had a very bent cop on their hands. So they want him bad. DEA is just drooling to lay hands on the mastermind behind the cave. He's a very popular guy. It's gonna be a real tangle, but I'm sure they'll all work it out."

Sheriff Clayton and Al stood on the porch, watching as the ambulance took off carrying Bart, handcuffed to a gurney, and two escort deputies. A sheriff's department cruiser pulled out after that. The car with two ICE agents inside fell into line next, though they and Jaime would have a wait before they got next to Bart.

Sheriff Clayton followed Al back into the house. He glanced at the shards that were all that remained of the door as he stepped through. Bonnie had cleaned up some of the glass and bits of wood, but the rest was a mess.

Inside the house, Maury was sweeping up some fallen

dust from the ceiling and wall with the vacuum. Fergie carried out two steaming mugs of coffee from the kitchen. Bonnie followed her with another three mugs. Maury turned off the vacuum, and it seemed suddenly quiet in the house, almost peaceful.

Clayton sat down at the dining table. "I'll be more than glad to share a cup about now. Maybe there are one or two things we can all catch up on."

Fergie and Maury sat down too. Bonnie held her mug in both hands and leaned against the corner of the wall that led into the kitchen. Al went ahead and took the other seat, across from Clayton.

"I'm sorry as hell your brother and your friends were threatened once again," Clayton said. "Jaime assured me he had this place sealed pretty tight. He does think a lot of you, Al, is maybe just a little scared of you. He has a crew on the hustle to come replace the door as we speak. Jaime says he'll be out this way early tomorrow to apologize himself once he's had a chat with Bart and let the city have a go at him. He says he'll be picking up a pie, so have a fresh pot of coffee ready."

"I think we may have to put Jaime in a class with Maury here," Bonnie said. "Man has a wandering eye, doesn't he?"

"Oh, I didn't know you'd noticed," Al said.

"Women notice a lot more than you think, Al."

Clayton took her in from head to toe, all bounce and pluck, and pretty in her own way. As Maury had put it, a dumpling. Once again Clayton didn't say whatever was going through his mind. He turned back to the others.

"This wraps up your case, doesn't it, Fergie?" Clayton asked. He looked over the rim of his mug at her as he took a sip.

She nodded. "You can't imagine how glad I am to have

this behind me." She looked toward Al. "I did need your help, as it turned out, but I didn't want to do anything that might seem to coerce you with what you would think were favors."

"Honey," Bonnie said. "I'd have coerced away until his eyeballs rattled."

Fergie shook her head but did manage a small blush. She turned back to Clayton. "I didn't think it was ever going to end well when Bart didn't turn up after all that fun in the cave."

Clayton nodded. "Tell you the truth, I didn't either. A smart man would have hightailed it out of here, not stayed to badger one of the finest men I ever worked with. Jaime says the same thing."

Al felt himself blush. He hoped it wasn't as obvious as it felt.

"I had a short talk with Bart just now, before they took him away. Did little good. Of course, Bart is being silent as a stone, and we have damn little forensic proof with the murders of Gladys and Darin, except what you all heard secondhand from Wayon. Pretty thin. We can tell the surviving sisters that Bart is 'allegedly' the murderer. That may give them some peace of mind. It's nothing I want to announce to the press. Between the DEA and the Austin PD, there's enough to ensure Bart will never walk the streets again. City should have a pretty good case against him." Clayton looked toward Fergie and took another sip of his coffee. "Do you know he even used their resources to find you were staying at the Cactus Flower Motel?"

"I didn't think I'd be so easily found by just anyone," Fergie said. She glanced toward Al. "I suppose some people who knew I'd stayed there before might have been able to find me."

"Why didn't you stay here?" Bonnie said. "I told you that you'd be welcome."

Fergie just shook her head. She didn't look at Al.

Clayton had been watching her, getting far more backstory than any of them other than Al might imagine.

Al's eyes narrowed. "You know, you seem pretty calm for someone who isn't going to get anything to stick on Bart. I mean, two pretty cold-blooded murders."

Clayton's head swung toward Al, his mouth twisting into a tiny wry smile. "You're a detective, Al. What do you think we've got? I mean, that would hold up in court."

Al shrugged. "Not much. Not enough. Just hearsay, really."

"But Cal Maxwell has literally tons of evidence, the kind that will hold up fine. He has a real itch to pile it on when it comes to Bart. The two DEA agents killed may not have been out of his bunch, but their deaths happened on his turf and on his watch. Just between us, Carl's a bit of a vindictive S.O.B. If anyone asks, you didn't hear that from me. If they can't put the screws to Bart, we can always play the kidnapping card for Bart snatching Maury and Bonnie. But that would mean court appearances and a lot of testimony under oath, by all of you. Talk about whatever happened to Wayon might come up, could get even closer scrutiny. I imagined you'd all just as soon not go that route as long as Bart gets some of what he deserves."

"So, that's it?" Fergie said. "That's all the justice those ladies will get for their sister and nephew?"

"I don't know yet." Clayton fixed her with a firm stare. "Thing about justice is it sometimes has a funny way of getting where it needs to go. You might've heard of a fellow named Jim Bob Grady?"

"The blue boat. Right?" Fergie asked.

Clayton nodded. "Well, earlier today, you may not have caught the news on this yet, Jim Bob Grady got released from his hundred days of county jail time. He was in the courthouse, getting reminded of the gritty on his probation. When he came out, there was a crowd there to meet him. The father of the boy who died and the boy's uncle were in that crowd. And don't you know that as soon as the bailiff's back was turned, Jim Bob Grady tripped and fell all the way down the courthouse stairs. Broke his stupid neck. Can you believe it? Surrounded by a crowd like that too. Gotta believe he just stumbled and fell."

"Are you saying it just happened, and no one saw a thing?" Fergie asked.

"Look, sometimes I'm not on the scene. I wasn't there at the courthouse myself. I can only go on what I hear from those I trust. More than half the time, it's all I've got." He stopped for a second and swept each one of them slowly with his penetrating eyes. He didn't have to mention anything about what went on between Wayon and Al down in the heart of the earth. "Sometimes I have to shrug and let things work themselves out. Anything else you want to ask?"

From time to time Al had noticed that Clayton could be more than a little old fashioned about justice, almost Old Testament so. Clayton seemed glad he hadn't been there to see Jim Bob Brady falling down the courthouse stairs the way he had because he wouldn't have been able to look the other way. But since he *hadn't* been there, he wasn't going to give it much of a stir now that it had happened.

"Nope. I'm all done." Fergie glanced around to the others then looked down into her coffee cup. Al couldn't tell if she was seeing it half full or half empty.

Clayton turned back to Al. "What I wanted to say, Al, is that I'd like to have you back in the department, at least for as long as it takes to replace Wayon. You could mentor the new guy or gal, too. I'd be grateful for that. You may stray from the path from time to time, but you get the job done as well as anyone ever could."

"I'll think about it," Al said.

"That's all I can ask." Clayton tossed back the rest of the coffee in his mug and rose. "I imagine you have a lot to think about." He glanced toward Fergie and Bonnie. "Let me know when you can. I'll be holding your badge for you."

He turned and lumbered toward the door, and to Al, he'd never looked more like a bear going back to its cave.

"You know, taking the job for a short spell might not be a bad idea, Al. I think you need people around you." Fergie's head was tilted an inch to the right, and her lips were pursed, somewhere between thoughtful and amused.

It was quiet around the table for a minute. Finally, Bonnie cleared her throat. "Here's an idea," she said. "I could take Fergie back to her motel in Al's new truck, and she could get her things. She could stay here a while."

"Well, I suppose I could let you ladies have the downstairs," Maury said. "I can get by on the couch for a while."

"Is that okay with you, Al?" Fergie asked.

"Sure," Al said. His voice sounded a touch scratchy. He was trying to picture the madcap days of fun ahead, and for the first time, all the chaos that had gone on down there in that cave didn't seem so surreal and unlikely. In fact, it seemed downright tame.

"Well, since we'll have the truck, we can pick up another bed. Oh, and some new curtains for down there," Bonnie said.

"I'm not fond of that shower curtain down there either," Fergie said. "How about a new one?"

"Done. We're gonna need your credit card, Al." Bonnie held out a hand.

Al dug it out of his wallet and handed it over. He stood up and ran his fingers across the stubble on his head. The two women, already on the move, paused by the door and looked Al over, like he was something on display in a store window. They headed outside through the gaping hole that had once been Al's door; both wore jeans with what they needed in their pockets, so neither needed to head back to grab a purse. Al watched the two taut, jeans-covered derrieres pass through the doorway. Once again, women walking away. This time, both sneaked a glance back to catch him watching. Their laughter and voices got more excited as they faded out of his hearing. He could hear his truck start.

"Well, now you've done it," Maury said. Al realized Maury was staring at the door too, his mouth open just the tiniest bit.

"Done what?"

"You've found two women out of the thousands out there who aren't put off at finding out that a guy's soft, fluffy exterior has a hard-edged, steel interior that can spring like lightning once riled. They're actually attracted to that aspect of you, especially Fergie." Maury sighed.

"You showed a little mettle yourself today, Maury. We owe you our lives."

"You should share, Al." He was looking at Al with two laser eyes turned up to an uncharacteristic intensity.

"Share what?"

"You'll figure it out."

"If there's anything to figure out, I imagine it'll happen between those two." Al waved a hand toward the front door.

"You're going to let them decide?" Maury's voice went up an octave.

Al leaned with one hand on the table. He tilted his head as he looked toward the door. There was a lot to mull over, but he was a detective. He would sort it out, in time.

"You'd better stick around for those guys coming to fix the door, Maury."

Al pushed himself upright and walked away from the table.

"Where are you going?" Maury said.

"Fishing. It's what we turtles do."

OTHER BOOKS BY RUSS HALL

Thrillers

To Hell and Gone in Texas (An Al Quinn Novel)
Island
Wildcat Did Growl
Talon's Grip
World Gone Wrong

Mysteries

The Blue-Eyed Indian
Bones of the Rain
South Austin Vampire
No Murder Before Its Time
Black Like Blood
Goodbye, She Lied

Westerns

Bent Red Moon
Bullets in the Wind
Three-Legged Horse

Young Adult Sci Fi

Inside Jupiter

ABOUT THE AUTHOR

Russ Hall is author of fifteen published fiction books, most in hardback and subsequently published in mass market paperback by Harlequin's Worldwide Mystery imprint and Leisure Books. He has also co-authored numerous non-fiction books, most recently *Do You Matter: How Great Design Will Make People Love Your Company* (Financial Times Press, 2009) with Richard Brunner, former head of design at Apple and *Now You're Thinking* (Financial Times Press, 2011), and *Identity* (Financial Times Press, 2012) with Stedman Graham, Oprah's companion.

Russ has been a nonfiction editor for major publishing companies, ranging from HarperCollins (then Harper & Row), Simon & Schuster, to Pearson. He has lived in Ohio, Connecticut, Florida, North Carolina, and New York, and he currently calls Texas home. Russ is a long-time member of the Mystery Writers of America, Western Writers of America, and Sisters in Crime. He is a frequent judge for writing organizations.

In 2011, he was awarded the Sage Award, by the Barbara Burnett Smith Mentoring Authors Foundation—a Texas award for the mentoring author who demonstrates an outstanding spirit of service in mentoring, sharing, and leading others in the mystery writing community. In 1996, he won the Nancy Pickard Mystery Fiction Award for short fiction.